Attention Please Now

Attention Please Now

stories by
Matthew Pitt

AUTUMN
HOUSE PRESS

PITTSBURGH

Autumn House Press Staff
Editor-in-Chief and Founder: Michael Simms
Executive Director: Richard St. John
Community Outreach Director: Michael Wurster
Co-Director: Eva-Maria Simms
Fiction Editor: Sharon Dilworth
Coal Hill Editor: Joshua Storey
Assistant Editor: Evan Oare
Editorial Consultant: Ziggy Edwards
Media Consultant: Jan Beatty
Tech Crew Chief: Michael Milberger
Intern: Christina Haaf

This project was supported by the Pennsylvania Council on the Arts, a state agency, through its regional arts funding partnership, Pennsylvania Partners in the Arts (PPA). State government funding comes through an annual appropriation by Pennsylvania's General Assembly. PPA is administered in Allegheny County by Greater Pittsburgh Arts Council.

ISBN: 978-1-932870-37-4
Library of Congress: 2009939878

for Kimberly,
who keeps my life lit with fortune

Acknowledgments

Stories in this collection previously appeared, sometimes in slightly different form, in the following publications:

"Golden Retrievers," in *Crab Orchard Review*

"Attention, Please. Now," in *The Southern Review*

"The Mean," in *Best New American Voices*, edited by Charles Baxter. It also appeared in the *Robert Olen Butler Prize Stories* anthology.

"Wanted: Rebel Song," in *Oxford American*. It also won the Salem College Center for Women Writers' Reynolds Price Short Fiction Award, judged by Ellen Gilchrist.

"Answers to Frequently Asked Questions," in *Colorado Review*

"Observing the Sabbath," in *Alaska Quarterly Review*

"Outpatient," in *The Madison Review*, winner of the Chris O'Malley Fiction Prize

"The Whole World Over," in *Colorado Review*

"Au Lieu des Fleurs," in *Witness*

"Kokomo," in *Inkwell*, winner of the Inkwell Fiction Award, judged by Martha Cooley

Writing this collection turned out to be less solitary of an act than I feared. One reason: the extraordinary books that I read over the intervening years. The authors I discovered—their characters, sentences and spectacles of imagination—have been vessels, carrying me into astonishments, and carrying me through my own doubts and misgivings. I only hope this work in some way honors theirs.

This book is also a shared endeavor thanks to support from the *New York Times* Company Foundation, the *St. Louis Post-Dispatch*, the Bronx Council on the Arts (particularly Leslie Shipman), and the Mississippi Arts Commission. I have benefited, more than I can say, from friendships made at the Bread Loaf and Sewanee Writers' Conferences. Thanks to Michael Collier and Wyatt Prunty for inviting me into the folds.

Support also came from fellow writers at NYU's Graduate Creative Writing Program, led then by the unflappable and incomparable Melissa Hammerle. I am indebted to the faculty I learned from there, and at the conferences mentioned above: Robert Boswell, Breyten Breytenbach, E.L. Doctorow, Fenton Johnson, Randall Kenan, Allison Lurie, Thomas Mallon, Paule Marshall, Brian Morton, Peter Turchi, and Chuck Wachtel.

Thanks to the editors who published (and improved) these stories, and the authors who selected them for honors and accolades. These include: Charles Baxter, Martha Cooley, Ellen Gilchrist, and Stephen King; Natalie Danford at *Best New American Voices*; Stephanie G'Schwind at *Colorado Review*, Bret Lott and Donna Perrault at *The Southern Review*, Marc Smirnoff and Carol Ann Fitzgerald at *Oxford American*, Ronald Spatz at *Alaska Quarterly Review*, and Peter Stine at *Witness*.

Thanks to Sharon Dilworth for her editorial cheer and gleam, Michael Simms, and everyone at Autumn House Press for bringing these words into the world.

Thanks to colleagues at Penn State-Altoona and New York University. To Heidi Zeigler for sharp insights sent from southern latitudes, and for her impeccable taste in best friends. Thanks to my in-laws, Dean and Kathe Miller, and to my family: my sister Sarah, brother-in-law Josh, and my parents Rhonda and Darrell, who taught me to savor good stories, then gave me a sturdy stage to tell my own.

To my daughters, Celia and Nina, who delight already in reading and being read to. And to my wife, romantic lead, and best friend Kimberly Morgan Miller: whose editorial eye deepened the work, and whose faith and support sustains me.

A final reason the collection feels like collaboration: your holding and reading its pages. Thank you.

Contents

I can't be in the avant-garde
because I cry when dogs die
in movies.

Bob Hicok, "Cutting Edge," *Insomnia Diary*

beautiful beyond belief at this passing
at this very passing moment that's just passed.

Wislawa Szymborska, "The Acrobat," *Poems New and Collected*

Golden Retrievers

Even before August, summer was smothering the dogs of L.A. June's heat wave shocked Orange County. The forecasters laughed it off. It'll peter out, they predicted; but it didn't. A tractor-trailer filled with Pacific fish jackknifed in July, leaving Hollywood and Vine smelling of mackerel and eel and smelt roe, a foggy, murderous scent the street cleaners couldn't erase. A scent the dogs could neither locate nor escape from. They ran down Gower beside their owners, actors trying to shed water weight in the heat. They ran across bridges which rose above rivers; when the dogs saw the barren riverbeds they howled. Their tongues swelled as they begged licks of Evian from their masters' palms.

Then came August 5th—and the meltdown of Susie Light's Hollywood career. On the evening of the 4th, Susie shut out the lights at Peticular Bliss, her kennel for the dogs of stars. She'd just finished preparing sixty meals: fifteen low-cal, eleven no-fat, nine vegetarian, and twenty-five more assorted rations, all done up with capers, coated with twists of lemon, and spooned into colorful, Fiesta-style ceramic bowls. The next morning Susie knew something was wrong by the smell outside the bedding area. Food. Food? But the dogs always ate what was given them. She unlocked the door. A pulse of heat lurched at her. Her hair fizzed, her lungs felt thin: The air inside was grim and splintered with stillness.

Susie walked the aisles, pawing fur, checking for heartbeats, holding her breath in hope of hearing theirs. A minute later, a recorded, eerily perky, female voice filled the otherwise silent room. It came from Ab's suite. Ab Doberman, a Pinscher belonging to an aerobics instructor who taped two shows for ESPN2: *Lose the Fat!* and *Living With Fat.* The instructor insisted that Ab wake up in the morning to her programs. Susie approached Ab: His rangy body lay stiff on the carpet and his face was a queer void, though his nose was still slightly moist, like a stick of butter left out to soften.

She bent down and petted his fur. You liked Desert Palm Bottled Water mixed with a protein supplement that made it look like split pea soup, and you liked to hear your owner feeling the burn. Could you be dead too, baby?

In the following weeks, Susie received measures of exoneration. The SPCA of SoCal and the LAPD reached similar conclusions: The air conditioning unit *had* been left on when Susie locked up the kennel; it had simply conked out during the night. Susie Light wasn't delinquent in paying her electric bill, or negligent in her duties. The city removed her license from probation.

The first September breezes redeemed the stale air; mercy followed. Most of the actors dropped their lawsuits against Susie. Others failed to show at the courthouse. Susie did show, each time wearing the same gray suit, a spindly yet animated frock, a lilac pinned to the lapel. In her mirror the gray seemed louder each morning she wore it, as though the fabric were feeding off her skin. She bought Snickers from a machine in the courthouse for comfort.

Though it was the stars who sued, it was the Jamie Farrs and Conrad Bains who seemed to suffer. Those who hadn't fared so well in the wake of fame— the actors surviving on residuals—who seemed truly disconsolate from the loss. They were the ones Susie couldn't face.

"I think I need to cut my losses," Susie was saying over iced tea to her old friend Clara, late in September. Clara was what Susie had longed to be: a television actress, only one step away from her dream of cinema. The other friends in their group from high school, all of whom had also wanted to make it big, regarded Clara with the very mix of awe and protracted envy she'd hoped they would. Only Susie had remained close to Clara: The others now felt puffy and bucolic beside her. Not that they were doing poorly. But L.A. is a town of earthquakes as much social as geological. Imbalances in clout are documented overnight, rifts in status between friends, institutionalized.

Clara smoked cigarettes with scrabbling intensity, like a dog stripping leftover chicken bones. She'd once been the group's prude, delusional with duty. Now she was wildest and fairest of them all. Her voice had gone gruff, and this drop in register gave her pleasure. The thinner Clara became, the more fiery she had to sound, so producers would know she wasn't just some softhearted fuck from the sticks they could push around. "I don't think you have losses to cut, Sooz."

"I agree," Clara's manager said. Clara had brought her along for advisement. "If anything, now's the time you franchise." The whole incident felt unreal, almost playful. Litigation in L.A. was like a bad review of a smash hit: not to be taken seriously. "We just gotta handle it delicately. Who was your biggest client? Your biggest *name* client?"

"Johnny London."

Clara's manager stroked the rim of her water glass. "London's tough. He's in Tunisia wrapping a picture, but he'll be back soon. I happen to know he shares a joint checking account with his personal assistant. And she owes me huge. I'll have her draw up a check for $10,000 to Animal Relief Shelter. I'll tip some hack at *Variety* to it, they'll write a big spread on Johnny's humanitarianism in the face of sorrow. By the time London gets wise to his pooch dying, his ass will be so well-licked from the good PR, he'll think it was his idea to kill her off."

London's pooch had been a basenji. Johnny had visited her at the kennel only once in a year. "Might I ask how you 'happen to know' these things?"

"Susie," said Clara's manager. "Take my hand, squeeze it. Trust what the hand is saying. The kennel mess couldn't have happened in a better climate. Politically, I mean."

"I don't want good politics. I think this is a sign to go. Get out."

"And do what?" demanded Clara, to no response. She stamped her cigarette out, eyes narrowing to the width of fingernails. Life here was tough on Clara, and would be tougher without Susie. She'd once told Susie she was too busy finding work to enjoy her own accomplishments: "I have to live vicariously through the people living vicariously through me."

Back in high school, Clara had also been the only one in their circle of friends to believe in God. Now faith had found the others—Gina with her prayer group, Kay and Ray with their AA. Clara claimed to have given up on the church entirely. "But I've been advised not to rule out Scientology," she had said. "It's like a pre-approved platinum card. You don't dismiss the offer."

Roderick Kim strolled by their table. He had blue eyes, a sharp chin, biceps that seemed to be fighting through his lemon-green T-shirt. Susie had been to his place once, to bathe his Australian sheepdog. This was years ago, when she told clients she had to introduce herself to the dogs on the dogs' home turf. Her method empowered and relaxed them. The actors lapped this up, the servile artistry of it.

Initially Susie used her house calls to reveal her acting ambition. She tried to work it in naturally, hoping the celebrity in question would ask what had brought her to L.A. But that never happened—so Susie resorted to reciting famous film lines to the dogs, in earshot of their owners. Or more transparently, leaving her number on the backsides of head shots. She often dreamt of how her discovery would unfold. With Roderick it went like this: She'd pick up the latest script he was working on—a romantic comedy set in Prague, perhaps?—its pages tossed everywhere. Roderick would be having ego clashes with his leading lady, and when he saw how naturally Susie read the lines, he would grab the phone, demanding the role be recast for her. He would lean into Susie on the couch—the flickers of candle flame flanking her face would draw him in—and he'd kiss her. The morning after they would laugh together gently, trying to recall each detail for the inevitable profile in *People.*

In fact there was no morning after, or night before, Roderick was in-between projects, and he used track lighting. His house was Venice typical, a chimera of clashing cultural milieus, party favors from the booty of various forgotten and ruined empires. One of his bookshelves was lined with editions of the "Idiot's Guide To" series; others were filled with the companion "For Dummies" volumes. Roderick recited Shakespeare at the Mark Taper Forum like a demigod; what a disappointment witnessing the dropped foliage of his original thoughts. Even his dog had seemed embarrassed.

Australian sheepdogs were the most perfect specimen, Susie reflected—but bloodhounds and fat bassets, oh, they were her favorites. She'd had four bassets in her care at Peticular Bliss. None had survived; they were heavy panters, which probably contributed to their death.

Clara checked her watch and nudged Susie. "It's time for the opening. We have to hurry if we want to be late."

That August night at the kennel, it had risen to 110 degrees. Only nine of sixty dogs had survived. Fifty-one dead friends. "Okay," Susie said, rising slowly. "How much do I owe?"

They drove south. As they approached MacArthur Park, Susie tuned out Clara's monologue; she watched joggers leave their cars at the park entrance, leash their dogs, and run toward the poplars and cedars. She tried to admire the leaves on the trees, aglow with sunshine, edges slightly polar with deposits of off-white pollen. But dogs kept catching her eye. She watched them all—some heeled, others throwing all of their weight and happiness into the run.

Clara's Jag idled at a red light one block from the park. Looking into the passenger-side mirror, Susie watched a mastiff move behind her. Its jowls jiggled as it strutted a slow line, like some prisoner at sea walking a plank with fierce, final dignity. Then it was out of sight, having suddenly dissolved behind the mirror's blind spot. Susie waited for the dog to reappear. It didn't. She thought she heard the mastiff's claws scrape the concrete, saw the flesh dent its ribs when the dog drew a deep breath, but of course she did not hear or see these things. When the light turned green, Susie scoured the area. There was no sign of the mastiff, no sign it had ever been there...

She might never forgive herself. What would that mean? Susie had failed herself before; all those mistakes eventually tunneled under the range of her consciousness. Eventually. What would it take to make this mistake seem insignificant, too?

"This is so exciting," Clara squealed. "I can't believe I'm about to watch a first-run film *beneath the earth*." Mann Underground, a subsidiary to Mann's Chinese Theatre and the Hollywood Walk of Fame, was opening today. It was indeed the world's first movie theater located inside a subway station. It had THX sound to block out the rumble of subway cars, and little windows in the doors, so customers could take a break from the film to watch people getting on and off trains—or so passengers getting on and off the trains could peer in and try to recognize famous people not watching movies.

Clara had been invited to the premiere, a remake of a 1979 disaster film. The two descended an opalescent gray staircase past the checkpoint. Susie hung back, making sure she seemed an innocuous "plus-one," not a lover (Clara's career wasn't strong enough to survive lesbian rumors). They strolled into the embassy of celebrity flesh, Susie drifting, Clara exchanging clerical kisses with her peers, throwing discretionary waves to the audience, which was held back by an embankment of bouncers.

Liz Phair, Beck, and members of Pavement were strumming guitars and drinking Coronas, secluded in a corner of the subway station. Liz sang harmony in burnt orange taffeta, to Beck's lead: *"You say I'm a bore / Not your cup of tea / But you've been an Elysian Encounter / An Elysian Encounter to me..."*

The premiere went off without a hitch, technically speaking. The soundproofed walls worked. The projector worked. The headsets worked too, though most of the guests discarded them early to talk shop. But halfway through the film, Susie saw something possibly terrifying beyond the theater window; trick of light, maybe, though it seemed real enough to smell. A murky bauble of bronze fur. A dog. But no one else had seen what she had. Had they? No. So she let the disaster movie play on and the players speak through it and the new L.A. subway roll on through all the satisfied talk and pomp of the Hollywood elite.

Susie found the incidental habits hardest to break. Ordering squeeze toys online. Running a lint roller over her clothes. Fridays—when she'd buy food for the dogs—were worst. Her life had made sense on Fridays, comparing vitamin supplements at Trader Joe's, watching baggers gather the purchases she paid for on borrowed wealth. She'd listen to the receipt churn from the register; spending so much on frivolities made her feel like an actress.

"Uh, ma'am? Excuse me. Your card has been declined."

She stared dumbly at the store clerk. He must be new. Trader's Joe's knew who she was. They knew Susie took care of Oscar winners' wiener dogs, movie execs' Great Danes. This kid needed a lesson in respecting clout. Then it struck her. She slid her hands into one of the bags. Her fingers traced the frozen liverwurst entrees, which prevented heartworms and contributed to coat sheen. There was no reason to buy this. It was September 27th; all the dogs were now ashes or buried bones, and reason for any of this had long since left.

"None of this is for them," Susie said. "None of them, really, are mine anymore." The store clerk trained a casual smile toward her; this must be how policemen look at the women who've just been punched blue and deserted by their boyfriends. She felt too embarrassed to return it all. She felt pressure to return the clerk's smile. She felt the thinness of the paper sacks.

October began cool. The temperature dropped (71 at night, 74 during the day). Softness resumed. Clara called Susie each day. Encouraging her to shop. Drive. "Walk, even, if that's what it takes."

"I'll be fine, really. My checking account's still pretty flush."

"This isn't a money call. If it were, then fuck, I'd just promote you to producer."

"I don't work on your show, Clara." Susie readjusted her phone. "What's this really about?"

"This is a health call. You need to let go. Inner turmoil doesn't cut it in this town. Confession and memory don't either: You have to explode. Do something flip. Show don't tell. Exaggerate your confidence."

"Maybe I should get back into acting." Susie was half-serious, though Clara often ran through the list of her friend's physical features—"sharply arched brows, eyes too dark and bracing, that whole *wise* thing you've got"—working against Susie, preventing her from having The Look.

Clara was worried for her friend. "I don't want you to be like Mike," she said.

Mike? Mike? The name lingered in her mouth—oh God, she meant Michael! Susie hadn't thought of her old friend in years, regarding him as some light confectioner's treat which gave her pleasure long ago. He'd been part of their group, the oddest and softest of them. And being a boy, the most useful. He'd been the one boy allowed to commiserate with the gaggle of girls. He'd given the girls' collective ego a knuckle; his devoted presence persuaded many a popular male senior that these were the girls to try and score with. The girls to blow part-time paychecks on.

When the girls became seniors with cars, they graduated themselves to the nearby college town, towing Michael along. A bright nervous face rushed suddenly to Susie's mind—Michael's, and Michael's quick, chattering feet— such a dancer! So good he prompted competition, prompted Chet Baker to cut in on the two of them one night at a frat house. Chet was dark and powerful, and moved with a rusty swivel to his hips, his groin hemming her in. Chet kissed Susie when he wanted to, his tongue darting down her mouth like a sloppy banana squeezed from the skin. From time to time she'd look up at Chet—named after the famous trumpeter, though his lips held no fraction of the skill, the dexterity, the tenderness. Still, Susie felt flush; she was a trophy of desire. His desire. She would let this man cave her virginity in, topple the last remnant of this stupid, boxy innocence she couldn't wait to rid herself of.

"How did you hear from Michael, Clara? Did you call him?"

"What are you, kidding?"

"Right, okay. Well, when did *he* call? What is he doing these days?"

"Stand-up. In Vegas," Clara said, sucking in smoke. "Vegas, can you believe it?"

"Do you have his number?"

Clara said she'd misplaced it. Susie could tell she *hadn't*—an actress is the sum of the style of her lies, and only the childhood friends of the actress were familiar enough with that style of deception to call it in the air. Finally, Clara relented. "I'll give it to you, but I don't think he's a person you should be speaking with. He's a real idiot mess."

"What do you mean?"

Clara blew a tray of smoke into the phone receiver. "I mean Michael's like a boy with a ball. He throws it, uh, in the woods, and it's lost. But instead of just finding a new ball, he chases it into the woods, uh, looking for it..."

Susie stretched her arms, the receiver still in her hand. She looked at the clock, wondering, if these were long-distance calls, how much sooner she'd cut Clara off during rants. Susie didn't care how far Michael had fallen, or what talent he was, in Clara's judgment, tossing away. He was just a name and a voice Susie had lost track of, and now wanted back. She sought only simple reconnection with the man, and that was all. Well. Maybe reconnection and a drink. And maybe a show. Maybe a dance; maybe. Maybe. More.

Though they hadn't spoken in nearly a decade, Michael answered Susie's phone call as if he'd been waiting on hold all this time. After three phone talks, Michael agreed to visit. They'd meet at Union Station; he refused to take a plane in from Vegas. "Flying into Los Angeles is like staring at your own smile in the mirror. You're seeing too much forced nicety at once."

Susie respected his complaint, at least associatively: To her, Las Vegas was a wasteland on life support, intubated on electric sunlight and slot machines, arid of charisma, underscored with a population far too vulgar to see that they were lost souls.

Michael stepped off the train and sniffed the air; Susie took cover in the crowd, in case she wanted to back out. An old valise hung over his shoulder, blue, half-empty, veined with wrinkles. She took in his faded penny loafers, the long shelf of his nose. She drew close to hug him. It was a long hug, one she refused to stop. Finally he pulled back, complaining his bag was too heavy.

"So where are we taking me?"

"Public premiere of a new subway stop in East L.A. The seventh mile."

"I thought L.A. was The Last Mile."

He was speaking with a hard tone, the clipped efficiency of a failed traveling salesman. But wasn't he here, weren't they together, because of how well the phone conversations had gone? She ruffled his head. "Your top is thinning."

"That's okay," he countered, maneuvering from her touch, "my bottom is thickening. Hey, thanks! You helped me walk right into that one. Truth is I've been killing myself for new material all summer, and getting *nada nunca*." Susie forced a smile. But she could see where he was headed: jokes. They began to compare fitness regimes, but Michael took the opportunity to toss off self-deprecating one-liners: "I'm so abusive to my body, my liver had to pick me out of a lineup. My only form of consistent exercise is passing kidneystones. When I tried to donate my semen to the sperm bank, they told me to take it to a pawn shop..."

She managed to stop him with a compliment. "I like that one best."

"Really," he wondered. "Because that one I'm still playing with the wording."

They continued toward the turnstiles. A tejano band struck up a ballad in the subway well. Susie gobbled up Michael's hand with her own; it felt more relaxed than she'd expected. "Still dance?" Michael shook his head. "Oh come on. Bullshit. A man can't teach himself to stop dancing once he knows he's good." She led him down the stairs, eager to grandly descend, but he wasn't kidding: He moved like a lumbering bear. "Michael," she said finally, eyeing his nose, releasing his hairy hand.

"I told you. I'm no dancer. I don't work out. I don't do anything anymore that isn't bad for me or good for tourism. Usually both. Susie, I'm not even Jewish anymore."

"What are you talking about?"

"No fooling." He showed Susie his Nevada driver's license. "I'm no longer Michael Yonah Resnick; meet Mike L. Resno." Three years ago the manager of the Mirage had offered him a spot opening for Nick Fike, on the condition he adopt a *nom de plume*. "My heritage threatened the goyim from Provo. They were all convinced that if the Son of God were to choose the Mirage as the site to stage His second coming, then the funny Jew onstage would find a way to stab Him before He could get His first parable out. So I've been offi-cially gentilized by Nevada." As he spoke, light flashed from around a bend; the subway was pulling in. When its horn blew, Michael pretended to have been shot: "Watch out! They got me! I'm coming apart, I've come unjewed!"

Susie backed off. Her brow furrowed. She was listening to Michael, Mike L., trying to figure out whether he was going to kiss her. Through his routine, she'd made a point of touching him, or pollinating his ego with well-placed laughter. In the crawlspace of time from the moment he stepped off the Amtrak to the first mordant rumbles of the Red Line, Susie recalled how starkly Michael had once loved her. In high school, in the mash letters he'd written then, and the increasingly desperate notes in college. And now here she was, pining for *his* affection to no avail, waiting with empty lips for a train.

As their train came to a halt, Susie pressed her front teeth against her lower lip. She wondered—would she see a dog again? The first time in this station with Clara, she had spotted what had seemed to be a golden retriever jump into the subway well, dart in the direction of the cars, only to leap from the well and over the turnstile, before vanishing. But it was all impos-sible. Some leprosy of her senses had afflicted her; she'd recover. Only it happened again. This time at the North Hollywood station, on her way to have her hair done. A different dog, darker, fuller plume in the tail, but still a retriever. It had sat patiently among the waiting passengers, not seeking scraps of food, attention, anything. Finally the train had arrived—and that was when the dog bounded into the stairwell and darted down the tunnel, trying to outrun the momentum of the train. It had left a calling card of hair and heat on the platform's edge. Surely it hadn't survived. But how had it gotten there?

Suspicious of her mind, but always a fan of a fair trial, Susie began to weigh the evidence. Perhaps it had been another kind of animal—a rat or cat, or just clothing blown by wind? Or some blasé promotion...light FX from the engineer's car, visual ad copy for a new family film? But the trades would've hyped such a stunt to death—she wasn't that out of the loop. Madness, above all, was the affectation of enhanced or depleted perception, corroborated by no witness other than the afflicted. Was she headed there?

Michael egged Susie onto the subway car. The Red Line shot into the tunnel like a panic, a slippery riot, bound for East L.A.

Michael proved a devoted companion. He took Susie's tension and doubt over her career and threw it far away. He kept her out of her house, kept her in the moment. In East L.A., they sat on a new bench already pocked with graffiti and knife grooves. They sat, just so, for two hours. The jet set arrived for the ribbon cutting, surveying the station. Some were there to have their hands immortalized in wet clay beneath the turnstiles. Michael watched, giggling. "This damn town. It kills me. It took me all of two months interning in 'the 'Bu' as Ed Frietland's piss-ant to realize I couldn't bring myself to live here... Why haven't you figured it out yet?"

"Michael, I love L.A.!" He eyed her. "Well okay, love is strong. How about despise affectionately?"

Michael sipped Sprite, waiting for more of an explanation.

"Have you ever had to stop yourself in mid-curse? Your whole day has gone to shit. Like anarchy had a fire sale. So you drive to 7-11. Maybe buy a scratch-off. You take your coin out, shake your fist and scream, 'If this Lotto ticket doesn't fucking come through!' Even while some of you secretly *wants* to lose, you're so used to it. But you scratch the ticket...and it's a twenty-dollar winner. L.A. fucks with my head and heart, sure, but just when I'm about to jaywalk across rush hour Sunset...Boom! It hands me a twenty." She toyed with the disposable camera he'd brought. "It retrieves itself to me."

"Retrieves. How do you mean?"

She laughed. "I said 'redeems.' L.A. redeems itself to me."

"No. You said 'retrieves.'" Susie blanched. She covered her face with the camera. Michael's face seemed small through the lens, distant and unattainable.

"So what's great about Vegas?"

"What's *great*?" He turned away and chewed his straw. A street vendor selling tapas made it halfway down the subway stairs before bouncers dragged him back up, kicking and screaming. Michael turned back around. "On any given night," he said, "someone else is a bigger loser than me."

The celebrities orated gangtags they saw on the wall with an errant flourish. "*Somos locos y que*," read a leading-man, leaning into his cocktail. "Such a beautiful language they have. So romantic, so peaceful."

"This is great; in weeks this station will be littered with undesirables, riff-raff."

"I plan to give change—but only to the well-spoken ones."

"Oh, me too."

Michael smiled as he eavesdropped, a forced, squirmy smile. "With all the free pub and cameras, I'm surprised I haven't spotted Clara. How is she anyway?"

Susie shrugged. Just where to start with Clara? The hit show? The Emmy nomination? The makeover and body sculpting? "Clara is, uh, in a word, superior."

"Yeah." Michael set down his Sprite. "And I bet she's the first to tell you."

"At least that means I'm the first to know." Now it was Susie with the squirmy smile. "But she worries these days about self-inflation. So get this... to stem her ego, she stayed at a monastery the other month."

"You are joking."

"Wait, it gets better. So she arrives, right, and from the moment she walks in, she's giving the holy men there all these assignments and special requests."

"Priceless. I can see her now. 'Uh, excuse me, Brother. Do you think I could possibly get my monasticism *on the side?*'" Michael shook his head. "So our girl Clara turned into one of these?" he asked, indicating the antics of the celebs.

"She's probably as close to a confidante as I've got, Michael. Her concern for me is deafening. She'd give me half of anything she owned." Susie mashed her lips. "Having said that—yes. She has. Clara is absolutely a Beautiful Person."

"What does that make you?"

"Lumped with the other ninety-nine percent of Los Angeles—Part of a Beautiful Person's Entourage. A sidekick."

"Don't sidekicks deserve sidekicks of their own?"

She looked at Michael. *That* was the kind of one-liner she'd been hoping to hear from him. Was it lust she sensed—hopeful, anxious, light flask of lust—peeking through all his talk of friendship and warm reunions? She'd lured Michael away from his world. Back into a city he hated. So surely, surely, the two of them should get a little sex out of this raw deal. Maybe, but she sensed something else: coarse enjoyment. Some part of him was glad to see her alone, aimless, spineless, confused. But his coldness only made her lean closer, splash hot breath against his cheek when she spoke. Susie believed the body more courageous than the mind. She'd dated a man years ago that she'd lived in fear of sometimes—but at night she never hesitated, in sleep, to pull the covers off of him when her feet got too cold. The mind slipped into timid lapses, rote response. But the body was tropical, dense and prolific. Ready, always ready, to churn forward, even at risk of her mind's protests. Though the mind thought all day, it took it years or, sometimes, a lifetime, to recognize what the body had known all along.

After Chet, Susie had lost the patience to seek out a mate who coddled, who offered up decency beyond the bed. After Chet, Susie begged off Michael and men like him, and found herself drawn only to lovers who could circulate damage. Lovers who cornered and claimed, spoke only when speech was the final alternative to sleep.

What was she chasing? What end result had she had in mind?

They bought tickets for the 3:15 show at Mann Underground. Susie sifted through her purse, in case Michael wanted to pay for both tickets—which he did not.

Maybe she hadn't sifted long enough.

Seven Ugly Sundays was playing. The plot was claptrap, something about buzzards carrying hazardous waste, with a bit of revenge and a girl sewn in between AK-47s and dialogue abstaining from plausibility. Michael pulled off Susie's headset. "Ever seen a grown man cry?" he whispered—though he didn't need to, everyone else in the theater was involved in full-throated discussions, trading up, making deals, wearing the mark of the good life on their faces. "One more 'violent male bonding' scene should just about do it to me."

"I've given you more culture than you can handle, huh?"

"Sweetie, Vegas is twice as medieval as this place." She watched him shift in his seat. His belly was round and soft, like a scoop of sherbet. "We better hope they never institute a reapplication process for statehood. Our domiciles wouldn't stand a chance."

"Hey, it's a smile. I thought you'd lost it."

"I still have it," Michael said. "But you're right, I usually save it for shows. It's a Mirage smile."

"You make a lot of money out there."

He let his hands nap on his belly. "I do alright." She asked if they tipped well and he nodded. They must love you, she said, you must be good. "They tip me because they would hate to be me." The sound of villains getting iced leaked from their headphones, a guttural sweep of exit wounds, claustrophobic gunplay. "I get money for the same reason Salvation Army Santas do: People pay me to remind themselves they're blessed. People pay for my life because they don't have to live it. I've got a career because I'm one of life's great washouts."

"I'm unemployed," Susie said, "because I take my job everywhere and can't put it down." They looked around; no one was shushing them, not a body in the theater seemed to care.

"So how about that job? Clara gave me her version of your story. Two versions, actually. The first just depressed me, the other made your life sound like a Kafka novel."

"Right." Was it Clara's way to exaggerate because she was an actress? Or because it got results? *The Drama of the Gifted Child.*

"So where's the truth lie?"

The end credits began to advance, the names evaporating in a crawl from the top of the screen. Never before had Susie wished that a movie like this, a piece of escapist trash, would stretch on. "Nowhere in particular. It just lies."

"Listen to you. Timing, cadence, killer material to boot! You could do what I do in a minute! Just the right blend of stage presence and eviscerated esteem."

Clara complained to Susie—each chance she got—that she was misreading signs. "He lopes in and dashes your heart apart every weekend. You keep dressing for a first date; he shows up looking like he's come to paint your house." But Michael had loved Susie once, a thing Clara didn't know. The feeling had gone missing over the years, true, but Susie was sure she could retrieve it.

In time, though, Susie grew less sure. Grew sick of Michael's sexless attention. She was tired of washing her sheets for his weekend visits, only to have him sleep on the couch. She was tired of him apologizing for bringing half-wilted flowers, apologizing for falling asleep in the middle of movies, apologizing for being the kindest man she knew at a time when she couldn't seem to recognize kindness; or worse, a time when she tried to stare kindness down, burn holes in it, ignite it into something else.

During Michael's last visit, they made the mistake of buying wine. Michael made the mistake of holding her hand all the way through a Police LP, the same one they'd listened to back in high school, in Susie's bedroom. She set down her glass; Michael refilled her. She was going to do it, touch him, just as soon as it got to "Invisible Sun."

"I think the rest of the band should've seen a messy breakup coming," he suddenly scoffed. "Anyone that willfully calls himself Sting vants to be alone."

"And I guess that makes you the reverse," Susie said, breaking away. "You gave up your goddamn name to get in bed with Andy Williams and Siegfried and Roy."

She checked the wine bottle: empty. The peace and pleasure they'd felt a moment ago seemed to have slipped away, a chained dog gone madly free from a tight backyard.

Michael turned the turntable off. Gordon Sumner's voice warbled to a halt. "What about you? You still call yourself Susie Light. I don't even remember what your real last name is. I mean, if you're really so okay with losing the kennel, and okay with your acting dreams sinking into the La Brea Tarpits while you prop her majesty Clara's head up for public appearances, then why keep the fake name? Why not give that up?"

Oh, why does anyone let dead dreams possess them?

Susie stood. She emptied her ashtray, a legacy from Clara's last visit. Clara had inspected Susie's house with disdain, scorning her efforts to spruce it up for Michael, scorning Michael for playing games with Susie, scorning Susie for letting Michael continue them. "I don't know—hope?" She wondered if he'd call this time when he got back to Vegas. She wondered if she wanted him to. She wondered why it was not in Michael's power, or hers, to take themselves seriously.

November fizzled on, for the most part, incidentally. The summer heat was a distant memory. A few celebrities wore white ribbons shaped like dog collars, or halos, to honor the victims of the kennel incident. But who could recall, exactly, who the victims had been? Los Angeles was perceived as a harbor for disaster; in fact it thrived on the contrary: L.A. gorged on recovery, it was in love with the belief that single acts of temperance could wash away all excess.

Midway through the month, the final lawsuit against Susie was summarily dropped. The actor's agent had caught wind that "granting forgiveness" was in with 18-24-year-olds. Johnny London sent a fruit basket thanking Susie for all the attention. Susie called Clara. "I don't want to do it, Clara, so tell your manager thanks from me..."

"Linda? You got it. See, what did I say? All woe works itself out here. Linda's a real golden retriever."

Had Susie forgotten to wake up this morning? "She's—she's a real *what*? I don't understand."

"Golden retriever. One of *those terms* you forbid me to use. It's LA-LA slang for execs who fetch the goods. The ones who roll their sleeves up, swim through the cesspool of a project everyone thinks is doomed, and surface with an Oscar between their teeth."

After the good news about the lawsuits, Susie found herself afraid to stand still. She feared she'd float away with the slightest wind. There was nothing to prove, nothing demanded of her. For the first time she had no ties to this city, and for the first time, she found herself truly terrified of it. She would have to find out if there was a sum to the parts of Los Angeles, any sum at all. Or was it just parts?

Only dogs stabilized her now. Cigarettes and dogs. She'd begun hunting for their sight. Their trace. Any dog would do. She loved them all so much—plaintive beagle eyes. The pugs' fractured mugs. The burning loyalty of setters. Scotties, those bluish blessings. How a boxer's stomach scratches across an uncut lawn, making the grass softly hiss.

When she thought of dogs she thought of Michael. How he'd come to L.A. without an agenda. How he'd left without a kiss. When he'd been here, much had felt right. She'd forgotten the weight that was supposed to have been pinning her. Their time together had been like some trailer to a kind of movie she thought she'd never pay to see, but found her heart racing for all the same. She'd always presumed she would use dogs as her key to stardom. They would unlock the door for her, and then she'd give them up. Someday she'd groom the right terrier, nurse an ill greyhound back to health, which would lead to a producer or casting agent re-sculpting Susie's life into the mold of instant fame. They would discover her. Conan O'Brien would marvel at how she got her start. The humble beginnings from which she'd phoenixed. *After seeing your movie*, he'd say, *I find it hard to believe you were ever just a dog lady.*

But she *was* a dog lady. This was the plot twist she hadn't counted on. The dogs were the sum of her parts. At some point, caring for them began to give her pleasure in a way that headshots and auditions no longer did. The narrow bend of her dreams had shifted without telling her first.

The day before Thanksgiving, Clara invited Susie to the Pacific Ocean. On the deck of a pier, another offshoot of Mann's Chinese Theater—Mann Overboard—held its Grand Opening. The banner struggled to keep still for the cameras as DC-10s roared above, rocking and bending it in rude salutation. Wind whistled in Susie's face. If it had been this cold in the kennel, even for an hour, they all might have lived to see morning.

Roger Hewlett strolled by to say hello, refusing to walk away until Clara and Susie congratulated him on his People's Choice Award. Craig Capshaw waved his fork, a triangular piece of flapjack at its point waving in syncopation, like some miniature windsock. Alsie Ajay, who later that month would insinuate Clara's lesbianism in *The Hollywood Reporter*, hugged her now through her stole, as though a warm embrace in the present could erase future acts of spite.

Susie peered at her food. Her crêpes were gray. The birch syrup was dimpled with bitter clots and tasted like mildewed chocolate. Clara hardly touched her soapy oatmeal and blonde orange juice, transfixed as she was in the meandering sophistication of this power breakfast. Susie clasped her hand. "Tell me again—why do we eat here?"

Clara thumbed through Susie's hair and regarded her as a piece of clay. "It's not so bad. What doesn't kill you only makes you stylish." That was the end of that examination. Over the years, they'd shared pointed words, moments where they seemed on the outbreak of discovering crucial flecks in the other. But it would never happen in front of cameras. Publicity's promise was a kind of alchemy, molding people into alloys of their purer selves. True stars knew how to walk a banana path to stay in focus for a camera. True stars followed Tinseltown's rules to the letter. Susie was not that—no matter how much she'd dreamt of becoming it—she was no true star.

A soft flash of color, a khaki gold, lit up beneath the table just in front of Susie. This was unsurprising. It would be a retriever. Pacing beneath tablecloths. It would go unnoticed but for Susie; it would seem to be in search of a toy or ball, something to fetch, but would soon grow tired, about to give up the game in disgust, its tongue hanging close to the ground like a flag at half-mast. Susie was used to all of this; the retrievers must belong to someone, but she'd stopped wondering whom—from fear the answer might prove too logical. She needed, in her life, leaps. Sighing, she gulped Volvic and watched. This dog moved with fantastic fluidity, maneuvering past celebrities in small steps like a typist tittering on a keyboard. He went unnoticed, and seemed to be everywhere in the room at once, a strange figure that didn't belong at, but couldn't be removed from, the party.

The patio at Mann Overboard was loud, but Susie's head was louder, flush with the quizzical diction of new knowledge. Some loss allows its victims to kick it under the carpet, to, thanks to memory's weak range, eventually lose the loss, and its nagging persistence. All other loss proves perilous when ignored; at every turn it demands resistance, stance of character, hope for better days far into the hummable beyond…

The retriever was at Susie's feet, eyebrows arched like broken dashes. Ignoring her crêpes, her syrup, but not her eyes. She nuzzled his soft curly nape with her lips. "Yes boy," she said, "oh God yes, bring him back."

Attention, Please. Now

You are familiar with his stance. His stroke. The way he stepped out of the batter's box when his team ailed for runs, stepped out and just stood still, arms crossed, until the ump urged him back. He'd return to home plate, all right, but only after ignoring repeated warnings. He took no practice cuts and made no adjustments, unless you count that hard glare he'd direct toward the stands. Like he expected the scoreboard to apologize. More than once you probably brought your mitt along to the game, dreaming of catching one of his screaming line drives. God knows he tried to make your dream come true. The guy was a baseball repellant. For so many hard-throwing pitchers it was a familiar failure: Throw Mr. Spalding into his wheelhouse, then say farewell—108 red stitches, instantly soaring. The staggering career numbers of Steve Sprissel are done up in a bow for the Cooperstown Hall of Fame: .308, 485, 1,441. These are statistics that can retrieve discarded childhood memories of Little League and freshly cut backyard lawns. Not one of those 485 homeruns came cheap, either. Sprissel didn't get cheated on a single swing. Thanks to that approach, some sportswriters believe he *did* get cheated out of some of his career. If Sprissel had ever learned to choke up, he might've not torn that tendon during his sixth season, or wrenched that bum shoulder the year he turned thirty-nine, the last year he could see his way clear to play.

By the end of his last season—which he mostly spent in Triple-A and which I was there to chronicle—Sprissel was so gimpy, our organist had time to play the entire opening theme from *M.A.S.H* during his labored shuffle from on-deck circle to batter's box. That's when I realized the inevitable was closing in. Sprissel must've known, too, only he wasn't about to let his dignity get leeched by some stilted farewell tour, receiving rocking chairs in Gulfport or bronzed cowboy boots in Tupelo. But Sprissel deserved to be heralded in *some* way. And as the public address announcer for the Spartanburg Stags, I was the one with the means. The one with the loudspeaker. But management had warned me not to tout Sprissel's major league feats during his at bats. And they nixed the video crew's plan of showing highlight reels of his best hits in between innings.

None of us in the publicity department could fathom why Sprissel's tour with the Stags was being played down. Not that we knew what Sprissel was doing in the minors in the first place, taking hacks with hacks. We'd heard that some of Steve's family—his mamma, and a sibling maybe—lived just a few towns over from Spartanburg. But being closer to kin hardly seemed to me like grounds for giving up the major leagues.

Sprissel's official story for knocking around Triple-A was rehab for that bum shoulder, his latest spring sprung loose. He was only getting his timing back while he healed. But it was late June in the Deep South—the heat and humidity cranking so hard it smashed mirages, forced you to consort with reality. I saw the way Sprissel listened to bats crack in the cage. The way he watched dusk approach during night games. When I saw him limp down the first base line like he was running in a sack race, I knew: Tendonitis had sunk its career-ending claws into his ankle.

Here I should make a brief comment about me: My life had gone well. Better than my friends had predicted. They judged me like you do an abandoned mutt left tied to a tree: Anything I did beyond surviving and finding a warm bed out of pity would be gravy. But I had this habit of heisting my own good luck, so I'd grown warily protective of my job. It was the only glorious thing in my life left to piss away.

And it *was* a glory gig. A job so simple I could do it drunk—and often did, guzzling Pisco sours between pitching changes. I hid the hooch in a cabinet and held my bladder until our latest loss was in the books (closest john was in the press box, a six-minute hike). However—and what story's worth telling without a however?—my glory gig was almost over. I could see the scrawl on the wall. The big-league club we're affiliated with was in the throes of a massive fire sale, dumping their big salaries and hot prospects, reloading for a team five years down the line to coincide with the opening of a brand new ballpark. That meant Sprissel was gone.

And so was I. Just before our July 4th game, a pal in human resources tipped me off. My contract, he said, would be terminated early, by the turn of August. Management had a damage-control plan in place: utter anonymity. They'd decided not to distribute lineup cards to fans for the rest of the season; the equipment manager had been ordered to strip the names off the backs of players' uniforms. Canning me would leave the fans with no guide, no one to identify which castoff players they should be booing, making their miscues less conspicuous. "Can't I sue for breach?" I asked. Sure, my mole replied, but it would be a wasted gesture. Material witnesses had seen me drunk on the job. Perhaps even photographed it.

Now, was it my fault the sport moved at such a goddamn glacial pace?

Besides announcing names, my main duty was to inform our drowsy crowds what each player had done (or more likely, hadn't done) in his previous plate appearances. On that July 4th game, two drinks already in my belly, I figured if I was going down, I might as well speed the rate of descent. Sprissel's last at bat had been awful. He'd struck out on a fifty-five-foot curve with the bases jammed. But I didn't want to dwell on that. So when he led off the seventh, I failed to mention his failure from the fifth. Instead I announced: "Your attention, please. Now batting for the Stags, hitting and playing third, number forty-one, Steve Sprissel. Folks, I have it on the best of sources that, during last week's three-game set with the Shreveport Captains, Steve ate every meal at the Jumpin' Jambalaya Diner. He always ordered the special, with extra cayenne, and sides of corn bread and collards."

For some reason, the few fans left in the stands hollered over my little factoid. Maybe thrilled to hear that a future Hall-of-Famer went to the same greasy spoon they did. Upon hearing my comment, Sprissel glared in the direction of the main loudspeaker. Shook his head, beat mud crumbs off his cleats, stepped back into the box, then turned on a first pitch change-up, handcuffing the right fielder on one hop. Single and an error, runner on second, nobody out. A rally was on. The Stags actually forced our scorekeeper to work that half inning, plating five runs.

We still lost, of course: 7 to 6 in 12. But what a game! It would've been over in 9 innings, or 10 or 11, but Sprissel kept things knotted by making great defensive stabs in each of those frames.

Moments after the final out, as I was scurrying to the urinal, the team's scrawny adolescent batboy flagged me down, still wearing his batting helmet and uniform, its belt hitched way too high above his belly button. "You the guy who talks to the crowd?"

"Yeah."

"Mister Sprissel wants to see you."

"Yeah? Where?"

"Down in the clubhouse. Over at his locker."

"Mind if I piss first?"

For someone I figured for fourteen, the batboy's grip on my wrist was shockingly strong. "Man," he croaked, "I don't give a shit what you do or when. But Mr. Sprissel told me to get you to that clubhouse in five minutes, no excuses. So you'll just have to hold it."

The clubhouse was still abuzz with the foreign thrill of almost winning. But as soon as the players saw me being dragged in, they turned off their hip-hop CDs, tossed armfuls of socks and balls into their duffels, and evacuated what was surely about to become a crime scene.

Sprissel stood in a corner, holding as many bats at one time as he could without his wrists bending from the weight. "You the announcer?" he asked. I nodded. "Heard what you said in the seventh. I don't like stunts."

He let go of his bat handles and a whimpering grunt, all at once. Pine and ash clopped against the gray concrete. Ferocious echoes splattered off of every wall.

"I do like good luck charms, though," he went on, kneading the muscles in his forearms. "And I had two straight hits after your little crack."

"Three circus catches, too," I reminded him.

"Bullshit." He spat a slug of chaw into the shower drain. "You don't get credit for those. My defense never goes through slumps." He gazed at an oval mirror that hung above the showerhead. His reflection, blurred by steam, seemed sympathetic. After a moment he turned away from it. His reflection had answered a question; he hadn't wiped off all his eye black yet. Scratching at it with a thumbnail, he kept talking. "Plan on keeping this up? Your running commentary? Tailing me into diners and liquor stores? You got nothing better to do with your summer?"

"I could ask the same question," I said, careful to put away Steve's equipment while I spoke. My dad used to tell me that well-timed charity always takes the edge off of tart remarks. I wonder sometimes what TV show he cribbed that line from. Does anyone know?

"I mean," I went on, neatly creasing pairs of Steve's batting gloves, "you and me don't have much in common. But one thing we do share right now is near-unemployment. My days in the booth are numbered. And it ain't any different for you on the field. It's in the papers. Big club's salary dumping like crazy."

"Maybe they are. So?"

"So what I'm guessing is, they've already tried to dump you, but no other team's willing to take a flyer on your health."

"I'll play until the color's gone out of my eyes, I guess."

"Stags are twenty-two games under .500, Steve; those eyes oughta be black-and-white by now."

He shot me the tucked smile of someone who'd nearly given up on striving for discretion. "Buddy, you a student of the game? Then you oughta know I spent five long years in the minors before I got the call. Every one of my coaches put in a lot of effort to nurse out my bad habits. And I was in no way a 'can't-miss' prospect. So who's to say I'm not here to mentor the new kids? Just be a shepherd for next year's heroes?"

There was one sentence more about to slip past his teeth, lingering, but he held it back. Instead he asked me what I was doing later that night.

"Why," I asked, "you want to wine and dine me?"

Sprissel chortled. "I host a Texas hold 'em affair over at my rental house every week, me and the rest of the infield. But we need a fifth. You any good?"

"Awful."

"Perfect. You'll come tonight, then. Bring beer. Poison Dart Pilsner, long-necks, not the cans. They're my favorite. Feel free to tell the crowd that tomorrow. You can also tell them how I vacuumed up your wallet."

That is exactly what he did. I folded early and often that night. It was like the other gamblers held marked hands and I had transparencies. When Steve's phone rang around 1:30, I was sloshed, broke, and grateful to back away from the cursed table to get it. Sprissel, who was calling on a hundred-dollar bet, grunted approval. Took me a while to stagger to the phone—I nearly ran into a jib door on my way over—finally picking up on the eighth ring, half expecting it to be my loan officer. "Sprissel's residence."

"Well *you're* new to his game," a voice said, followed by a string of silence, and then: "Don't you know who I am?" Instantly I got conscious of the crackling mosquito zapper outside. Apprehension doesn't figure into my drunkenness often, but this woman's voice, as light and piercing as a needle, had done the trick. "I'm Steven's mother."

"Oh, OK. Steven's here, I guess." I looked down the hall. "Though kind of busy." Sprissel was talking trash about someone's hand. Not knowing if this woman would want to hear Steve bragging and loaded, I flattened my hand against the mouthpiece, stalling. As if he could sober up while his mom and a total stranger made small talk. "You want me to bring your son over to the phone?"

"What I want," she said, "is for you to send my son back home."

"I don't follow," I confessed.

"Course you don't, Mr. Voice of the Stags. Listen, just announce this. Tell him I'm off the clock. And tell him I already inherited enough trouble with the child I got; I won't baby-sit his trouble, too. Either he picks his kids up from my house, or the state does."

The next day at the ballpark, a memo from the front office awaited me. Stag management had approved, vigorously, of my unique approach for plugging products before player at bats. In fact, they'd left me lists of brand names and local businesses I should feel free to "work in" during this month's games, "or perhaps even longer..." Biting the ends of my sunglasses, I savored that ellipsis, its flirting suggestion that the demise of my job just might be negotiable, if I was willing to do the sponsor song-and-dance.

The Stags took the field that day looking as solid as toast in water. Each player seemed both thirsty and bloated. Apparently Sprissel's poker game wasn't last night's only source of entertainment. I knew I'd need great material to keep the fans from fleeing the stadium early: This game was going to sting. Our foe was the Royals' top farm team, and they were headed to the playoffs. Their catcher ran faster than our shortstop when he wasn't hungover. Our outfielders were fumbling fungoes and popping antacids; our first baseman was kneeling on the bag, blinking his bloodshot eyes and trying not to get sick all over his mitt. Only the most catatonic of ground balls wouldn't pierce our infield today.

In the first inning Sprissel came to the plate with one man on, one man out, and first base open. "Your attention, please. Now batting, number forty-one, Steve Sprissel... Hey Steve, after the pitcher intentionally walks you to first base here, your mom would like you to take another stroll. Seems you have a couple of small packages at her house you need to pick up."

Both pitcher and batter took umbrage at my poke. The pitcher disobeyed his manager's order to intentionally walk Sprissel, throwing one right down the heart of the plate instead, heavy on pride and light on gas. Sixty feet six inches later, Sprissel, whose bat had been sloped over his shoulders, crushed that ball into dead centerfield. A crater of hot, empty bleacher seats filled up suddenly with happy, boozy fans bolting for the souvenir ball.

I went easy on Steve the rest of the game, and even managed to start shilling from management's list. "After each and every home game, folks, Steve Sprissel reaches for the penetrating relief of BENGAY. Got big pain? Better call on BENGAY."

In the ninth, Sprissel's second homer broke a four-all tie and the Stags' long losing streak. Still, with baseball, one streak snaps and another flies on: The clubhouse batboy again was sent to fetch me to the locker room. This time I followed without resistance.

"The team's gonna start getting the wrong idea about us," I told Steve, watching a few of the players bolt. "Think I'm coming down here for conjugal visits or something."

"Dammit," Sprissel said, shaping his hair with a wet comb. "Don't touch my life. Don't bring up personal shit in front of twenty-five thousand fans."

"You get a look at that crowd?" I asked, glancing at a photo taped in his locker. "We probably drew less than twenty-five *hundred*. Besides, I didn't say that the packages were your two children. All I said was your mom wants to see you..."

"I don't mean that crack. I'm talking about the one from the fifth."

"The BENGAY remark?" I was incredulous. "But it's true. The trainers practically cure you in that stuff."

"No one needs to know how broke down I am."

"Steve, what difference does it make, if you're calling it quits after the season?"

He slapped his chest. "*I* decide when I call it quits!"

"Got your per diems, folks. Per diems." It was the clubhouse attendant, an old black man with spindly forearms, a faded tattoo of either a trident or a rake on one of them. He was handing out hotel and meal money for the players' upcoming series in Tupelo. Sprissel took his pay stub from the attendant and pierced it through one of his cleat spikes, which hung from a hook in his locker. It reminded me of shrikes, those birds that prepare for winter by hunting down bugs every day, impaling their surplus onto barbed wire fences, leaving those bugs behind until they are truly hungry.

Steve had laid down the gauntlet: Any mention of his decreasing skills would land me in his doghouse. Everything else, though? Fair game. Each time that I mocked him, I thought Sprissel would erupt, or at least shoot me that disgruntled frown of outfielders who run out of room chasing what they'd thought was a harmless fly. But in fact, the harder I hit Steve over the PA system, the harder he hit back at the plate. His average soared, courting .300. Fastballs he had been late on were now finding their way into the parking lot. He still trotted like a three-legged dog, but he was grinning while he did it.

It stayed that simple for a few weeks—that is simple's shelf life—where I kept going to poker nights, losing hands and stocking up on fresh piles of Sprissel's dirty laundry. Because we were gambling and because we were drunk, most of the material I gathered was on the blue side. I used it all anyway. "Your attention, please. Now batting third and playing third, number forty-one, Steve Sprissel. Steve Sprissel, folks: One satisfied girlfriend called his tongue a 'tool of the devil.'"

Then I started laying into other players. "Now batting, first baseman Edgardo Rios. Heads up, ladies. You'll know Rios is in the room when you hear his lone come-on line: 'Think it's too late for me to become an artist? 'Cause I just found my inspiration.'"

"Attention, please. Now warming up for your Spartanburg Stags, pitcher Dan Boyd, subject of tonight's trivia question. What do emery boards, nail files, and steel wool have in common? All three items can be found at your local Tall Order hardware store, or beneath the bill of Boyd's ball cap." Then our organist would rip out a verse of "Your Cheating Heart."

I always worried I'd crossed a line, but the players ate up the attention. The only complaints came from guys who had yet to receive my signature intros. They'd buy me beers after games, plying me with their skeletons and personal vendettas, written on old scorecards and Gatorade cups. These were men, for the most part, with no vertical movement left. Some had already been to the bigs and hadn't blossomed. Some had hit the wall of their talents too early. Triple-A was their last stand. What I offered them was a beam of recognition, and they soaked in the rays. When I revealed that one of our starting pitchers (a lefty) kept count of the road kill he ran over in his pickup truck, our audience burned him with boos. He only waved his hands towards his face, as if to summon the flames closer.

For fans of a team low on talent, gossip was as welcome as a game-winning hit. Attendance rose; turnstiles clicked; our house of worship was once again alive. My job security grew stronger; my name started making rounds. The Orioles invited me to audition for the big-league club, come spring. *This Week in Baseball* wanted to run a segment of my best clips. How 'bout that?

While airing out players' charms and vices, I would sometimes wear earplugs to drown out the crowds' fugue of cheers and catcalls, and just gaze at the shapes their mouths made. When they booed at my intros, they looked like they were about to apply lipstick; when they cheered, it looked like they were flossing out food lodged in the crags of their teeth.

And our Stags? They were playing more like a team. Long tossing before games. Extra batting practice. One outfielder tutored another for hours on how to shift weight with two strikes in order to protect the plate.

Our poker games grew more frequent, and each night we played, Steve's mom would call sometime after putting the girls to bed. I imagined her stretching the elastic corkscrew of the phone cord as far as it'd take her, so she could talk where the kids wouldn't hear. Probably the bathroom. Our talks would last anywhere up to an hour. By August I was spending more time on Steve's phone than at his table.

"I'll get it," I said one scorching night, after the phone's first ring.

"Get a number and a reason," Sprissel barked. "Cause I am *not* on the premises."

"I know the drill, Steve," I sighed. "I'll take your message."

"Our little houseboy," Rios remarked. Laughter trailed me down the hallway. I wondered which of them had played the role of mother-interceptor before I came along. Phone in hand, I strolled to the porch and climbed into Steve's hammock.

"Evening, Mr. Voice," she began, using the name she always called me by.

"We're speaking early tonight, ma'am," I replied, riding the hammock's waves and consulting my watch. "Have the girls been falling asleep sooner?"

Instead of answering, she asked, "Steve winning the pot tonight?"

"Not so much. He may pull even before the night's through."

"Then he's still got me beat." I heard tinging; she was arranging dishes or glasses. "I got his goddamn check in today's mail. Tell him that, could you? Tell him his sister wheeled on over to the mailbox and got it herself."

"Did she use the new ramp Steve had installed?" To my dismay, I was getting good at neutralizing Mrs. Sprissel's anger. All I had to do was pretend to stick up for Steve, and she'd get lost again in her own brown study. I'd still never met her, but had seen her in a photo taped inside Steve's locker door, a shot of her slouched on her couch between her granddaughters. She was wearing a shift, blue snaps down the front of it, her auburn eyebrows carefully drawn as if she'd soon be taking them out somewhere. During our phone chats I'd learned a lot about Steve's life, and her lack of one. I knew, for instance, about the accident Steve's kid sister Laurie had been in two summers ago. One weekend, drunk and hungry for privacy, Laurie and her boyfriend had skinny-dipped past lake buoys. She'd popped back up from a deep dive directly into an outboard motor. Left her with a severed spine.

The year before that accident, Sprissel had become a father. "I asked Steven, had he used birth control with the woman," Mrs. Sprissel was saying to me now. "And you know what he answered? 'Guess I just had *faith* that God wouldn't give me a baby.' And he was right. God didn't give him *a* baby. He gave him two. Then Steve handed them right over to me."

Not quite true. Steve had given it a go with the twins' mother. Before I knew him, I'd seen the couple together some nights confronting each other under the concrete tunnel connecting the dugout to the clubhouse. The pipes above them were sibilant with pressure from the hot shower water. The echoes sounded like joints cracking. Sprissel and the girl would get tangled up in a way that suggested half Nelson as much as lover's embrace. "Steve just wants you all to be provided for. That's why he still plays."

"He told you that, huh?" Mrs. Sprissel asked, pouring herself water. "At first we had no idea. How much cash we'd need for his sister's hospital bills. The physical therapy. But now we know we got enough. *He* knows." I heard the sound of a tissue being yanked through a plastic slit.

"When the girls' mother skipped out, Steve asked me if he should quit. Point blank. Should've snatched his bait. But I didn't. Now he's had time to see how it is on my end. All the work that goes into it. Think he likes what he sees? He wants to pretend he does this for nobility, fine. But he just don't want to leave the diamond. Once he does, he's stuck here with me."

"Season's almost over. When it is, maybe he'll be ready to retire," I suggested, the shrug obvious in my tone. Steve, more and more, was talking about rehab, advances in medicine, the prospects of latching onto an American League club.

"*Retire?* Mr. Voice, if you're scared of the cold and dark, do you leave the campfire? Remember that game last week in Georgia? I watched every out on the closed-circuit TV. Steve got a full-count curveball. Pitch buckled his knees. It was sneaky and perfect, and the umpire was ready to punch him out. But then Steve spun around, glared at the ump, and that was that. Strike three became ball four, and Steve was free to take his base. That's what he can't give up. Those free bases. That royal treatment. People waiting in line to tell him his feet float six inches above the turf."

"Everyone's always talking about Steve's patience at the plate," she continued. "Know the difference between a single to center and striking out to end the inning? Point-oh-oh-three. Three one-thousandths of a second. That's not patience. It's reflex." Mrs. Sprissel exhaled heavily. "Painful physical therapy, two hours daily. Dressing and feeding three girls in the morning, and barely finishing the job before lunchtime. *That* is fucking patience."

After dashing off Mrs. Sprissel's latest message on Steve's dry erase board, I checked my watch. We'd play maybe six more hands of poker. Then drive home drunk from local bars or Steve's house, justifying our decisions not to spring for taxis because downtown was so deserted. The town lights would smear like drizzle as we drove by them. All four wide lanes of state road 56 would be empty except for our cars. How bad a shape would we have to be in to crash with all the lanes to ourselves?

When I returned to the poker table, it was gamy with dried beer and everyone was relaying their off-season plans. Greg Langford, our shortstop, was going to take up golf. All the players in the show golf, he reasoned bitterly.

He wanted to find out which courses. Which clubs to buy. What to wear. He was going to start acting more like a pro when he stepped off the diamond. "How 'bout you, Sprissel?" he asked. "You about to start the longest off-season of all. What's the first thing up your sleeve once you retire?"

"Shit. Do some autograph shows, I guess. Just kill time in New York or Florida or Vegas until deer season. I want to bag a ten pointer this year."

"Heard you was pulling offers to join broadcast booths. Even maybe manage."

"Yeah, well," Sprissel said, grinning, "it'd need to be a good goddamn offer. To take me away from cleaning out all your guys' pockets week after week." Steve picked up an empty Pilsner bottle, turned it upside down, and began to swing it like a miniature bat. "Tell you what, though. And this is no joke. Seattle's ball club is gonna be hunting for a new DH this winter. Been thinking I might do a couple years there. I could get used to all that smoked salmon."

"What about your family, Steve?"

Sprissel checked his swing, staring at me over the green bottle. "What do you mean?"

It was like he and I were suddenly looking at the same thing, a bomb strapped to the top of a drifting ferry, and as slow as it was going, there was nothing we could do to stop it from docking and detonating. "I mean your daughters. Lynne and I mean Nina. Your sister. Your mother, Steve, for God's sake."

Rios pointed at me from behind his fanned-out straight. "Cool it. We all got a right to get temporary amnesia from our problems."

"No," said Sprissel, puckering on a lit cigar. "Keep at me, kid. Pot's getting bigger, and my fortunes always seem to lift off once you start dissing me."

"All these women," I began, only to stutter, "who've been w-w-waiting out the year for you." I had him frozen at the plate. Only I was like the ump in that game in Georgia—had my hand up but couldn't bring myself to punch him out. Sonofabitch, it'd been great, those few weeks, hanging with this almost Hall-of-Famer, sleeping untroubled sleep, with no anguish about where the money for my next light bill would come from. And I just couldn't do it, shoot my good luck in the foot again, even if this time I had a reason.

So I shut my mouth.

Or rather, I kept it occupied with Pilsner, so it didn't have the chance to sabotage me. I folded for the night, drank myself onto Steve's couch, becoming so much dead weight Steve didn't even bother trying to move me until morning.

29

By noontime, when Steve drove me to the ballpark, it'd already climbed to ninety degrees. I started on my workday Pisco sours far too early, before the first inning was even in the books. They rolled down my throat readily as raindrops, cooling me in a way air conditioning just couldn't. During the game I ably hawked our town's pharmacy, bowling alley, and two antiperspirants. Then it was time to do my eighth-inning guest interview: Louie, head mechanic at Loyal's Auto Body. The back fender of my Bonneville was crumpled, and the idea of getting a discount fix from a mechanic lifted my spirits. I darted to the toilet before the interview, leaving a note for Louie on how to announce the players himself, something I'd been letting the guests do on their own lately. Made them feel important, and maybe gave them incentive to up my local business discounts. As I walked out, our cleaning lady slipped in, her two young kids following close behind, little helpers holding trash bags and that dustpan that's got a kind of metal jaw. It surprised me seeing her in the eighth—usually she waited until the game was over to pick up and dust—but what the hell, I figured, this way I'd come back from the john to a clean workplace.

After doing my business in record time I raced right back to the booth, but apparently not fast enough. The mechanic stood outside the booth. His face looked perplexed. "You aren't announcing the players, Louie," I observed, grinning. "You aren't doing your duty. What, you catch a case of stage fright?"

"Holy goddamn," Louie at Loyal's said, breathing frantic, like he'd just been in a fender bender himself. "Dude, tell me you got a fucking key to that office."

"Sure I do, Louie, sure I do," I said, though I'd lost it months earlier. "But we don't need it. Cleaning lady's in there. She'll let us back in."

"Buddy, she's the one what locked us out." I stared back, not comprehending. Louie pointed inside the booth, and I saw that it wasn't the cleaning lady at all—it was Steve Sprissel's mother. And she was passing my live microphone back and forth between her two grandkids. "Haven't you been listening out there?" Louie demanded.

"To what?" I asked, reluctantly, like I was about to tip the first domino in some amazing labyrinth. Louie at Loyal's grabbed my wrist, the way that skinny batboy had done, and dragged me down a tunnel. When we reached the end, I could hear the same sounds everyone in the stands was hearing. The sound of Steve's two kids, alternating and amplified, shrieking out to their daddy to *take us back, please, take us back* over the loudspeaker. The players, umpires, fans, and coaches were all frozen. Our entire stadium was silent.

"We gotta do something man," Louie yelled. "Gotta break that door down."

Before we could, though, Sprissel had emerged from the dugout. He climbed slowly up the cement stairs, and hobbled right out onto the field, taking these slow, lopsided steps, not stopping until he reached the middle of the diamond. Red-faced, he put a hand over his heart, tipped his cap toward the booth, and, after a few moments, gave his mom the OK sign.

"It's over," I said, realizing with a chuckle my pants were still unzipped. "Steve's just come through. The lady's gonna let us in now."

Louie leaned in. "I don't really pay attention to the Stags," he confided. "I'm a golf man. But that's not typical baseball. Right? I mean, what the hell *was* that?"

"Patience," I said, "paying off."

The next inning was the ninth. With the game tied, Steve was due up second. During what would turn out to be Sprissel's final professional at bat, he was plunked by a tight fastball. Dinged right off his funny bone, and it had to hurt bad—this was his only plate appearance, as long as I'd seen him play, without elbow pads and body armor. But he didn't call for time. He winced, laid his bat down, and took his base. Then took a healthy lead off of first, which the pitcher allowed: Steve was no threat to steal. On the very next pitch, though, I swear, Sprissel scored all the way from first base on a long single that caromed wildly off the right field wall. Not one person partial to America's pastime could've expected that kind of dash, not out of those legs, and that's just why Steve's wager worked. The right fielder got flushed and missed his cutoff man by thirty feet. Two infielders swiveled away from the oncoming throw, like they were the finish line tape breaking in some race the baseball had just won. It may have been the most mad twenty seconds of our entire season. Caught up in the play, I clean forgot to check for the third base coach's signal as Steve ripped around the base paths, but I do like to think the green light to head home was not an order, but an instinct.

The Mean

Twenty after four on Tuesdays, the chimps went berserk. Their mayhem followed an arc (source, midpoint, apogee, to trace it on a rose compass). First the troop would pet the safety glass lightly, as though consoling it. Then they'd prowl the perimeter of their cage, feet and knuckles skimming concrete. This was a warning—it meant their hearts were getting hotter, meant they were close to getting mean. They took it out on the bars. The chimps rattled the iron, clamping down, wailing to be let in on whatever secret it was outside they could smell and hear but not see. Sometimes the head zookeeper would forget to put up their toys. That was when Tuesdays howled. The primates would hurl Wiffle balls, spinning tops, rattles, and building blocks at the bars. The noises were spiky, arrhythmic, and relentless. The chimps wouldn't let up for hours.

By then, Charles Shales and his high school students had killed their joints, cached their pipes, and vacated the hideout. By then they'd left the Milwaukee Zoo, gathered their paraphernalia, having taken pains not to leave behind any trace of their festivities under the scaffolding behind the Monkey House; they trusted the harsh winter winds to scatter the scent of drugs by morning, and the chimps' memory of the commotion to dull and fade. The group would ask Shales if he wanted to hang with them, but Shales would decline.

He'd have to come home and get his head unclouded in a hurry. Shales would have work to do in preparation for tomorrow's remedial algebra classes—maybe, say, a hundred papers to grade on the associative property—with a blue pencil and a bag of salt and vinegar potato chips as his only anchors. The high from the joints would be all but dried, just a small static gristle scatting somewhere in his head. But the pain wouldn't be back yet; that was the main thing. He figured he could barrel through most of his stack before the pain supplanted the pleasure.

After washing the skunk and zoo from his hands, Shales would pop in live bootleg tapes of Liddy's band, Some Assault. Would listen for her crisp drumwork, urgent four counts, and harmony vocal. He would bend over and tap his fingers against the speakers, head bobbing. The band was confident, brash, numinous.

They sounded—just as rock should—like polished hell.

The first ten papers Shales graded would actually be fine. But then he'd come to some kid who argued, say, that the associative property made every integer negative, once what was outside the parenthesis multiplied with the numbers inside of it. But this kid wouldn't call the process multiplication; he'd call it "claiming." He'd write for his sample problem: $1 (4 + 1) = -5$, and then explain his reasoning: *"When the first one is claimed by the four and the other one, it's all bad. The first number is now a minus, and so's the second. Whatever number's are inside the parenth thesis have control over the other number. No matter how much bigger that other number is."* And Shales would check the kid's name on the front of the paper and wince. "You're wrong in every way," Shales would write, "but you show your work well." He'd draw a C. Then a twinge would kick up, just beneath the skin. He would try not to look at the clock, mentally punishing himself when he took two glances in the same minute, wondering when Liddy would be finished with her show, when she'd slip into his room and climb in his bed.

Wednesdays they held faculty luncheons at the high school. These were designed for teachers to relay disturbing student behavior, or to reveal any intimate grievances the students had confided. Usually everyone just swallowed their cafeteria food and left. The only real issue they wanted to discuss was, "Higher wages or we walk!" But they gave wide berth to *that* subject; the district superintendent was always in attendance, ass pressed against the radiator. Shales imagined that, at the first sign of teachers talking contract negotiations, the superintendent would press some button with his butt warning the governor and, that night, a midnight law would be pushed through the Wisconsin legislature declaring faculty luncheons off-limits to everyone but students.

After lunch Shales spotted Mary grading quizzes by the water fountain. He darted through the crowd to stand by her. "Hey Charlie," Mary said, picking sesame seeds from her undersized yellow sweater. "It's been many bells since we've been together."

Shales affirmed. The motor in the drinking fountain turned over. The other teachers filed out from the lounge, dumping their food trays. The smell of burned chicken patties wafted up from the trashcan just inside the door. Shales and Mary stood without saying anything. When Shales had first moved to Milwaukee, Mary had made overtures of friendship, had checked up on him. Since he'd gotten sick, most of their interactions consisted of long, desiccated silences.

"So," she finally asked, "how's your weekend shaping?"

"Oh, I can't think about that on a Wednesday." Any time other than the current moment felt far off to him. The weekend was an aeon from now; yesterday's high, the Pleistocene era.

She pointed to his eyes, which he must have forgotten to dab with Visine. "Looks to me like your weekend's already begun."

"Student papers. Can't get enough of the little geniuses. What about you? Are you doing something, going to a show?"

"No more movies for a while," Mary said with a laugh. "Not with 'the Spoiler' lurking."

"The Spoiler" was what the newspapers called Vondra Popeil. She had been haunting Milwaukee's largest cineplex since midsummer, gaining notoriety and ire for standing outside the main doors and giving away the resolution to every new movie. "They get married, have two children. It's van Heuk who wrote the ransom note. Penny dies courageously, her mother gives up crack, they leave it open for a sequel." Since she was purchasing tickets to the movies, the police couldn't pick the Spoiler up for trespassing.

"It's too bad, too," Mary said, as if answering a question. "I could use more stories without endings. If she'd only cover my eyes and ears *before* each picture ended, I'd laud her with lilies." Mary was an English teacher, and Shales loved her turns of phrase. He loved how she could get words to do what she wanted—she probably didn't see it this way, but she'd tapped into a formula. She could create a little beauty with her metaphors and rhythms, a beauty that seemed to intercept the misery of time. In her own way she was preventing endings.

On the Thursday before the last Tuesday, Liddy came over to Shales's apartment after a bad practice. She was wearing a tank top with an iron-on peanut butter cup on the front. "I can't do this much longer." She clutched her hands, folded her knuckles—this was to work out the tension in her fingers. She gripped the drumsticks too tight, always too tight. "Charlie," she said, "you can only tell your friends they suck so many times before it puts the friendships in jeopardy...Maybe I should just give up and join the marching band."

He thought of her group, five of them, a prime number, indivisible. Then again, so was one. "If you join the marching band, I could come watch you play. In fact I'd get paid for it. But honestly? I hate pep rallies and the marching band gives me chiggers."

Liddy laughed and pulled off her shirt. Her breasts were rosy, the skin hot. She placed her arms around Shales, still holding the shirt. He could feel the fabric and the drying sweat on his neck. This was normal, he told himself, her coming over and peeling off her clothes. His listening to her discuss her career as a rock star while his cells tore one another to pieces like feral dogs. "So do you really want to do that? Quit? Don't you want the band to reach its full potential?"

"I am the full potential," she declared, rolling into bed. "My beat's the only good thing about us." She swallowed six pills, three shapes, four colors. Shales had asked her once why she never smoked with him. "Where you're going's good for you," she'd said. "I need a higher high."

"So what was the problem tonight?" Shales asked. "Same as always?" Liddy thought the guitarist played like one of those solo-hogging dinosaurs from the seventies. "Jilt's really getting to you. I've seen the way you look at him the day after a show. Like he's stolen your best friend or your diary."

"I don't have a best friend," Liddy said. She darkened the room by pulling the sides of the pillow over her face. "Or a diary." She placed her hand in Shales's, into his grading hand, and let it lie. His lesson plans fanned out onto the floor. She'd be asleep inside of two minutes. It wasn't like before, though before wasn't so long ago: They wouldn't have sex, probably never would again, and this suited Shales, because when they did have sex he felt he had something to live for. It wasn't that it was so good, or so thrilling. It was that it was irrevocable. No matter where Liddy went, what records she sold, or what shelters she wound up scurrying in and out of, she would remember him inside of her. This thought was one of the few that still made him feel vigorous.

"It's not like Jilt's not replaceable," Liddy mumbled, more asleep than not. "It's his stash we can't replace. If he wasn't connecting us he'd be gone. I mean it, if what he was giving us wasn't helping you, he'd be a fucking antique."

She poked out from under the pillow when she heard Shales set the alarm clock. "Three hours' sleep. Can't you let me stay the whole night for once?" Shales ignored her bait. He wasn't going to get drawn into this argument again. They had agreed to these terms: She could stay over, but they had to get her out of Shales's apartment before first light, before his neighbors rose for the day.

Friday morning before the last Tuesday. The oncologist greeted Shales warmly, not a good sign. His crinkled midwestern accent was based on inverse proportion: The more dire things had become, the less urgent his inflection. It's metastatic, he said. It has spread to the liver. Does he want to be put on a list for something experimental? Or does he want to double the chemotherapy? No. To both.

The doctor's voice glazed over—grew so calm Shales wondered if he should expect to die this very moment. Shales has had breast cancer for nine months. He has been given an LHRH, administered cyproterone acetate; tamoxifen; chemo in tandem with CAMs; and of course the antacids, Alka-Seltzer, Tums, false trails leading nowhere. The only things that haven't let him down are the fat joints and the short nights with the seventeen-year-old stray who plays drums in bars. The seventeen-year-old he just dropped off, who by now is behind the McDonald's Dumpster puffing meth, killing hours until the school bus comes.

That night Shales went to the Cineplex; *Hit and Run* was showing. He could smell chocolate being munched, could hear the parents brushing Kleenex below their kids' leaky noses. He turned and looked, directly and earnestly, into the projector. By then *Hit and Run* had thoroughly annoyed Shales. Some facile load of bullshit he could've guessed even if the Spoiler hadn't screamed it in his ear earlier, where the rich girl and boy live fickle lives but learn about themselves thanks to the drifter they accidentally hit while driving their convertible; where the gentry falls on hard spiritual times but is repaired, ultimately, by this poor drifter who shows them how much they've been neglecting. When the end credits scroll, the gentry is more compassionate and the unemployed man has become the gentry's new caretaker, and there is a sense of justice, a sense that light rewards the lost.

The reels of his own plot were what Shales wanted to pick through, anyway.

On Reel 1 was Liddy—thin girl with dark-dyed hair, wet-looking like a tarmac after a rainstorm, knobby elbows, pale pink gums, small teeth that were sharp and told a story, tight stomach, trace of fat at the hips, wrists wrapped in white tape. The day of the first semester final exam, she'd worn a jacket with the McDonald's logo, a Taco Bell T-shirt, and a Jack in the Box necklace. She kept her bangs out of her face with a hairpin shaped like a carrot that had come from a juice bar. Shales approached her as he passed out ScanTrons. "I like the accessorizing." "Thanks, Mr. Shales." He had been Mr.

Shales to her then. She had been the girl who kept dropping her pencil during the exam. Playing him for a fool, dipping down for quick peeks at a cheat sheet pressed between her sock and her boot. He told Liddy to stay after class. That was when she first called him Charlie.

Their conversation was initially gummy and awkward. I wasn't scheming, man. You were just dropping your pencil? Just dropping it. I drum, Liddy said. Beat skins. It takes a few days to recover feeling in my hands after shows. Against better judgment, Shales gave her the floor. She explained how good it felt, splitting time, or resurrecting it, as though it were dead, with booze and X buzzing in her at one on a school night. And Shales must have grown concerned and told her to go see a doctor, or at least the school nurse, about her hands. Then he must have slipped and mentioned himself. Mentioned, in passing, everything. He must have felt exhausted keeping secrets, must have been drawn to the prospect of giving away his secret, unburdening himself of it. Or, he was looking for another identity to climb into. He told Liddy he'd pass her if she wrote an essay defining the mean. She agreed and clasped his hand, and told him she was sorry about the cancer, Charlie, and there's something I can do for you, if you want.

Next Reel: Liddy gets on Shales's bad side. She doesn't show for a conference. He looks over her essay as the light outside weakens. Winter comes early in Wisconsin. She clearly has problems explaining math concepts in print. She thinks the mean is the number that occurs most in a given set. She's fairly bright, and he doesn't want to fail her, so he agrees to let her explain it to him orally. But she doesn't show, making Shales late for chemo. Shales decides on humiliation tactics. He takes out a Rolodex and calls Liddy's parents. A nightclub manager answers. He is amused to be speaking with a math teacher and is mentally recording every word Shales says for later tonight, when he'll retell it over a few cold ones. Liddy's the little wispy piece, yeah? Yeah, I think you've been had, teach. I may have three or four kids running around I don't know about, but Liddy ain't one of them. Parents? Don't think she's got 'em, truthfully. I think one died and the other dropped her. Beyond this I don't know, and since I'm not social fucking services I don't need to know, yeah?

Third Reel: Liddy walks in during conference hour the next day. High. Got my days confused, she giggles. I heard you spoke to Mom and Pop, and my uncle Jack Daniels. She giggles. I played last night and my head is still on naptime, so I guess you can flunk me. But Charlie, I really don't care. Last night we played great. I played great. I pounded so hard I couldn't say if it was the sticks cracking in two or my arms. She giggles. I'm no student. Fuck school, I'm a student of life. Too much life. Shales listens and nods, not with the consternation he thought he'd feel. The girl has guile, noise, and not a prayer of living past thirty at the rate she's going. She's his hero. She has talent—although most of that talent is anger, and will burn away as she forgets the family she is angry at. Liddy sighs: Am I expelled, Charlie? He rips her essay in two. I'll be dead inside a year, he says. That's an extreme. You live like Dionysus, that, too, is an extreme. The mean is balance. The mean is when both of us are sleeping. Any questions? Liddy says no, and Shales prints an A on her hand, on the spot where the stamp for last night's club is rubbing away. She pushes close to him and draws sticky, sweet breath on his face. I told you I would help you and I mean it. Can you smell this, taste this? This is what I'm good for. Prepare yourself, she whispers, for a little peace.

Shales found himself in the Cineplex parking lot, warming his Buick. He had no idea when he'd left the movie theater, or if *Hit and Run* was over yet. The car heater churned, biting into the accumulated sheet of frost. What if the Spoiler had approached him years ago, offering to tell him the ending he was living now? What if she'd told him that right out of engineering school he'd be designing Apache rotors to be peddled off to unconscionable regimes in shaky state-sponsored auctions? Or had told Shales that eventually he'd muster the courage to quit that job and leave California, where medicinal marijuana was allowed, for Wisconsin, where it wasn't, but only then would his body fall apart? Would he have believed her?

But there was no one to tell him the state of things, only X rays and biopsies...he was getting ahead of himself. Trying to finish the problem without showing his work. An equation was just a story condensed into one sentence, or a narrative in reverse. With a narrative, a reader waded through rows of flowery words hoping to come away with one core truth—with equations, a reader picked over the core truth, and then revised it, plugging in factors and numerals, deciphering, extrapolating, justifying its presence to make sure it belonged at all.

Reel 4 was Shales in transition, resigned to his desperation, letting it take charge. Reel 4 was when his view of life reversed: Until now he'd been a disciple of moderation. He had tried to exist in the mean: meaning balance, meaning restraint, meaning a lapse in judgment in one thing—say junk food—could be remedied only by a stricter regimen in a corresponding situation—say ten minutes longer on the stationary bike. But as the pain intensified, all that sentiment broke down. Shales sought out extremes. He told himself he was still sticking to his philosophy; it was just his body was so wracked and torn apart that he had to respond in kind; the more apocryphal the sources the better. Shales tried support groups—a half dozen, until he forgot which building and which night and which of his peers were in remission and which metastatic. He sought out a therapist but couldn't afford her human kindness. He tried acupressure, shark cartilage, gin, and Dramamine, tried to take up the clarinet again, tried a whorehouse for the first time since the Army, tried mistletoe (which actually did keep him sedate through mild pain...could be just the act of chewing, or the unofficial theorem that enough shit flung results in some of it sticking). Then there was that night he drove over to Madison—on a recommendation—and was buzzed into a warehouse with an awful draft. Shales didn't remember it all, but the process involved having his head swaddled in a tunic, and resting his chin inside what amounted to a large rubber band suspended from the ceiling. He felt hands; they smelled of camphor; he heard chanting in French. All the while Liddy and her offer were looming, dilating, looking less crazy.

So the deal went down. Liddy arranged to be caught with a note in class. Shales pretended to catch her and confiscate the note. The note was from Jilt, the guy who had the stuff, and it contained the details of the deal. *Meet at 2 sharp. You dick us you die. You squeal you die. You late you lose. Milwaukee Zoo. Monkey House. By the bush's. Don't look like a teacher. But don't look like a teacher trying not to look like one.* Shales tried to catch Liddy's eye to confirm these strange directives, but she refused to look up from her desk. Shales left school before noon, feigning nausea in fourth period. He was sure it was a set up. He wondered if he should buy a gun at Wal-Mart. But he wound up bringing nothing but the hundred, in twenties, specified in Jilt's note. Oh, and wide-ruled paper, in case they had nothing to roll the pot into. Shales took back roads to avoid being seen, long and vacant streets in the industrial zone, Devore Drive, Jackson Circle Park, past the old cinema where he and Mary—before he got diagnosed—used to watch films together, past the alley behind the Pink Rink, closed now for six years, and so on and on.

It was bitterly cold but the sun was bright and feisty. He realized why this spot had been chosen. Sheets of blue tarp covered cranes and bulldozers: Construction was underway on the Monkey House, and the grounds were closed to the public. The area was abandoned. Shales stood in one spot, just behind a pile of pallets. His brow was moist and he felt more nervous than he ever had before a CT scan, or lying naked on tissue paper in some featureless examining room in Oncology. As he waited he watched his squat shadow lengthen in front of him, flatten, as though the sun were beating it submissively into the concrete.

The kids showed precisely four hours later, two hours late. They walked not toward Shales but past him. He didn't turn to mark their progress. A minute of silence passed, another, and another. Finally he was sent for. Liddy emerged, took his hand, and led Shales beneath the temporary scaffolding in back of the Monkey House.

No one seemed happy to see him. Of course, he was the variable in this equation. They had all done pot before. They had been doing pot four, five, six years: as tagalongs to older brothers, at school dances to relieve the awkward roaming in the gymnasium, in bathrooms, in basements, in bed, taking a hit or two to help them relax before big exams. They had built this routine at the zoo—it was their textbook—and they were wary of allowing intruders in on the magic, especially middle-aged teachers in sweater vests. But Liddy had vouched for Shales and had, apparently, sweet-toothed Jilt.

Then Jilt reached for his inside jacket pocket, shoulders wide like he was baring his chest for the world. As he made these motions the group gathered round. Since there'd been nothing in the way of formal introductions, Shales listened closely for names: he knew Liddy and Jilt, Mikey had dropped out of his class the year before, there was the guy in back not speaking or being spoken to, and another one, either Claude or Claw, Shales wasn't sure which.

"You score kind?"

"Shit. Naw. DeJuan tells me like ten seconds ago he won't deal us out no more. Shit is that?"

"Shit."

"He try to up the piece's price?"

"Naw naw, check it out. DeJuan's a pussy, simple as that. Told me he cut out on school, cut out on dealing, all so he could work on his game at the yard. On his game—he's five foot *seven*. Can work on his game all damn decade, he's still gonna wind up just another unemployed nigger with a crossover dribble."

The quiet one, the one in back, looked at Shales for the slightest fraction of a second, to see if Shales was cool. Shales was cool. Shales was fighting pressure that was bench-pressing against his organs. He was cool with anything that would take that away.

"So then where'd you get the shit? Secondhand?"

"Would I fuck you like that? The shit is à la Ray's brother."

The dim thin eyelids rose. "Ray's *brother*?"

Mikey held his arms triumphantly overhead, bent at the elbows. "Touchdown!"

"Yeah yeah, but smoke good. Proceeds from this afternoon will contribute to posting bail. Ray's brother got DEA'd hard."

"Shitting?"

Jilt shook his head. "Real. They spun him, spun his house for six and a quarter. Spun dry."

There was a moment of silence to mourn the loss of Ray's brother to the Milwaukee penal system. Then the quiet kid approached his old teacher. "Shit Shales, this is your lucky day!"

The kid took a hit off something, and Shales stopped sweating. It was the first time in fifteen minutes they'd addressed him, and he figured if he didn't speak now, they'd forget he was here. "I don't know if you've been filled in on...what you've been filled in on. But I really want to try some of that...I'd pay...name your price."

"Name my price what *I* got?" The kid moaned ruthlessly. "Well now, let's see..."

"Kyle!" Liddy screamed. "He's a first-time customer. Just like anybody else. First-timers are always right; don't be a fuck."

Shales turned to Liddy, trying to beg her off. "But this is what I want."

Mikey grabbed Kyle's joint. "No, see teacher, time to get schooled. This shit is just that, shit. What you want is what my man Jilt's got under the jacket. I'll translate it to math terms. Kyle's joint is addition and subtraction. Any penny you pay for that weak-ass, beaned, grown-in-a-tub shit is a penny too much. Kyle knows that, but Kyle knows he can't get high off anything anymore, and he just smokes for the recreation. What's in Jilt's jacket is logarithms and cosines. Hard-to-fucking-get."

"See what you want," summed up Claude or Claw, "is the kind."

Again Shales looked to Liddy for guidance, and again got none. "I'm sorry. A kind? Kind of what? Kind of brand?"

"No," said Jilt, impatient at how long it was taking to hammer home the lesson, "the Kind." He pulled out the first bag and held it to his nose. "The Kind. You can't think about it this much or the shit won't feel good when you finally get around to doing it."

"Well, I have the money, old twenties, pre-1990, like your outline said. So can I buy some and..."

"We're waiting," Jilt said, checking his watch. "You should wait, too. You've waited this far for your hit. You might as well wait for 4:20."

"What's 4:20?"

The boys snickered, embracing the power of slang knowledge. "It's a special time. A minute we all hold dear." Later Liddy would clarify: 4:20 was ceremonial, teatime for stoners. Then she would step in before Mikey could take Shales's money to test the alleged Kind, and make sure they weren't beaning Shales. Liddy was his protein and his protector that first Tuesday. She knew Shales needed her and shocked herself by rising to the occasion.

Shales doesn't really remember the details anymore of the actual smoking; time wasn't passing, just sensation. Like the first time he'd had the courage to suck up all the way, and it was like he was breathing a garden. Or how Liddy's hair glinted under the sun, a color that couldn't have existed except in magazines or under black light—waxen, mordant magenta. The sight of mechanical lungs Mikey produced from his backpack—"This is how you use a bong, man"—and how the smoke from the Kind he paid for waved feebly through the bong's chamber, like the hands of a man tentatively poking ahead in a pitch-dark cave. Shales's lower jaw muscles fibrillated between hits. He pinched his skin for the friction. The magic had come: It was now dullness in Shales's skull, not pain in his stomach, claiming authority. The dark pearled eyes of reconnoitering seagulls, settling on the zoo grass, a stopover on their way to Lake Michigan—the birds stood at their stations, tensed, and took slow, deliberate steps toward the humans, eyes surveying the sub-rosa scene point to point like Secret Service agents—filling him at once with both paranoia and peace. Come to get him. The monkeys hitching up their noses and moaning from within the cage. Come to get him.

After a few hits Shales decided to ease himself into the conversation. The gang was talking about pranks—pulling the wool over authority's eyes, getting one's way despite the system, all that kid shit that really was cool. He would play it cool too; he wouldn't just start in. He'd just add a few *uh-huh*s or *right*s every now and then, until the others were comfortable with his presence. Then it hit him. No one was talking. They were busy smoking, or inspecting each other's skin for veins, or doing these things and looking at Shales. It was him; he had been the only one talking all along.

So it didn't bother anybody when Shales just started a new story, the one he'd been planning to say while busy listening to, and trying to politely interrupt, himself: "So I mean, just because someone's good with numbers doesn't mean they won't fuck with you. You know that Catherine the Great's math tutor, guy was Swiss, Euler, Leonhard Euler? Euler once tricked all these wealthy, erudite Court philosophers into accepting the validity of a higher power. Know how? Just wrote $(x + y)^2 = x^2 + 2xy + y^2$ on a blackboard, drew a line beneath it, and added 'Therefore God Exists.'" Shales drew in some more smoke; the old stuff was clinging to his throat. "So I guess what I'm saying," he said, giving everyone a moment to rein in their laughter, "is that this is really nice."

After Catherine the Great he was in. A procession of Tuesdays followed. The kids were inquisitive, asking questions no one else in Shales's life had, or would. What was the Hemo-Vac like? Did it actually suck up blood? Why aren't you bald? How much time do you have? They began making sure he had better shit than the rest of them. They dropped their cost. Everyone wanted Shales's last hit of the day to be off their joint—they wanted something to remember him by. Shales knew all this—but he was getting more to smoke in the deal so he let it slide.

Besides, he was participating in the nostalgia, too. Watching how the boys stood, like cantilevered sculptures, one bent at the waist trying to cup a flame, another's legs sailing wide apart. Jilt, getting funnier and more confident each week. Liddy was different. She was still beautiful but in the way of worn brick, not so much for her strength now as for her strength then. On the last Tuesday she was wearing houndstooth pants and Shales's Space Camp sweatshirt, wasn't doing much at all, just packing on the vein leading to her elbow. It vaguely disturbed Shales that he couldn't bring himself to tell Liddy to stop. But she wasn't his kid anymore.

It was closer to say he was theirs. Now, it was closer to say this. They spoiled him. Mikey blocked the January, then February, now March, winds; Kyle patrolled the grounds more often—as the days lengthened, and the construction crew started putting in more appearances—so Shales didn't have to look over his shoulder. Jilt, like a grandfather, always had something special in his jacket pocket for Shales. The Tuesday episodes were feeling less like drug transactions and more like holiday reunions with family. Shales gave them updates on his treatment; the others stood and smoked and shot up, rapt, listening to him.

And Shales was astounded by their game of numbers. 1011, 808...Mikey can't make it today. Oh wow, why? 611. They'd picked up the codes of offenses from cops that had busted them, or friends of theirs. Rote memorization impressed Shales; he had a soft spot for attempts at order. Actually, he was prepared to call the group quite smart. They didn't possess dented vocabularies, so much as...specialized ones, for the benefit of their own comprehension only, all ties to classical expression severed.

"We gotta get nake sometime, baby," said Jilt to Liddy. He was playing with her, of course. By now everyone in the group except Claw (it was Claw) had slept with Liddy. Jilt was trying to get under her skin, but the only thing that could these days was the syringe—and bad shows, and when she heard Shales vomit from a bathroom or behind the forsythia that lined the Monkey House. Anyway the teasing was for Shales's benefit, too, to deflect the awkward silences. He was close to finished. He looked beaten even when grinning. His decline was clear to them all—maybe even to Shales a little less than the others. They blew out smoke but with little verve. You could hear the monkeys groom each other and hum through their flat noses.

Then Jilt said, "Man, we want to *tell* you something."

Shales looked up from Claw's bong. The circle tightened. Jilt cleared his throat and reached into his pocket. He pulled out a sheet of paper, looked it over, and glared. His ever-present smile went into hiatus. "It's wet."

Kyle: "What?" Jilt: "The page, dipshit! The page we wrote for Shales at lunch. It's fucking soggy!" Kyle: "Don't look at me." Jilt: "Who should I look at? Who else had to take a hit while we were writing and forgot to dump out his bongwater before he put the bong in my fucking pocket?" Liddy: "So just say it, Jilt. Say it to Charlie." A pause, because Jilt was collecting himself and one of the chimps had unraveled a hose and was whipping it into the safety glass. Quiet. Jilt: "Fuck. I forget every damn word." So they offered to walk around without Shales for a while, and try to come up with a new page, but Shales did not want to be left without them.

"In this problem, solve for *y*."

Shales stepped back from the blackboard the following morning, wiping chalk dust from his hands. He let silence take over. He watched the second hand on the hall clock sweep past twelve. He gave the integers time to sink in. Not one of the kids made a move for pencil or calculator. When he called on students for the answer in a minute, the faces would be blank and stiff, as though a military superior had entered the classroom. That was all just fine. Shales was rapt with two girls sitting in front. They were smacking gum—grounds for detention according to the rule he had floated months ago, when he cared about such distractions. The taller of the two girls had constructed a fortune-teller, one of those pinwheel-shaped puppets. She picked a number and used that number to guide her friend's fate, concerning who would ask whom to the spring dance. Shales couldn't stop watching. They'd written the names of two boys, Billy and Ryan, on all eight of the fortune flaps, and it was clear they had crushes on both boys. The whole thing riled him. Who were they kidding, giggling deliriously when they drew one of the boys' names? As if they were playing with chance, as if they had no idea how things were going to turn out. They were stacking the odds and pretending there was still something at stake. Look at them. Fingernail polish the color of grime, infantile light in their eyes. Giggling at their good luck. That's not probability. It's a mirage.

Shales insisted on the Wednesday matinee. But neither he nor Mary were dressed for the Cineplex, which was kept uncomfortably underheated. So Shales draped his arm around Mary like a stole. She let his fingers nibble below her left shoulder. Mary looked around. The screen was frightful and enormous. Though this was the movie everyone was hyping, and this was its premiere, hardly anyone was watching with them. Morning weekday shows were always this sparse, apparently: About ten ushers sprawled out along the back row, watching as spectators, and they seemed to be so comfortable as to forget they wore Velcro cummerbunds, or that their fingers were artificially buttered.

Shales and Mary stepped into the lobby. Shales took a long look at Mary, waiting for her review. "Well, you know, it wasn't bad," she offered. "But if I'm going to get fired for insubordination, I expect an instant classic." Shales thrust his hands into his pants, scanning the lobby. He seemed intense but in control. Not like the man who'd appeared in her classroom just hours before, who'd called Mary out of that room with a whisper. Who'd said he needed help, needed her, could she grab her coat and leave with him, right now? She could drive his car, he'd said, providing keys. There was no question: She could imagine him seized with pain on highway 94, car sliding over the yellow stripes, the road slippery with ribboned snow, on the way to Racine.

But then in his car he told her the pain was clearing. It comes, it goes. Shales asked if she would instead take him to the Cineplex, to see the matinee premiere of *Princely Sum*. And it was a good movie, just not what she'd expected. "What has that actress been in?" Mary asked. "Where I have seen her before?"

"Where is she?" asked Shales, stepping outside.

"That's what I mean. She absolutely rings a bell, but I don't know from where..." Mary looked up. Shales had stormed over to the box office window: He was screaming at someone there, a woman who had just bought a ticket. He was making wild, circling gestures with his arms, and his shirt collar fluttered as he wagged his index finger at her face. The woman cowered before Shales, ticket wrung in her hand. Mary stepped forward, peering into the confrontation. "You dumb bitch," Shales said. "Listen good. Here's how it goes, here's how it ends. He doesn't get the girl. Okay? And when he slips into the coma? Slipping into the coma was the best thing he ever did."

The Spoiler stood quietly. Her face seemed tight below the nose, as though she were having difficulty clearing her throat. Her lips parted slowly, unspooling. Her ticket for the next show dropped from her hand and blew down the walkway. She chased after it.

Mary watched the Spoiler try in vain to snatch the ticket off the ground. But each time she caught up to it, it spilled forward in the breeze, tumbling beyond her tightened fist. Mary approached Shales, gazing at him: His teeth were clenched, his breathing abbreviated and heavy. Mary touched his hand—it was as if his heat had all coiled there. She began to laugh. Shales turned toward her, startled by her amusement.

"What, what?" she asked, still laughing. "What do you want, for me to send you to the principal's office? It was enterprising revenge!"

Shales wondered if he should let go of her hand. If he did, she would ask him to take her back to school. But if he didn't, he could prolong his day with her a little more. A pair of brakes squealed just then. An elderly couple had pulled their car to the curb. They were studying the marquee, straining to read the show times, hashing out what to see, whether they would see anything.

Mary called out to them: "It's safe to go in, in case you're wondering. No one's going to ruin your ending. We have this guy to thank for that."

Shales smiled. "Yeah. I mean, that's not why I came here." Mary studied her ticket stub as if appraising its future worth. "You have to believe that. Whew. For a guy with nothing left, I feel pretty clear."

"Well bravo, and I mean that. But your summary was shaky, Charlie. What film were you watching in there? He *did* get the girl."

Not the one he thought he would, and not the way he thought he'd get her. But somebody *should* be getting something in the picture. Shales did the math. He considered his will, funeral arrangements, not yet finalized. It wasn't like it wasn't his body to do with as he wished. He didn't have to put his family's concerns before his, just because that was the standard thing. Fuck the visitation. He wanted to be broken down, become something else. He could have himself placed in an urn, to be signed for and picked up and carried off by Liddy. She could take his remains behind the forsythia at the zoo to smoke up the ash, suck up a high, some clutch of pleasure to trap momentarily between her teeth and throat, letting him escape, ring by ring, through the lips.

Wanted: Rebel Song

(Translated from the Bittae-Ogro)
It is high time melody accompanied our yearning and rage. Our peoples' struggle given shape by suling, trumpet, gong, and guitar. This November will mark thirty years we have waged war for our independent state. Our fervor has never been higher; our morale sings through the fields. Our cause deserves a national anthem to score its righteousness.

This was the announcement I and the other Ministers of the Cabinet sent out, via pamphlet, from a humble billet—but had we controlled the broadcast towers, we'd have happily transmitted our call throughout the fatherland. It has been a watershed year for us rebels. In the first decade of our liberation effort, the state held us at bay with rebukes, with threats. They took brazen comfort in torturing us. We agreed to a ceasefire, which they cravenly broke. But this past summer we at last proved triumphant in battle. The state's army has fled from the island's northern coast, ceding that remote crescent back to us. What's more, our military victory has bred another: credibility on a global stage. Other nations have awoken to our cause, and are demanding to know from our oppressors, *Won't you recognize them? Won't you grant them their own sovereign voice?*

What better way to declare that voice than in song? We have already adopted a national flower. Our flag stirred pride in a generation of children, myself among them, who lived in squalor while the state gorged on our labor, goods, and heritage.

As Minister of Recruitment, I convinced the Cabinet to hold an open competition to compose the official anthem of our separatist nation. It would inspire our people to know a kinsman had labored over the notes, just as our infantry labors in battle and mothers labor for their young. The homegrown song would stir not only battle-weary loyalists, I argued, but would also help me enlist sorely needed fresh blood from the hovels and shanties.

We encouraged our musicians to come forward and perform songs of 16 stanzas. Lyrics were to be written entirely in our indigenous tongue, the true peoples' voice of Bittae-Ogro. The competition's jury, of which I was a member, would audition all hopefuls, and then select the winner on the final day of November, which marks both the onset of our holy month and a Day of Contemplation for heroes fallen.

But the state marred the auditions with suitcase bombs and air strikes. Their violence beat the sunrise out of bed. By noon, reports of garlic in the air prompted our Minister of Health to evacuate the marketplace, but it was too late: WP, the new napalm, had ignited everywhere. Instead of song, agonized screams sheeted the town square. White phosphorus set its flag that day into the melting flesh of three-dozen farmers.

Could you ever acquit an army that employed such artillery?

Random blockades turned away droves of would-be performers. What's more, the oppressors locked down their own university, where we had hoped many minstrels, and learned scholars sympathetic to the separatists, would respond to our appeal. Other music makers had previously withdrawn their names from consideration, claiming they couldn't complete usable music within the deadline's confines. And our most accomplished woodwind player had already been lost—shot dead in a raid the previous night, protecting our printing press.

As a result, the field of surviving compositions was fallow. Hours of chaff. I will not deny, brothers, that as we jurists sat through auditions our spirits sank; chastened hearts are just as transparent as joyful ones.

"Number 12's song was vainglorious," proclaimed one rueful panelist, as we sat in conference after auditions had ended. "Not even a single mention of a rebel triumph in battle."

"Not as insulting as #40," I argued. "All about redress in the hereafter. Why should we have to wait until we're buried in the ground to be rewarded with light?"

Our Minister of Religion, who had a highly trained ear, cackled. "Many of these pieces cheaply cobble from songs of the past, and not just any songs: One composition used snippets of the Ganikan anthem—our initial colonizers—as well as the Kettish—our bloodiest colonizers—and even the Bukonese—our de facto colonizers. How can we claim a song as a mirror of our people's soul if we have robbed other nations' notes to make it?"

"Was anyone moved by #37? Good rhythm on that, I thought."

"The clockmaker's piece? Yes, the percussion was direct and sharp, you're right. But it soared without a threat. Can you imagine it inspiring anyone to take up arms, or spend the fruitful years of life hidden and isolated in the high mountains?" ·

Our ears roared with clash and clank—ugly notes, ramshackle motifs. Not a single song was suitable. Most vexing of all was that these verses, penned by native kinsmen, fell short, far short, of the ones contained in the state's sprightly national song. Our Day of Contemplation was almost here. And after our very public decree, the absence of an anthem to unveil would humiliate us, severely daunting our course.

But then the next day a cassette arrived. None of our couriers had delivered the parcel. Amazing then that it arrived intact, with no outward signs of mishandling. More amazing still that the composer had taken the risk of sending it through normal channels: All anthems intercepted by the state's postal service were considered acts of treason.

As for its contents? Well. The music started out deceptively light—like a lonely lit match in a forest. But soon enough we knew the song was no idyll, but a burning, defiant declaration, of love of country. The song had no lyrics, and the tape cut out after five verses. Even still, our ears were ravenous for its next tone. We knew we had our rebel song. Our aspirations had been distilled into this anthem, the way a single newborn's face can distill one's hopes for all humanity.

We jurists drank that night. Drank joyously, drank voraciously—each sip enlarging and adding octane to our hearts. When we convened the next day, I proposed that we agree to terms at once with the composer. Only Colm, the Minister of Culture and Arts, disagreed. After last night's revelry he had scrutinized the tape. "If I am to believe my ears," he explained nervously, "this composer cannot be a rebel. That descant melody rising above the main one relies on an instrument long-banned from our villages. And those acoustics, gentlemen. Such balance of sound cannot be faithfully birthed in a basement or barn. Only one site on this entire island could cradle such notes with such gentle care: the Capitol Conservatory." Colm then opened a window and drew in a gulp of sea air; a thing I'd never imagined could seem doleful until I saw him do it. As a young man, Colm had been the island's foremost musician until the state's Exalted General plucked him from the Conservatory. *You will create a song for army rallies,* the General had commanded, standing so close that Colm swore he felt embers on his eyeball from the bastard's cigar. *But I only perform,* Colm pleaded, *I cannot compose.* A plea he repeated for ten days in the fetid, frigid darkness of his catacomb cell. By the time the state finally got around to releasing Colm, three of his fingertips had gone green, numb and useless.

(These days of course, our people have been quarantined from the capital's cultural center.)

Our dilemma suddenly was not whether we could track down this composer, but what would be the consequence when we did? Was the state sending us a Trojan horse, a sublime artist doubling as an agent of espionage? Was it a dilettante in the student movement, whose longing fickly wavered between revolution and inheriting his family's sugar mill?

As Minister of Recruitment, it fell on me to seek the answer. My communiqué to the composer received a quick written reply: The gifted musician pledged at once to take the next ferry to our billet. So far, so good. I would interview the composer, then inform the Cabinet of my endorsement or warning of him. At the appointed hour of our meeting, though, I found only one small woman in my office vestibule. All of fifty, she was frail beyond her years. She smiled as I paced the hall. An utterly horizontal smile, even as a ruler's edge, with teeth shining like polished brass. The look that appears on some women's faces the instant after they've acquired something. I tried shooing her, but she stood her ground, insisting I let her into my office. "Who are you here on behalf of?" I demanded.

"On behalf of this," she said, and gently lifted a stringed instrument from its case. After a few swift turns of its tuning pegs, she strummed the initial chords of the winning anthem. Live, the measures sounded softer, and all the more affecting. I lowered my head to beg the composer's pardon, but she dismissed my gesture.

"My time is too precious to spend wallowing in your apology."

Though her rudeness took me aback, I was perfectly aware of how prickly artists could be; I offered her a plate of fresh squid and let it slide.

After a few moments of interrogation, it became clear she wasn't well spoken in Bittae-Ogro, so I shifted reluctantly into the distasteful, dominant language of our colonizers. "We're pleased you could make the journey here so hastily," I told her. "And Miss, now tell me, which province were you born in?"

"Province? Not any you'd recognize the name of."

"I am the Minister of Recruitment. My business is replacing fallen heroes with fresh ones. By now I imagine I've scoured every inch of the broken country."

"This country, perhaps."

"Do you mean to say—to say you don't hail from our nation? And yet you've submitted this song for the rebels' use?"

My mind spun giddily, wondering if this woman's intent was to defect. It would be a welcome coup, whisking the writer of our national anthem from another homeland. "Then where was this composed?"

"A railway depot in Port Balboa," she replied coolly, after reflection. "Or no—let's see, this one? Possibly it came to me in Khinpura. Yes, that's it. Khinpura. While shopping for scarves." Off my off-put look, she added: "Don't worry. You can claim to your countrymen that the anthem was inspired as I gazed out over your most magnificent bluff, or watched you impose your will on a weaker people, or whatever…"

"We have never conquered another nation. What's more, we don't desire to."

"Of course you do," she answered, examining her instrument's bow, lank and curved as a spine. "Freedom is far more fulfilling when you have another tribe under your thumb. Think of the Kettish. They once fought for home rule against Belakhstan, and, after obtaining it, searched for their own nations to enchain, such as Nilaysia and your own. So human governance goes on, a repeated motif of rising and falling misery and cruelty, endured at one moment, and inflicted at another."

"All we want, Miss," I assured her, bristling, "is our little crescent, our Northern shore. And if you were more well-versed in the history of our liberation, why, I'm confident you'd be eager to help us write the remaining pages."

"God, no! I hold no home in my heart for you separatists. Oh, I did once. I was a moon-eyed schoolgirl when your insurrection began. But tell me, what was your last 'brave' action? Assassinating the Exalted General's wife at a religious feast?"

"We struck at him through her. Out of necessity," I insisted, pursuing a resolute tone that I truly didn't believe in: This was a rebel action I had deeply disapproved of. Still, I had a duty to continue my argument, so I did: "The general is a butcher who keeps hidden inside his tank and compound, while she strolled the streets unguarded. What we did was no worse than their acts of torture. The way they violate and then abduct schoolgirls, right in front of their mothers."

"Not worse?" Eyelids lowered, she pondered this. "That's true North of your moral compass? Pity. No. I'm not here to receive your indoctrination. Just my earnings."

She pressed a sealed note into my palm. "This is the going rate for an anthem."

We had stipulated a monetary prize to the winning composer. But how could the jury justify giving winnings to a mercenary who rejected our calling, our very essence, who wanted only to peddle her song for a price? What would it say about the new sovereign state if its first official act was to purchase music meant to reflect our pride? Wasn't that more humiliating than presenting no song at all?

"Bear in mind," she added. "I charge a little less for songs used only at religious ceremonies, or sporting events. I've composed such work for Izmirana, Portania, and New Oster. Of course I've forged many anthems besides yours. You have heard my recent handiwork in the national songs of several breakaway republics. For privacy's sake I leave these clients anonymous—as I will with you. No one will ever know you retained my services; it will be as if a ghost of your choosing wrote the piece."

Your fee, I told her finally, is untenable.

"Timelessness has its price. And be assured I have other offers. Producers of a major action film have inquired about the very verses I sent to you. There is no ceiling to their desperation or their funds. Makers of a headache remedy also wish to negotiate." She helped herself to the cold marinated squid I now wished I'd never offered. Native fishermen had caught those squid, after spending days at sea, tossed in a rowboat nearly rent in two by rocky waves. And now she was smacking her lips on their catch, hoping we'd wrap up quickly so she could lounge her weekend away on the shores of Bournebrough.

Once, as a child, members of the state's Security Service forced my family out of our small farmhouse at gunpoint. For entire weeks we slept in the pen where we kept our dogs, and their marrowbones. That whole interminable winter my family indulged the soldiers' every demand and vanity. Fed, housed, even cleansed them. The months remain an abscess in my memory. And before marching on, the soldiers scorched what little remained of our crops, so we couldn't give them to insurgents. And now this bandit before me, popping squid into her mouth, was trying to rob my fellow rebels just as the state had, and would do forever, until we rose up to their rule.

Infuriated, I unsheathed my gun and leveled it against the composer's hand, a spot I imagined, for her, to be wholly vulnerable. I was proud to see fear throttle her body. "Compose a new anthem for us," I demanded. "Or never play another note." When she flinched, I fired at my desk, missing her by inches. She took up her instrument and strummed a few plodding measures. The music of statesmen.

"Just play what you sent us!" I barked, thinking perhaps I'd spare her life but steal her song. I would record the anthem in its entirety, then cleave one of her fingers. But her notes now sounded sour and scattered. The hole in my desk sizzled. Though I knew it was fear, not impertinence, causing her to fumble, I was still enraged, and swore to have her remanded to a filthy windowless cell.

"Will you?" she asked, again flashing her straight-edged smile. "For how long? Until your Day of Contemplation passes? Until you happen to locate a random soldier whistling a song to himself that's as strong as mine?"

I thought of the woodwind player we'd assigned to protect our printing press, the night before auditions. Thought of the wan music our countrymen had brought before the jurists. And while I suppose there is a sort of music in the harmony of a hundred rebel tents being pitched on a clear night, and a beat that persists in one's brain after narrowly dodging an infantryman's grenade, it is not the kind of music composed by victors.

Our musicians were, and would need to remain, our defenders. And so perhaps they would always remain on alert, incapable of commuting from a state of terror to one of reflection. This despised woman could make the music our people could not, because each hour was for her assured; a safe blanket. A rebel of her own sort—entering enemy airspace with no weapon other than time, and no diplomatic immunity other than the fact that she is a virtuoso and we are a country too beaten down, from years of war like lashes of the whip, to write anything but the most feckless of notes.

"Hide your smile," I warned, as the heat of the gun barrel warmed my palm. "Your composition? What do you call it?"

"'Hymn of the Itinerant.' Of course, I cede the right to the title once my fee has been fully secured. Once this happens, I'll deliver the remainder of my stanzas."

"Before I arrange for your departure, we must convince the Cabinet you're in the fold. We will need to embrace, warmly, at a ceremony this afternoon."

"For photos," she answered, nodding. "I understand. But you will never post this evidence to the world. None of my clients do. It's an admission of..."

"I know what it's an admission of," I snapped. "I'll destroy the camera later. And the money and music will be exchanged privately between you and me. But no one else can know the cost of this song. So I expect more than your standard anonymity pact. I will escort you to the marina. Explain later how you were assassinated by the state while putting the finishing touches on your anthem."

She nodded, and rose to follow me.

Once I successfully recruit a new soldier into our ranks, the separatist custom is to present the rebel to our Minister of Defense, and several ranking officers. A kind of combat christening. I had brought so many green rebels down this corridor. Each one petrified—but when they entered the Minister's office, swelling with the sound of our heroic veterans applauding their sacrifice, a sense of calm caught fire on their faces. The moment of brotherhood enjoined them to bravery. And now I would be tricking our loyal officers into applauding a mercenary. They would cheer her for embracing our cause, and cheer me for finding her. Send her off with hoots and hurrahs to be fitted for a standard-issue army uniform.

I was aware of the countless souls her song might stir into service. How the anthem, in years to come, will inspire many real rebels to step forward, and labor for our shared dream. And yet, how ashamed I was that day, gaining clearance to submit myself before the Minister of Defense. When I knock at his guarded door after enlisting new recruits, I always ask for entrance by saying, *"Sh'lin mu deendha"*: "Believe me, brothers."

Goes Without Saying

His eardrums surly and clopping with temporary tinnitus, brought on by the night's CD release party, Stir trudged from his apartment's front door to the kitchen, in search of a fizzy drink. His young son Philip sat beside the TV, hours past bedtime. He didn't even twitch at his dad's arrival, enraptured instead by ADtv, a network with no original programming, airing ceaseless commercials from the past. A vintage spot of twins throatily giggling at their reflections in bowls of Jell-O. Morgan Fairchild modeling Capri pants on a set salvaged from H.R. Pufnstuff.

"Not loud enough?" Stir asked Philip irritably, standing behind him. Clutching the remote like a rope, he amplified the set's volume from 19 to 90. Philip still didn't acknowledge Stir was in the room. *"THIS NEW YEAR'S,"* warned a thin-lipped uniformed man, identified onscreen as Sgt. Marsh. *"REFRAIN FROM FIRING PISTOLS IN THE SKY. BECAUSE YOU KNOW WHAT? BULLETS LAND."*

Stir boosted the bass. Above his convection oven, a mobile of scuffed CDs shivered. Waves of sound pitched the discs together. "Still not enough for you, son?"

"THE ONLY ORANGE JUICE PROVEN TO FIGHT HALITOSIS."

Stir fished a lemon wedge out of his drink, squeezing it so its acidic spray would catch Philip in the eye. "Pay attention to me," he muttered.

Philip flinched, then shucked the juice off his face, but otherwise remained as he had been, sitting zazen through thumping jingles, until his father admitted defeat, took shelter in his seltzer water, and left the room.

Most of the CD release party's memories already seemed dim. How long did the band play? Did Stir ever grab dinner? The facts were defiant suspects who wouldn't pull forward in a police lineup. Stir remembered his wife yelling at him when he'd left for the party. All evening he'd clung to the club's open bar. Shut his mouth between sips. Slipped to the john just before leaving. When a cell phone rung out in the bathroom, Stir had frisked his jacket. But of course he'd ditched his cell behind. The thing would've been a house arrest bracelet: Melanie calling every half hour, apologizing, venting, then demanding apologies.

It took five rings to understand where the ring was coming from. A chorus from the 1960s—"*Do You Believe in Magic?*" or "*Did You Ever Have to Make Up Your Mind?*" Not that those dreary ring tones soared like songs anyway; they were barely taxiing on the sonar runway. Didn't matter. Only one party attendee used The Lovin' Spoonful for a ring tone. Even before Stir checked the voice mail, he had a fair inkling why he'd had to retrieve his boss's phone from the bottom of a trashcan stuffed with soapy hand towels and beer-dampened napkins.

"Alistir, can I refill your glass?" The offer was for show, as was Stir's mulling of it. Arnie had clearly wished Stir hadn't stopped by, especially not with the discarded phone in hand. "Got pepper-flavored Stoli in my icebox. They don't even distribute this stuff stateside."

"When were you in Russia, Arnie?"

"Wasn't. This is bottled in Kazakhstan. Went over for our second anniversary."

Stir had nodded, while appraising his boss's loft. Arnie, VP of A&R at Opening Act Records, had worked with sound all his life, but except for a piano relegated to the corner, dull with dust, subservient seeming, like a busker begging for tourists' tips, there were no traces of music. No street noise bled through Arnie's arched windows, and the low-beamed ceiling made Stir feel he'd stumbled into a Buddhist temple, that any idle talking would be a transgression.

"Helluva trip I bet," Stir remarked. On his way over from the CD release party he'd played the cell's voice mail; all international calls from Arnie's third wife, Azita. So—the circulating office buzz contained real blood: Azita *had* left Arnie, and *was* living on some remote island; just packed her bags and retreated from the shaky marriage.

"Every trip with Azita is a hell of a trip." Arnie slunk toward his liquor cabinet. His sullen temper was notorious. But still, Stir didn't think this visit would lead to any trouble. He'd done the right deed by retrieving the phone. Besides, as Opening Act's lead talent scout, Stir had steered Arnie from far too many contractual icebergs for one fuck-up to seal his fate. "You sign that girl group from Milwaukee yet? Summer Salt?" Arnie yelled from down the hall. Stir didn't reply. "Alistir, close the deal. Shira and Glen tell me this act is a slam dunk."

"Shira and Glen didn't talk to the drummer. Girl belongs in Bellevue. She keeps—I wish I were kidding—a jarful of some guy's ashes by her bass drum." Stir glanced again at Arnie's dusty cornered piano. A stack of bound journals rested on its bench, each covered with dried flower petals. Stir undid the spider of rubber bands fastened around them, peeking at a random page: Azita's handwriting. He recognized its restless curling and curves from Arnie's 60th birthday party invitation.

"My point is we're not the only label cruising them. If EMI poaches them, I swear...." Arnie's voice grew diffuse; Stir guessed he was being spoken to from the loft's opposite end. "Next topic. What's this demo you dropped in my inbox?"

"Band's called Rare Blood Type. Sony cut them loose, inexplicably. Third track's got sterile production values. It's an otherwise promising single."

"Let me guess. They want an 'engineer' in the studio, not some name producer."

On Arnie's flat screen, topknotted actors in samurai outfits swiped swords through six-packs, shouting, *"WHO WANTS BEER WITH ITS HEAD CUT OFF?"* Stir knew Philip was at home now, awake, watching the same images snap from the screen. Unable to hear the screaming samurai, or the goddamn donut jingle that followed. Since birth, Philip hadn't responded to any of the thousands of words and tones tossed before him. To him, sound was a foreign language. Check that. It wasn't a language at all.

Stir still held one of Azita's journals. How had he found it on the piano? Perfectly square? Tilted? While considering this, Stir realized that against his will, or at least his reason, he was stuffing it into his portfolio bag. Arnie hollered that he could show Stir photos from a jazz festival, and Stir replied, sure, if it's no trouble. It softened the thievery, somehow, to hold a conversation with his boss while stealing from him. As the piano player chimed Middle C twelve times to mark the time, Stir again declined another Stoli. *"'The hour is late. I feel I've got to move.'"*

"I know that song," Arnie answered, re-entering the room. "Don't give me a hint. ELO? No, fuck, of course, it's Rush. I told you how I met Geddy Lee?"

Stir shook his head, covering his portfolio bag with his feet. One of the journal's flower petals had fallen off the cover. It matched Arnie's cognac colored hardwood, more or less. Stir hadn't stolen anything since college. Had he pulled off this theft cleanly? Finished zipping before Arnie returned? A moist sweet scent like pear flesh dangled in the room. Stir recognized it as the fragrance of his fear.

"Antique bookstore in Toronto. I wanted to beat the traffic back to Niagara Falls, but Azita dragged us in to buy a book on African dialects." Arnie balanced Miles Davis pictures on top of his already half-empty vodka. "And there's Geddy in the corner, reading about Egyptian aqueducts. God, what a shitty band. Nice guy, though."

Stir flipped through photos of Miles, stoking his trumpet as though blowing on a cold fist to revive the feeling. Stir's ears had begun to ring. Could Arnie see the photos twitching in his hands? Of course. Then had he seen him swipe the journal? Flames in the fireplace spooned under the logs, flicking red and orange like lizards' tongues. "Arnie. Should I not have brought the phone?" Arnie shrugged several times. But with each shrug, he seemed to mind the question more deeply.

Ten minutes later Stir was back on the street, loose sacks and escapee soda caps tumbling alongside him; trash day tomorrow. Somehow Arnie had made his disinterest in Azita seem normal. He'd even shifted the focus of their chat to Stir's dimming star at the record label. *You're no longer looking for songs that bristle and jar*, Arnie suggested at one point. Stir had, after all, advised Arnie not to sign the band they'd held the party for, a band whose debut had pre-shipped twice as many units as predicted. *That's natural. You're a new dad. Only music you probably hear at home is Mozart on Marimba, right?*

Stir had nearly decked Arnie for that remark. But Arnie knew nothing about Philip's condition: no one at the label did. Stir never brought Philip by the office.

He'd guarded that side of his life from others. Including his wife. Philip had become their 800-pound gorilla. Only they were shoving the beast from opposite ends: She embraced deaf culture, while Stir backed the cochlear implant option, or cranked the TV, hoping to get Philip to jerk back from explosions and laugh tracks, convinced all he needed to do was route the right signals to his son's sense of hearing for it to function.

Now it's now, the next morning, Saturday, and as a college jazz station incongruously plays Herbie Hancock's "Tell Me A Bedtime Story," Stir calls out over the phrasing for his wife, not expecting or wanting an answer. Melanie goes to Grand Central Thursdays and Saturdays, takes the train to a Scarsdale learning center, for half-day sign-language intensives. This gives Stir two hours, if Philip naps until noon. He opens Azita's journal to the first page and begins reading the account of her exodus.

Third full day. Curious frilled lizards climbed the hut to take in the smell of eggs cooked in fish oil. In the morning we established the words for oil, for flame, for heat. But when I tripped up on "egg," the old woman, nicknamed Throso, smacked her hands. A gesture of frustration, of which she has many. I spent much of the day learning how the clan assigns names. This went well. Babies go nameless for a week. It's believed that one god, controlling light, tries to steal our shadows each day at noon. But if the infant casts a shadow after the seventh noon, it will survive. After that, it can be named. Even still, everyone in the clan goes by a nickname. Nicknames refer to ugly objects or qualities, and are used to deter evil spirits. Throso, I think, is the word for laziness. At one point the lizard ran in ribbons around a banyan tree and I asked, "How do you call this?" Throso bent her head and tittered tiredly at the ground. "My head is too slow now. But I'anye could tell you."

That's a refrain I've heard repeatedly since arriving. I asked Throso when I could have an audience with I'anye. It took an hour for me to comb through her response. I'anye is her grandson. He came of age recently, an event the tribe commemorates by sending young men on their first fishing trip. He is out at sea now—most expeditions last for two weeks.

So, we'll wait. Because I'anye may be the only living clan member with the sheer stamina to field our team's queries about verb tense, tone, structure and syntax. The clan's use of the genitive case, for one thing, has baffled us. Tom and a few others believe that when clan members ask how to get someplace unfamiliar, they refer to the location as though the person they've asked to guide them there possesses it. Can this be correct?

Young clan members no longer speak or write in the old dialect, getting by with a pidgin dialect, working for coastal hotels or boat rental companies. The elders know it best, but most of the elders who are still living are not living well. They're fighting typhoid, cholera, infections of the lungs.

We can't even count on Throso's cooperation: today she could barely lift herself off her bed.

Stir shuts the journal and pops in a CD: Wayne Shorter, low and soft. He never paid Azita much mind at business parties. Sure, he made paltry efforts to talk her up, but always wound up wandering to louder conversations, colleagues' tales of can't-miss bands that did nothing *but* miss, anecdotes of women getting baptized by Al Green just so they could put moves on him. He'd always found Azita haughty, too earnest, the first to hail a cab home. Besides, he didn't need to ride the coattails of her good graces. Stir already had her husband's ear, had it, in fact, more fully than Azita.

But now she's got Stir's ear, and so he continues ferreting through the pages.

Once again I fall behind the learning curve. I never studied French, German, or Portuguese. I'm fluent only in English, Bengali, and Farsi, of course, my native tongue. Proficient enough in Hindi and Urdu to dwell on my deficiencies. I dabble in a dozen other dialects, each more obscure than the next. One college friend called me a linguist's equivalent of an e.r. doctor, devoted only to resuscitating languages at death's door. And that's at least a little true; it's exactly what I'm doing here. My form of triage is abstract: Try to document and record this dialect, and save it from extinction.

Stir's really done it now: laughed at a colleague during the Monday development meeting. A junior rep is selling Arnie on the rich future of Midwestern college towns, where a mash of roots music and white-rap (WRASP) is all the rage. Stir feels all they do at these meetings is play out the string on existing trends. It reminds him of lawyers filing appeals with no merit, just to cheat sentencing a little longer. "Lawrence, Kansas," the rep proclaims, "is well on its way to being the next Athens, Georgia."

Later, when she calls Kansas "profound with talent," Stir chuckles, recalling the phrase "profoundly deaf." That's how the audiologist had diagnosed Philip, to explain why the hearing aid hadn't helped, and why the cochlear implant was a long shot. Stir's boy was "profoundly deaf": Now how could you *not* lose yourself laughing at that phrase, as if wisdom were only acquired by those who lost a sense completely, as if only those who can't fully interact with the world might ever come to understand it?

Once the meeting breaks Arnie pulls Stir aside, summoning him to his loft for the evening. Stir blinks, glancing at a framed Mugwumps poster. A few thousand blinks later, Stir is riding Arnie's now-familiar elevator, funneling through a mental Rolodex. Trying to remember which labels might be hiring: Nonesuch? Vagrant?

He knows his job performance has been slipping for some time. Phone calls—he staffs out all but priority messages. Lunches—he shifts and reschedules. E-mails—gnats at his face. Wave at them for a minute, then move on. And today, he tops it off by seeming to laugh at a colleague. Now he's about to get the hook in Arnie's home. Maybe he *has* been quick to dismiss the edgy music he once embraced. Maybe advising Arnie to pass on the new Klezmer act was where his career soured. "It's not Jewish blue-grass. The revival's been exaggerated," Stir had sworn at the time, though the music's mystic joy had moved him. *Vessel of song,* the term meant, and Stir liked that too: As though all the world's opuses and power chords were already adrift at sea, and so each time a musician played a note or drum fill they were simply netting them from the waters.

At the loft, Arnie dispenses Stoli and flings a thick envelope onto the sofa.

"What are we toasting?" Stir asks gingerly, lifting the envelope. So this is how much severance weighs.

"Me," answers Arnie. "For the lifeboat I just threw you. Those are tickets. Fly out Tuesday night to Milwaukee. Quit loafing and sign that damn band."

Stir nods. Is he relieved about his reprieve? He isn't sure. He used to pray for demos like Summer Salt's to fall into his lap, songs that didn't sound like they were drifting in and out of creative comas. But ever since listening to the band, he's been at a loss on how to market them. Their music yaws with discontent. Poppy, but too strident for a mall crowd. They amplify instruments with condenser microphones, giving the sound a shaggy, far-away feel. And then of course there's their crazy rhythm player and leader, Liddy. When he saw them play Beloit College, she wheeled an upright piano onstage. Sawed in half, standing on casters. The keys removed, Liddy had played it by plucking and strumming its strings. It didn't sound like a harp, no longer sounded like a piano. It was like listening to a thunderstorm while attending the opera.

"Sure you want me making the trip now? Band says they won't sign until they all turn eighteen."

"You really haven't heard the rumbles, have you? Glen's gotten chummy with their manager; sends the girls swag bags. He's scheming to ink them himself. But Summer Salt was your find, so it's your get. And I've got com-plete confidence you will get them—as long as it happens by week's end."

The curtains beside Arnie's open porch door billow. An evening storm is taking shape. One night, collisions of thunder had filled the sky; one loud clap startled Philip, and he'd made a terrible, alien yelp. Stir was so grateful the thunder had gripped his boy enough to even *make* a sound of his own.

"You could've given me this at work," Stir points out, pissier than intended.

"Could've, yeah, but there's something else. Shoulda mentioned it when you were over on Friday. That cell phone you dug up? It's personal. Deeply so." Arnie strikes one palm against the other, as if to jar ketchup from a bottle, or burp a baby. "And it goes without saying I want it to stay that way." When Stir nods, Arnie does the same. What have they agreed to? Has Arnie promised to protect Stir's job, so long as Stir doesn't breathe a word about Azita?

Whatever; his boss is smiling now, fetching cognac from the other end of the loft. Stir seizes the moment, heading over to Arnie's upright, slipping Azita's journal from his overcoat and swapping it with the two others. This one in his hands covers her preparations for the journey, and her first two days on the atoll. From his readings, he knows Azita and Arnie fought over her taking this trip. He knows what Azita is doing—trying to document Bit-tae-Ogro, a rare dialect spoken by a speck of a fishing community. But he doesn't know which island she's on, and why she had to go right now.

This time, the pilfering hardly feels like a crime. It feels like his due. Stir wonders if adulterers go through the same shift: guilty on those initial clandestine meetings, but later shameless, thick as thieves, certain that what they're giving their new lovers more than justifies what they've done to the jilted spouses. Marital strife—Stir is learning what it can do. Melanie seems resigned to Philip's eighth nerve being damaged. She mastered in music education; sang to Philip daily as he grew in her womb; doesn't it bother her to cut and run this way? When they fight about Philip's diagnosis at dinner, she disconnects at some point, starts slicing open mail with a brass-plated letter opener, a sound that used to be their sexual tripwire. They'd met while working as interns for another record label, had first kissed in a mailroom. Now that sound meant nothing.

Stir pictures Arnie and Azita together. She's no stunner—lanky and rabbit-faced—but she is exotic, and young. Probably Arnie had been drawn to her vitality. He'd hoped for a happy hostess, and got a humanitarian. Stir imagines their travels. At first light Azita would tie her hair up hastily, rent a Vespa, and seek out a local to take her into bazaars and down alleys Arnie wouldn't be caught dead in.

Arnie would be a guy who'd prefer to sample from cultures as though they were trays of passed *hors d'oeuvres*. Who'd want to live in four-star hotels and receive first-class treatment in third-world nations. They'd take their summers abroad, only to turn foreign to each other the minute the plane touched down.

"Walls here are unusual, huh?"

Off Stir's blank look, Arnie indicates the spandrel between two arches. "Their height, the way they curve. I've been watching you watch my walls during your visits."

"Arnie, I know squat about architecture. But I'll take your word for it."

"My realtor said this loft was *remarkably* unusual. Such low ceilings in a place so high off the ground. I picked it to remind Azita of us." Arnie then tells the story of their first date, with what's left of his hair lying trampled against his skull. "I left the details entirely up to her. She had all the control. She had us eat an early dinner, and then we spent the next hour standing in the Whispering Gallery."

Stir smiles back with clueless curiosity.

"You don't know the Whispering Gallery? In Grand Central, next to...oh Stir! You gotta go. And go with someone. You'll be able to hear the other voice speak to you clear as day, even when the person's standing in another corner, even in a crowd. I'm telling you, you will never hear a human voice sound so...frictionless. The father and son who built it didn't plan it that way. The design was accidental. We barely spoke above a murmur, Azita and me, but still, I could make out her every word. Our voices just lifting, and. Curving around the ceiling. And this was during peak hours. I don't know how it works. Something about the way they built the low arches."

"Well, that's definitely an offbeat date. Couldn't call it romantic, though."

"You're wrong." Arnie caps the bottle of cognac, and sets it aside, though there is only a dribble left. "We never spoke to each other so well again."

Pearls of sunlight crack through the hotel curtain, as Stir checks the wristwatch he meant to remove the night before. Housekeeping is stocking milled soap bars in the bathrooms, and the city block outside his window has brokered a thousand transactions since dawn. When he wakes so late, he feels the world has given him up for dead. In an hour he's meeting Liddy at a bar serving Red Bull for breakfast, and gray granola in wooden bowls. He got in late to Milwaukee, fell asleep reading Azita's first journal. Now he considers her first entries after arriving on the island as he considers his face, and whether its stubble will make him seem older or younger.

Made it. Blurry with jet lag, hair catching the spray of waves beating on the rocks. There is protocol to follow. Wash perfume from my neck. Don't bristle when men won't shake the hand with my wedding band. Don't act as if the village is damaged, though of course it is. The atoll's northern crescent was hit with the brunt of last month's tsunami. It reminds me of a favorite bowl I broke: I scoured the floor for its pieces, until I realized I'd never find some shards no matter how hard I hunted. This isolated culture has been shattered beneath sheets of seawater 100 feet high. This chain is known as Tailor's Islands, since an aerial view makes the atoll seem like a string, the mainland a thick knot in its center. But that isn't what this tribe calls the chain, and that's why I'm here. To learn what this tribe calls everything.

A boy who mistook us for reporters climbed over sharp friable rock to greet us at the shore. He threw a stone at our luggage to see what it could withstand, then peppered us with questions while cadging socks from our duffels. He laughed when we uttered tribal phrases at him. "Only shriveled clan members talk that talk now." No one your age speaks the dialect? I asked. "Probably only I'anye. That old-time shit used to interest him."

Eye-YAHN-yeh. Great.

First Morning: Overslept—rude. But dawn, in my defense, never quite broke. The tide of light didn't roll in. Even at noon, as our team toured the village, clouds covered us all, opaque as streaks on a wineglass. When we approached the beach, we came across scattered airplane models the clan made from straw, with ten-foot wingspans. They also erected an ad hoc mock-up of a temporary triage center built after the tsunami, praying the medics and NGOs would return. It's a modern-day cargo cult, in the style of those I read about from the 1940s. The rest of my team trudged on, but I hung back, where I watched a man beside a makeshift shrine, hoisting a newborn infant over his head. His voice cracked in two as he screamed in anguish, "A shadow. Give me a shadow."

I'm nearly sure that's what he screamed.

Facho means bowl; trin is the tribal word for rice; *Sh'lin,* believe. I learned some words this afternoon, thanks to Throso, the only elder who agreed to meet with me. Some words are poor relations of nearby dialects; a few are used for local color by the colonizers. Others echo familiar languages: *yumai* means dream, very close to the Japanese *yume.* But it's taken so much focus and time to learn a few basic sentences. Do I need to admit I'll never account for all the shards?

Caught up in the journals, Stir arrives for his breakfast with Summer Salt's drummer late and unprepared—something Liddy senses inside of ten minutes. He's acting too mannered before her, a boy granted an audience with Santa Claus who doesn't want to blow his chance at landing the best toy.

"I'm thinking now we may just self-release the CD," Liddy warns, splashing in the mess she's made for Stir. They've never spoken in person. Her body's slightness shocks him; the stage makes her seem larger. "Our bassist has a treasure chest trust fund that's ours once she turns 18." She pauses, toying at her pair of green wool socks. "Or maybe I'll ditch the group, break up our little hive, and go solo. Only then I'd lose the label's promotional muscle, wouldn't I?"

Stir turns an ice cube over in his mouth. She isn't really speaking to him, he decides. She's dropping bait. His job is to not bite down.

"Something's got to give," he says. "When we're each so desperate to blaze our own trail, and equally desperate to have a flock of followers."

Liddy grasps the napkin next to his plate, coughs into it, then pops eight pills down her throat, rationing her water perfectly, sip for pill.

"Street drugs work better with granola?" Stir asks.

"Granola won't work without the drugs. Oliv—that's our bassist—tells me you were the one to sign Kafka Is Dreaming?"

Stir smiles, delighted Liddy knows about this feather in his cap. He inked the Kafka deal back when Melanie was pregnant, back when he imagined driving the freeway with Philip years from now. They would've sung along to the band's single "Flipped Off," and seen them backstage, Philip adorned in a tiny CBGB shirt. That shirt's now stuffed in a footlocker, and CBGB has been shut down. "Early on, I had to slog to get believers for that band."

"Real? Well mission accomplished. Now they got believers in droves."

"Pretty much. So how many albums do you owe your current label?"

"Two. But that's no hassle. The guys there love us to death. They'll let us jet."

Was she serious? It was naïve to think breaking a contract was as painless as getting an extension on a college paper. Then again, it would be naïve of him to let her know this. "Once you make the switch to us," Stir assures, "you'll have total creative control. It'll be your music, your language. I'd make it my job to guard the studio door from any label interference. Goes without saying."

When Liddy uses her right hand to sweep crumbs off her left arm, Stir frowns: She's inadvertently making the sign-word for music. He hates that he knows this.

"Well, congrats. I will admit you're the least revolting A&R asshole of the bunch. I want to hang that Glen guy by his gonads. It's time you met Charlie."

Liddy hoists a scuffed chrome urn onto the table. It knocks into a wooden bowl. Asteroids of granola spill onto the Black Flag decal pasted to its base. "Charlie plays Magic 8 ball on all my major decisions." When she removes her shades the bright sun barks at her; her mouth tightens as though the light is a poison. "I always carry him with me. He's never missed a show."

"That's a little grim, isn't it?"

"I'm staring down the barrel at a guy twice my age whose job security depends on me. Now tell me which of us is leading the grimmer life."

I'm not twice your age, you twit, Stir thinks, inhaling. On the exhale he says, "How about this. Let's write up some terms, but keep it casual. What do you say?"

By breakfast's end Liddy's signed a deal memo. It's a binding pact, a fact she surely doesn't know. He should alert Arnie before his plane is airborne, but can't. She's signed her art away, and Stir never acknowledged it. He leaves his cell off as he fastens in for the ride back.

He wants to read Azita's voice. It relaxes him to have her final journal keeping him company for the flight. It's her hopefulness he finds himself craving, her appetite for the foggy future.

Day Twelve: Team is excited. When I'anye returns—his fishing trip ends tomorrow—our ears will be warmed up on basic vocabulary, my tongue won't be tripping as much, and we can skip the preliminaries. "We all use hands and *mumble* to *mumble* the dirt and *mumble mumble* during the rainy fall season."

"Slow down, dear Grandma," I pleaded with Throso, in jerky Bittae-Ogro. Today she sounded worse but spoke to me more, surely anxious for her grandson's return. "Start again," I said. "Tell about the harvest. Please, though, slow down this time."

Telling Throso to slow down is like telling a mob trapped in a burning building to take an orderly path down the stairs. Throso views time as a spear, taking constant aim at her. If she dies, her language could go with her. This isn't a curio to her. It is the speech that sang her to sleep as a girl. That taught her how to weave.

From his airplane seat Stir flips to the next page. But it's blank. Though most of the book remains unfilled, the entries have stopped cold. He feels irritated by the abrupt absence of words. Cheated. In his mind he and Azita have been conversing these past few days, much the way Liddy spoke to the guy in her urn. Like Stir and Philip were supposed to do. Before the birth, Stir had dreamed of Philip someday shadowing his career. But there won't be any shadow, and so this job, and all the energy Stir has poured into it, seems now to have drained away. Imagine having a son, he'd imagined asking Azita, who can't seize any of the sounds you rely on for pleasure and purpose.

Once during a summer visit to Venice Beach, Stir heard a man playing trumpet on the boardwalk. Playing wasn't the right word: it was more like a chorus of rusty swing sets squalling in the wind. Stir learned that the man had woken one morning, deaf, and decided at that moment to take up the trumpet, terribly. On rare occasions he's been known to stumble into a pure note. And when he does a passing pedestrian will fling him a buck, and he says he feels valued. Stir had felt a twinge of envy.

And though there is no reason to feel any envy now for Azita, Stir can't help it. A woman isolated from her spouse, widening the emotional distance with physical miles, but a woman expressing hope for resuscitating a language, hopes Stir is barely holding onto.

A note saying little sits up for him on the stereo equalizer. *Welcome back from Wisconsin,* Melanie writes. She's supposed to serve on a Mozart Appreciation panel today, sponsored by area magnet schools. It slipped her mind, so she's rushing to do that. Philip is with the neighbors in 6-G. He has an ingrown nail they should look at tonight. She suggests dinner out, maybe the Austrian place (Mozart has her in the mood). He keeps reading, but what Melanie *has* written shrinks before him, replaced by words she didn't write: how her job conflict means she can't make today's sign language class, and how she wishes she could ask Stir to take her place, and know that he would.

Stir fetches Philip from 6-G. The neighbors' clean apartment stands in crowing contrast to his own. Even Stir's aquarium looks more like a frat house on Sunday morning: strewn with streaks of angelfish shit, scum around the bowl, food flakes floating unswallowed at the surface. And here is his beautiful boy, staring at the aquarium and inching one finger up the glass side, because he thinks the angelfish will mistake the finger for a worm and flutter over.

Of course the boy is not perfect: It's holy Hell getting Philip to bathe. He has a habit, beyond the boundaries of a "phase," of poking women who wear ruby lipstick. And—he is not perfect because he cannot hear the dishwasher hissing, and is liable to open its door during the drying cycle and get scalded by steam. And—he doesn't hear the shrieks of hypersensitive car alarms he touches in parking lots; the neighbor's kid yelling goodbye in the hallway. Or any of the beloved songs Stir knows note for note.

Sorting the stack of accumulated mail, Stir comes across something from Arnie. He tears the envelope with a single slice. The only item is an undated letter, written in the small swiping script Stir knew now at a glance as Azita's. For one irrational moment he thinks she's written it for him.

Couldn't sleep last night, it reads, waiting for I'anye—so I replayed our tapes of Throso speaking. Most of it was still over my head, but at one point I caught a phrase I didn't understand. She was talking about I'anye's trip: *The waves that brought him to the sea cannot carry him back.* Over next morning's breakfast, I watched the shaman wipe crumbs of rice to the floor, for the dogs, and thought, how quick it must have come, the tidal wave that sent infants and adults tumbling off the earth forever. Voices gone from familiar to extinct in an instant. I got a sinking feeling as he scraped the plate, but had to ask the shaman about that line, and why she had said it. The shaman told me the fishing trip has long been over, much of the catch already cooked, other fishers have been back all this time, but not, and never, I'anye.

His first expedition: untrained, no experience. He hadn't anticipated the force of the aftershock-fueled waves. Had made a misstep in the boat. Something: how it's happened is all wasted guesswork. He didn't survive the trip; the sea took him.

Stir folds the letter. So—Arnie knew all along what was missing from his loft. Why hadn't he canned Stir? Punched him in the jaw? And why on Earth has he sent him this? Azita's last journal entry was dated three weeks ago. His thoughts roll back to Azita's last voice mail on Arnie's phone: how she'd said that "despite it all," she'd stay at Tailor's Islands. Finally it's clear to him what that message meant. She no longer has anything on the island to work for. And still she will not be coming home.

Stir heads to his fax machine, letting Liddy's deal memo hover over the trashcan, poised for a moment to release the band from terms they have no clue they're committed to. But in the end he lets the message go through. He faxes it to his staff at Opening Act. In the weeks ahead Liddy's old label will demand a sizable slice of Summer Salt's royalties. She and her cohorts are about to learn how much of an "advance" winds up retreating from you, and into the hands of others. So what? Stir's job depends on this deal. So does Philip's welfare. Life was full of hidden costs that washed you away.

Stir pictures Azita on the northern shore of Tailor's Islands, after hearing about I'anye's fate. She wants to scream like that aggrieved father she'd spied on her first day. But she doesn't—the scream stays inside. Her eyes pan the tauntingly calm horizon. Surgical gloves, bedpans, and assorted medical supplies stack up on the sand like so much beach trash.

Suddenly, she walks away from the shore with purpose, catching the boy she met on that first day by his arm. He's late for his shift at the hotel, but she blocks his path, so he has no choice but to face her. "What happened to I'anye?" When he doesn't answer, she presses the issue. "No one in your village mentioned his drowning, no one mourned. Even Throso never brought it up. Doesn't she feel sorry she's lost him? Sorry for the lost language?"

"Feel sorry. Again, please say?"

She fumbles for a moment. "Remorse? Do they feel remorse?"

"Ah remorse, I know this term. Even without I'anye I can tell you: We have no match. No word for it in the language."

No remorse? Each day without him, Throso's face grew slacker. She lifted herself off the bed less often. But she wasn't ill. It's his loss that left her this way. Remorse may not be a word the tribe ever voiced, but not saying it can't prevent its effect—it has been in every word she's said to me.

First things first: lunch. Before taking the train to the sign-language class, Stir conducts Philip through Grand Central's food court, where he longingly studies food platters behind the Plexiglas as though they were pups in a pet store. Stir strains to hear each incidental noise: a grill's sizzle; a gimpy fly foraging by a cash register. Sounds his son will never know.

Food in hand, Stir heads upstairs to purchase tickets for the Metro North. Philip points at vending machines along the way, escalators, the opal clock face in the Main Concourse, but Stir can't explain what any of the objects are. At the ticket booth, Philip wrests free of Stir's grip to study the floor tile, forcing passengers to alter their paths. Out of reflex, Stir calls to his son to come back. The passengers grumble as they move around Philip. To them he's just an oblivious kid who won't take dad's commands seriously. This makes them want to jostle Philip, toddler or no. But Stir lets him continue to play, since he isn't causing any trouble—just letting a train schedule cascade down like a Jacob's Ladder.

The ticket agent questions Stir in a lethargic mumble, as if she just woke from a surgery with her jaw wired shut. Stir asks the agent to repeat herself in the microphone, which she does, this time in blaring mumbles.

They stagger syllable by syllable through the transaction. Yes, two tickets.

Yes, paying with cash. Sorry, I didn't catch that? Yes, both to Scarsdale.

"Right," Stir replies. "Both round trip. Wait, I'm sorry. Actually it's only for one full fare. My son's coming with me, but he's not old enough to be charged."

"Fine. Let me see him to confirm he's under five."

Stir says no problem, only when he turns to fetch Philip, there is a problem. The traffic in the terminal has thickened, arrivals rolling in at once from the uptown 4 and 6 trains, the 7 from Shea, and a commuter rail from Chappaqua. And somewhere within the waves of people and noise, Philip has vanished. Stir's eyes sweep the area, and then he darts downstairs, heading back to the food court, which is now so clotted with convergence that he doesn't know where to focus. What would have made Philip up and leave? Dear God—was he taken? Stir retraces their steps. At the ticket booth, he remembers Philip wasn't holding his favorite children's book, *The Cross-Eyed Rabbit*. He probably returned to where he was when he lost it. But had he left it on their table, or at the register? Dropped it while ascending the staircase, or washing at the bathroom sink? Stir stands in a corner to retreat from the noise, collect his thoughts, his shallow breath. That fearful scent of pears is back on his fingertips.

It is then that he hears a pleased playful sigh, no louder than a turning page, though it seems to sweep the corridor. It is his son, softly celebrating his reunion with his favorite book, standing at the opposite corner of the Whispering Gallery. A noise unmistakable to Stir and unheard by his boy, Philip's high murmur, somehow has carried above the crowded bustle and thick complaints of Grand Central Terminal, to reach his father's ears. Philip sighs a few more times, each one an assuring blink, a dash of code for Stir to gather in, and follow back to the source.

Answers to Frequently Asked Questions

A: The see-saw of oil drills in Tyler Texas, the sea salt abruptly absent as he gained distance from Galveston, the disappearance of perspective, as the Oklahoma flats pierced him head-on with their unrelenting expanse...

Q: Specifically where, Benny, did you lose your mind missing her today?

When Benny returns home from his latest cross-country photo shoot, Kate is not there to welcome him. His face goes rigid. His hands curl beneath the breakfast table. She's left him for another man. Probably the Spanish guy. Kate has had enough of their mass-transit marriage, the sham of their side-salad days. Their place is cluttered. Everything in stacks, clusters of junk loitering in remote corners. Hexagonal Ritalin pills are sprinkled atop their bed. Overturning a throw pillow on the windowsill reveals the source of a putrid smell—a glass of milk left out all day.

Benny flashes an antiseptic stare at the apartment. He finds a two-quart saucepan and pours in two servings of instant mashed potatoes. He doesn't panic; he plots. He remakes the apartment in his own image. Nix those saccharine Matisse prints, he figures, those posters advertising Upper East Side benefits for endangered species, union rallies, the rainbow of good shoes Kate is famous for slipping into, the causes she's carted into their lives. He'll put his golf trophy on the sill where the snow-globes now rest. What else can fill the space? Sally Mann photographs, maybe his Ansel Adams—no, she'd bought him the Adams, he can't put *that* up. How could Kate have left the place this way, left him to sort through every object, left him behind in a museum he can't leave?

Who was it? Probably the Spanish guy from her office. Is she with him now? When he's here does he use Benny's comb in the morning? And at night does he use this wall to support her back and her ass while he gets ready to slide in?

Ten minutes into this, potatoes boiling on stove, the phone rings. Kate's voice is thin and soft.

"Where are you?" he asks. "Why aren't you here?"

Her Uncle Ted has suffered a massive coronary. Benny blows his relief into the phone, a gluey gasp he hopes will sound like sympathy. She's calling from the Airfone, can't talk long—they're about to begin their final descent. "Will you come," she asks, "to the funeral?" Though Uncle Ted hasn't died yet, tragedies of the past have shaped Kate's family into a finely regimented unit of pragmatism. They've already made a down payment at the mortuary. The funeral will be held in Tucson, where Kate's headed now; a long distance for most of the family to cover, but Ted would have wanted it there. Benny can't help but think that the family needn't leave it to chance—there's still time to ask Uncle Ted what he wants, directly.

"Listen, Benny, I made a list." She tears a page out of something, maybe an in-flight magazine. "I left some things undone at the house that need tending to. First off, move the car so we don't get ticketed. And see about holding our mail—is it still before five there, anyway? If it is, deposit my check that's pinned to the corkboard. It's signed and ready to go. Oh, and the plants, obviously. Water them all, except..." He hears her crumpling the page. "You know what, forget all that. Just get here. Get here, okay?"

Benny tells Kate not to worry about arranging his flight. He'll take care of everything. And on some level he means precisely what he's said.

Two airlines do not allow cats and dogs in the cargo holds. All of them permit firearms. Waiting on hold for twenty minutes, and these are all the answers Benny has to show for it. Every two minutes he hears the prerecorded mantra of customer service: "Someone will be with you shortly," and it soothes him to believe this is so. It also puts him at ease when he's told that "operators are standing by." Either phrase is such a relaxing alternative to, "Sucker, don't hold your breath."

Benny studies the window facing the Verrazano-Narrows Bridge. The sun tracks along the horizon, and leaves a dusty filigree in its wake. The longer he waits, the testier he gets. Why couldn't Kate have waited for him to get back before leaving? It's been a week since they last shared a whole weekend. He reaches for his wallet and takes out his copy of her credit card. Since they got married, they share it all: credit card accounts, grocery lists, tax returns, closet space, absolutely everything but each other.

He pulls back from the name on the card (her first name and middle initial, and his last name—their last name—Daubach). "Why couldn't she have waited?" is not a fair question. He knows how important Uncle Ted has been to her since she lost her father. Family ties seep deeply into all aspects of his wife's life—when one is severed, they all are—and this is something he both admires and envies. The only corollary in his life comes in the darkroom, how if the thinnest slice of light slips into the room, all his work is lost. The truth—the truth, that is, if he'll just be honest with himself—is that he was shaken up long before today. Things had begun to shake at the same moment they seemed to be going well. And—the truth again?—Kate's tight family ties don't help. Benny resents hearing all the Ted anecdotes, resents how she's managed to maintain a relationship with her uncle over thousands of miles, but not with her husband.

"Have you been helped?"

It shocks him to be spoken to, after going through a whole Muzak concert. "Sorry. Could you repeat the question?"

Faced with delays from the start, it's the magic hour before Benny's plane finally boards, the time of dawn when sunlight complies most with the physics of photography. The sun is positioned perfectly. In the distance its beams strike the canny, swooping curves of the TWA terminal. Mesmerized, Benny stares at the glare as he hands over his boarding pass and heads down the corridor.

It's a full flight. Benny sits next to a couple with a baby girl. She lies in her mother's lap, her limbs enacting some sort of giddy pantomime of carpentry. First she hammers the air with a happy closed fist. Next she saws a piece of imaginary timber with her left leg.

Benny badly wants a drink. Just one Dewar's to nip at. He could at least order Bloody Mary mix for the approximation. Flight attendants pass by any number of times, but he never pulls one aside. He doesn't want to alarm the family he's sitting beside, make them think their newborn is just inches from a drunk. So he flattens his face to the cold window and hopes the visions of ascending altitude will repress his desire.

The plane glides across the sky, curling around a squall line. The clouds in front loom like dark, cocksure waves. Behind him the formations are colonies of harmless snow.

Turbulence straps the hull; the baby starts to cry. Her voice cracks nearly in time with the thunder. The mother apologizes. "Her first time in the sky," she explains. Benny takes a sideward glance; the father has finished his Pepsi and is working on his wife's cup of milk—the cluster of little bubbles atop its skin sit like arachnid eyes.

The mother's hair is unwashed. It smells of carrots and countertop cleanser. She holds a copy of *Teen People*. The father is dressed in beer slogans; exhausted, his eyes quiver like fumes on a hot highway. How young they are. Benny notes that they aren't wearing rings. Just goes to show; it takes more than a marriage license. The hungry, haunted heart can outwit a license. But a child keeps a couple together. Benny wishes he and Kate had slipped up on contraception. Wishes there was a baby between them, forcing them to strip down their lives. Things would be complicated, but these complications would begin and end at home, not be fanned out like prairie flames across the entire continent.

"Don't feed her *that*, Carol!" the husband admonishes, snatching a spoonful of applesauce away. "Fruit passes through her like a fucking sieve," he laughs, tugging the brim of his cap. "If I were smarter, I'd have bought stock in Pampers and Huggies." He fixes his rueful stare into the fabric pattern of another seat.

The baby coughs up a nickel of spit, orange and flaked, like sink rust.

"Uh oh. Bad color. We'd better...honey? Don't you think?"

"Excuse us," says the father. He struggles to dislodge a small canvas bag from the overhead compartment, then follows his wife and child to the lavatory. As he swivels out, his fanny pack brushes against a woman on the cabin's other side. She stirs from her shallow sleep. Her lips tap together. For a moment her almond eyes open. Then close again. Her eyelids are flat and full, shimmering as two fish afloat in day-lit water. The whale-moan of the turbines catches up to her: her head lops back onto her shoulder.

Q: How did Kate sleep before you got the job?

A: On her side. Her body was like the slat of a Venetian blind, bending to my touch, but springing back straight the moment I let go. Right hand behind her back, forearm beached on the hip. Her chin a little lifted, as though expectant for a kiss, a whisper, some physical token to take into the netherworld.

Q: And now?

A: Now she sleeps on her stomach. Hands sprawled flat. Taking up most of the mattress. By the time she's adapted to my presence in the bed, and has switched back to her side, I have to leave again.

The storm front has caught them. Lightning flashes strum the wings, as the pilot works to maintain cruising altitude. Benny looks up. The thin roof above him is the last roof left in his world. Above it only stratosphere remains, cold, colored like quicksilver, brutal and enormous. Benny looks across to the sleeping woman. Imagines the plane being struck by lightning—things set in motion by the gift of finality—and reaching for her. Would there be enough time to grab her, lock eyes, tuck his fingers beneath her jacket, begin to kiss, fuck furious with urgency, divorced from tact, eager to dismantle regrets in sexual consumption's bright, searing release? He tends to his breathing. How is it, my brain, in moments of worry, flocks toward such selfish carnivals?

Time passes neither swiftly nor smoothly, but they land intact. The couple wraps the baby in a blanket. When she flings her pacifier, the father is ready; he catches it brilliantly.

Q: How many bags do the airlines allow passengers to take?
A: Delta permits two carry-on items (with ten exceptions), while Northwest permits three (with six). The FAA standard for checked luggage is three pieces per person. I've coaxed my way into getting five bags in the cargo hold, and three more carried on. I've fashioned the plane into my own mini U-Haul.
Q: Could you just leave Kate by attrition? Take a few bags here and a few there, nothing too visible until the last trip, leaving only furniture and a page-long letter?
A: No. If he's going to do it he needs to do it now, do it quickly, in just one shot.

Just as the warning is issued that items may have shifted during the flight, Benny lifts the handle to the overhead compartment, and is hit squarely on the head by a piece of pottery. His knees buckle, and he slumps to the ground.

The young father is the first to see, or to respond: "You okay there, buddy?"

His wife: "Benny, Doug. I think he said his name was Benny."

Someone else: "You got knocked pretty hard."

Mannered voice (flight attendant?): "You feel okay, sir? Want us to send for someone to take a look at that, or have the ground crew bring you by cart to your final destination?"

Benny smells the heroics. Everyone wants to look good in an emergency, and this is close enough. "My head is fine," he says, gritting. "And this *is* my final destination."

The passengers begin to break away. Yesterday, during his shoot in Philadelphia, Benny watched a woman feeding pigeons. The peppery mass surged when she held out her hands and dropped pieces of bread. They fluttered away when it seemed she'd spent her supply. Only when she produced another chunk of dough from her pocket did they inch back. Maybe it could work that way now. Maybe the passengers would stay and listen if he told them that while, yes, he could recite his name and social security number, and count backwards from ten, he could not name the last day he'd gone to bed confidently beside his wife. What if he mentioned he was leaving Kate, and using her dead relative as a coupon to get a cheaper fare? Or that the piece of pottery that just clipped him on the head—a garish clay duck with a bright-green bill and a tuft of yellow fuzz on the top like a mound of grated cheese—was the same piece of pottery that Mexican customs had claimed from Kate and Benny during their honeymoon? That they'd never gotten it back, and so there is no way Benny could have packed it in the suitcase out of which it's fallen? Then would they flutter back? Well, maybe they would, maybe they wouldn't: Benny isn't holding any food.

The airline representative at O'Hare looks at Benny's ticket funny when he asks for all his bags now. "Sir. You know your itinerary has you bound for Arizona?"

He shrugs meekly. The woman's thick eyebrows arch at the middle, like dorsal fins. Her barrette clamps her hair into crisp, military lines. "Listen," she says, "I'll take care of these for you if you want to run to Gate 26-E. I can have them hold the plane..."

"I know what I'm doing. I just want my baggage."

She holsters her walkie-talkie and lets him pass. "Fine. Your loss."

Travelers sweep smoothly around baggage claim. They yank their duffels, totes, and hanging bags with efficient, parental jerks. They glide along conveyer belts carrying them to other gates. He cannot smell their deodorant, beer breath, sweat. Suits are pressed. Stockings have no runs. Mints are melting against their tongues.

He holds the clay duck, studies it. He really should hand it over to the lost and found. He had forgotten, after the clunk and tussle of deplaning, that the duck must belong to someone else. It's certainly chintzy enough to be mass-produced. It's the only logical explanation—it had been taken from them months ago, so Benny clearly couldn't have packed it. He hails a cab to a hotel and pays for his room in cash.

He calls Kate from the busy lobby so it will sound like he's in O'Hare changing planes, and not in a hotel, changing lives. Things are hectic in Tucson. Kate apologizes. "I got grandma duty. I'm obligated to drive Nana whenever and wherever Nana wants. So I'm not sure I can be at the airport the moment you arrive."

"That's fine. Do what you have to. I won't expect you."

Kate asks how the first leg of the flight has gone. Benny decides to keep it light. Not tell her about the turbulence. "What about," she asks, "your trip to Pittsburgh?"

"You mean Philadelphia. Philadelphia was fine." Except it was gray. Grave with fog. Most of his shots would turn out poorly. He doesn't want to talk about his job. Or how he's missed another important moment in Kate's life. He realizes he wants to talk about the duck (which he's been holding since he left the airport). He remembers the spot in Saltillo where they bought it. A tourist trap outside of a cathedral. They'd been wed two days and this was their first souvenir. Her breath was happy and heavy with *tacos al pastor*. They bought sodas from a vendor who convinced them to drink out of plastic bags so he could keep the bottles and get reimbursed for the glass. So she sucked oversweet Coke from a bag and looked straight ahead into the plastic. "Look at this," she'd said. "Look where I'm looking." He bent to gaze through the bag: the edges of the cathedral wiggled and waved and blinked, like a plastic castle within a fishbowl. The city seemed submerged. They were lost at sea. They closed their ears to the spitting cars, their noses to the aging street refuse, and built their ocean. A shredded T-shirt hanging on barbed wire became seaweed. The cacti looked like anemones. The cathedral posts were filled with encrusted barnacles. Kate had just landed a position in press relations for the Audubon Society; Benny's luck had followed right on the heels of hers, a job shooting photos for a real estate firm. They toasted their fortunes, bumped plastic bags, and sucked down the rest. They became the worst kind of gringos, insufferably happy, laughing loud, pretending to swim, to be crossing an ocean floor as though atop a balance beam.

But if he speaks about this, he will have to tell her everything. He doesn't have enough strength to tell her everything.

"Benny?"

"Hmm."

"You okay, quiet man?" He mumbles something about needing coffee. "No...I know what's bugging you. The place was a mess, and I wasn't in it. I know that feeling, I don't like that feeling."

"Kate, it's me. Really. It's me, not you."

"I should have left a note."

Benny stares into the weave of the metal coil below the pay phone receiver. He realizes he hasn't asked a single question. She has had to manipulate the conversation, pretend he has asked questions, so she can tell him the information he needs. He hasn't even asked when Uncle Ted finally died. He must have sometime during Benny's flight, because now Kate is talking firm dates and flowers.

Quiz shows have been Benny's steadiest companions in recent months. Since he took the digital photography job, his success in answering their questions has had a soothing effect. It makes him feel relevant to harbor answers to the contained mysteries of life.

His own life, their life, has fallen into a bleak formula: he gets sent away in the late afternoon. The travel agent at his company, Manifest Destiny, calls to tell him where he's needed. He counts the number of time zones his latest trip will distance him from Kate. Each one is like a high hurdle. But he agrees and hangs up. He has to agree—he is going places. They are both going places. The worlds they work for have recognized their ambitions and talents and have raised the stakes. If they fold now, if they learn to say no, then the offers and phone calls, the gratification, stop coming. His bags are always packed. His wingtips face the door, his toothbrush and deodorant are the only things he unpacks from his Dopp kit.

The hours between four and six P.M. become important. At home, this is when he waits for the call, to be sent away to some corner of the country. Usually he is still reeling, still tense or tired from the previous trip. He shoots pictures of real estate for Manifest Destiny, plots of unplundered land for developers to drool over. He captures images of potential paradises for others to sell. He has to make the unkempt grasses and quagmire fields seem appetizing. In Hawaii, Iowa, Jackson Hole.

Normally he would arrive at his locations late at night, wake just below the ceiling of dawn, shoot two-dozen rolls, and drive the rental back to his hotel. As he drove, he'd flip the radio dial until he found a quiz show. Benny competes. He does very well. Facts and minutiae, all of it staggeringly trivial, emerge from his brain with an endorphin rush.

He has become obsessed with playing them. He has become such an expert that, over time, the games began to lose their challenge. When that happened, Benny began to make up his own questions. He tries to identify the last five disinfectants used in the rental car: pine...vanilla...coconut... apple...new car; a hard game, since they mix and match, a scented gravy. He stops at a 7-Eleven, Drake's, Stop-N-Go—which will come first?—for a juice or water. At a McDonald's drive-in: will they ask if he wants to supersize it? Somewhere on some road, he lowers Zoloft on his tongue as gently as the neon mints placed on his hotel-room pillows, and tries to reconstruct his wife's face from the ashes of twilight.

Later, as his business trips became more frequent, his separation from Kate more constant, Benny began talking to himself. Not in the usual form—cursing himself for missing a turn, singing to a jingle—instead, he started his own quiz show. Trying to keep in touch with an unformed life, testing his ability to recall their routine back in New York ...only they haven't had time to build a routine in the first place. The questions come regardless of whether he's agreed to join the fray of the game. The lightning round proceeds without his blessing.

What kind of vegetable does she insist on removing from sandwiches?
Which colors does she wear together on rainy days?
What is the name of the condition her health-care plan won't cover?
Who is the guy she shares office space with? The one she refers to a bit too often? The Spanish guy?
What time of the month is she fertile?

These are questions Benny has, in the past nine months, forgotten the answers to, in order of increasing frustration.

And then there is the affair. The indiscretion. Whatever it is, he has to answer for it. When he met Greta in Alameda, Benny somehow found it easy to forgive the sex (short, inattentive, unremarkable). He found it easy to forgive himself for standing up naked and talking to Kate in his hotel room as Greta traced a circular path along his knee with her thumb. Writing to Greta is what he found the most unforgivable.

But that's exactly what happened. He spun out a note to her, another, then two in one week. Still—the transgression seemed less severe when he did it at hotels in daylight. He was putting a mistake to bed. That was the story he wedged into his head, like a crowbar forcing itself into a space. But when Benny began writing Greta at night, at home, in bed, in plain sight of Kate, he knew his life was smearing.

"So get another job," Kate spits out from time to time, in answer to his gripes. It's not a demand—she never demands—they don't really know each other well enough to demand. But he doesn't trust his employment value, wants to keep going until he's promoted. So when he says no, she pulls back and grabs her jacket, maybe takes a walk to cool down, but not too long, because she's running out of hours before Benny's next departure. She comes back conciliatory—a trait that doesn't suit her.

He thought about bringing it up with his therapist. But he is afraid of his therapist. His therapist likes to make small talk about hockey and do Nicholas Cage impressions. When his shrink does talk like a shrink, Benny giggles, because the words come out with a Bronx nasality. Neurosis? Yeah, new roses. Same garden, though.

Sick of his hotel room, Benny is drawn to bodies. Leaving the duck on his nightstand, he takes the El to Finishers, a dance club near Wrigleyville he hits each time his work brings him to the Windy City. Inside the club a spinning disco ball whirls, producing an effect like fish on a racetrack. The dancers make small, vibrating steps that seem to lack true motion. Benny chucks Kipper, the bartender, on the shoulder. Kipper has a crooked smile, a shaved head, earlobes fenced in with metal hoops and studs. His every fourth word is "fucking"; his every fifth, "cunt." Kate would not like him. Benny frequented Finishers before it became hot; in gratitude, his first drink is always free. Benny is all too happy to make that first drink a double.

The hours dance away. The fingers of whiskey get longer. He makes friends with the dancing bodies. Moving from one to next as though trying out beds in a mattress showroom. One body dances with particular fierceness. She's in a fight with the bass line. Her eyelids flick open and shut in time to the beat, like a splash of flesh. The sweat glistens from her skin, collecting at the neck on the knot of her fichu. She curls a finger at Benny. Me? But it isn't a question. They are far too drunk, their minds too discontinuous to bother with questions. Benny is for sale.

The woman again flings her finger at Benny. Downward this time. As she does, the ring she is wearing falls off. It spins along the floor and bumps into his feet. When Benny stoops to picks it up, his mind floods with memories of his proposal. How the ring he'd given Kate was the wrong size. Loose on the fourth finger. He'd asked her not to wear it until he made an appointment with the jeweler. She'd refused. She displayed it everywhere, tugging on the bottom of the band so the top held tightly, creating the illusion of a perfect fit.

As Benny scans the floor for this woman's ring, his eyes get lost in a pond of darkness and shoes. By the time he finds what he's looking for, she's out of sight. He has to get this back to her. He slaps a twenty on the bar, then sees all the empty glasses surrounding him. Twenty won't cover this wreck. Does he have enough to cover? Maybe Kipper will let it slide.

"B, you okay?" Kipper has come over. He is trying to help.

"Did you she where see—see where she—went? The beautiful woman. With the ring she fell off. The ringer fell off. Her finger." His drink feels heavy in his hand. Like baggage. This tiny glass is making his ligaments deaden. The deejay stopped playing Poi Dog Pondering; now he's spinning a house mix of "His Eyes Are on the Sparrow." "Did anyone see her?"

"Did we see the beautiful woman? We're *all* looking for her!"

"Yeah, and if you find her, find out does she got a sister?"

"You find her sister, find out will she *do* her sister?"

It's a mistake expecting answers from people on the lam. The alcoholics continue to speak in spoonerism. Later each man will drop his hotel keys and pick up someone else's set, exchanging rooms for the night.

"Tell me again where you are."

"Stop yelling," Benny pleads to Kate, standing just outside the club.

His motor skills are beached. It took six minutes to succeed in putting the call through. His fingers kept fumbling, he kept getting automated bemusement ("I'm sorry, but I don't know what you dialed. Try your number again."); what happened to "Someone will be with you shortly"?

"No one's yelling," Kate insists. "*Someone's* been drinking, though."

"It's true," Benny answers. "It's all true."

"So what the hell is your status?" Kate gets confidential with the phone, speaking too close to its mouthpiece. A snapshot flashes in his head: her burgundy lipstick pressing against the telephone. "You're what, on standby to Tucson?"

Finishers' last call lolls onto the street. They play games with oncoming cars. They scream that they are the kings of Chicago, and also the most misunderstood fucks on the planet. Is this really what they think? "I'm on standby to Tucson."

"How can someone flying to a funeral be put on standby? Did you complain?"

In the background Benny hears Kate's mother giggling to a comedian's stand-up act. "Kate," he says, "I'm tired of complaining." He has to speak to her. He has to divulge this other life. He had prepared notes for it, but now he can't remember what he's supposed to say. Maybe there is no other life. Maybe there are no notes.

She laughs.

"What? What?"

"Oh, it's…" She trails off. "The comedian's talking about losing wallets, keys, phone numbers. How when you find the thing, other people feel compelled to ask where you found it. Like it isn't enough *that* you found it, like they're planning on losing something there themselves in the near future. And just how…"

"Yeah?"

"Never mind. You had to be here."

Q: Why do I want to hang up right now?

A: Because you hear something in her voice that sounds like a runner giving up midway through a race.

"Hey," Benny asks, holding the phone even closer, "what is it?"

"Since I got here we've bought all this stuff. Food for the service. Wine. Boxes of lilies from the flower market. We got Nana new black pumps and arch supports. I had to get my hair done."

Q: Get it done how?

A: I don't believe it. Do not think of a question like that in a moment like this.

"And I can't remember if all this is supposed to make us remember or forget him, but no one else in the family seems to be talking about him now that we're so busy. I need you here to tell me it's okay that his being gone is all I can think about."

Q: Now I've been told by our producers that your wife is tuning in from another city. Do you have any messages to give her?

A: Hi Kate.

Q: Judges? Sorry, more specific, please. Any regrets to convey?

A: [Inaudible]

Q: Our microphone didn't catch that—can we have your final answer?

A: [Throat clearings] Being married to, and not known to, each other, and being married longer and not knowing more, and having not waited longer and having not known better.

Four in the morning. Stucco. Benny stares at the dried paint on the ceiling, cratered and cracking, like something lunar. He thinks in the dark about Gene Autry.

When Gene Autry died, Kate couldn't reach Benny. Benny was working late in a darkroom in Denver. There had been a mishap with the chemicals. She didn't have the number to the darkroom; his pager was at the hotel. When he read about it the next morning, he tried to call her from the room, but she'd already gone to work. Autry meant nothing to Benny, but he meant a lot to Kate. She loved the Singing Cowboy because her father had, and her father had loved him because he had been the only hero her father and her grandfather could share.

Maybe Benny shouldn't have felt so guilty. Maybe he shouldn't have overloaded on drinks on the plane ride home, doubled his Zoloft dosage. Maybe the clamp of the wingtips shouldn't have pinched so much. But he should have found a way. He never did comfort Kate about Gene Autry. By the time he got back, the gesture seemed ridiculous. On that plane ride home, his mind wound tight, and five-dollar vodka couldn't loosen it. His attempts at being a friend to his wife were crashing at his feet.

Q: Have there been other Autry moments?
A: Hell, yeah, high count. The day of Kate's six-month job performance review at Audubon. The night of the Lucinda Williams benefit concert she coordinated. I've missed more moments than I've made.
Q: Couldn't you have been somehow responsive?
A: I was. Not to her, but to myself. I startled myself with surrender. Had a stupid affair, began writing love notes to a girl I shared nothing but sex with. The letters to my wife were too painful, the raw bad habit of our solitude, and they served as reminders of how little time we'd spent together since the wedding, how seldom our paths converged.

Benny's pager vibrates on room 1622's black Formica table. He reads the LED with a sense of relief. Kate. He dials slowly. His fingers feel punchy from the alcohol. Two rings cut the silence. A male voice answers. "Yes?"
Benny grabs the hotel bedsheet and makes a hem. "I'm sorry. I must have the wrong—"
"Daubach? That you?"
"Yes. Who is—"
"It's Sal, from work. Listen, when you're done with your family mess, we need you. A shoot in Spokane. The developer is already losing money…"
Work. Had it been work that called him? Not Kate from Tucson? No, he couldn't get an area code wrong. He just dialed work by mistake. "But listen, Benny, I got you a nice setup. Drinks are on us. SelectaVision at the hotel. And I don't know if they have riverboats there, but if you want to gamble, go ahead blow a hundred, and we'll take it out of petty cash."
Benny hangs up and turns off his cell. He is nervous that Sal will just call right back through the hotel switchboard, but then remembers he has paid for this hotel room with his own cash. He's untraceable. His whereabouts are, to everyone, a question.
It's light enough now that the blinds don't matter. Benny can see the room's every ineffectual detail. The lace trickling down the curtain like a waterfall of salt crystals. The wet bar with its paper seal guarding him from the insides. And that lamp on the nightstand. That lamp. A tacky faux Tif-

fany. He steps to it cautiously. Investigates its glass shade: silver and ruby moths joined at the wingtips, circling the skirt. And there, plain as day, is the crack. It's the same faux Tiffany, the very one, that he broke in his hotel the night Gene Autry died. The morning after Autry died and Benny couldn't reach Kate. He had wheeled his elbow into it, cracking the outer glass, making a bullet hole break in one of the moths' thoraces. He'd tossed it into a Dumpster, saying nothing to hotel management. And now it was here, in front of him. The same lamp, same break, different city.

He pages Kate with his room number. Looking at the white, comatose wall, Benny waits for her to call back. Even knowing what he has to say, he anticipates hearing her voice.

"Asshole. I know all about you."

Benny swallows at Kate's opening line. But it's a confused swallow. Because this was the reaction he might expect from her, only he hasn't told her anything yet. And because her tone sounds less like she's lashing him and more like she's—well—laughing.

"I just signed off from your company's URL, Benny. You've been keeping secrets."

"Our Website? What were you doing there?"

"I couldn't take any more chauffeuring. Nana's had me drive her to five manicurists. So when she finally went in for her appointment, I just drove to an Internet café. And, you know, surfed your site. And you..." Her voice slinks into a huskiness he doesn't recognize. "You've been keeping secrets from me."

"What secrets?"

"Don't play. You've posted pictures of our apartment on your company's Sites for Sale page. Pictures of our bedroom, our fire hazard lobby, the dining room we spent six months picking out china for, and that we've had a meal in together—what?—six times?"

He had done this months ago but never told Kate. He'd taken pictures of their apartment, every angle in every hour of light, rolls and rolls of evidence that he could go back to with the click of a mouse. So that no matter where he was, he could see where he wanted to be.

"So should I be worried?" Kate asks, and there's that laugh again.

"Worried?"

"Does this mean you put our place up for sale?"

"No. I plugged in a phony reference number. Even if someone saw the listing, was interested in buying our place, and *did* call, they'd reach a voicemail that doesn't accept messages."

For the first time in months he knows that Kate is crying with a smile on her end of the phone. "But what if someone from work found out you were posting a fraudulent listing, or...Benny, you're not going to get your fucking promotion from that place, you're going to get your fucking walking papers. Why would you take a risk like that?"

"What can I say? Twenty-four hours. I needed some twenty-four-hour connection to you." He places the clay duck upright in his palm. Its fuzzy hair is thinner and more orange than the flame of a tiki torch. "I needed souvenirs."

A place to return to and be vigilant for. Otherwise, he knows only the uninvited country. The convenience store on Route 10 in Piedmont, where they keep live bait next to the ice cream freezer. The coastal towns alight with clean parks, groomed gardens, and other well-placed fingerprints of urban planning. The naked and nameless Midwest, with its skin of grass and wheat, dull as a hangover. The truck stop in Whately, Massachusetts, where he can tell what kind of service he'll get from the counter waitress by the way she has worn her hair. At first all of this had charmed him. He thought himself part of a wider field of vision. But these were all just patterns. He quickly saw what he was losing. The souvenirs of his homeland, the raw and complicated memories—the call letters of the jazz station they like to listen to on Sundays; the scent of the brackish bananas Kate insists on storing on top of the refrigerator (though Benny says the Freon kills them); the tripwire of their bed, the spot where when you roll across it, a loud cricket creaking sound begins. Kate herself, not lost at first, at first just transformed into a series of frantic phone calls, then sad postcard reports, lately, something more distant even than that: a woman he'd once been in love with and was beginning to lose touch with.

Just as he'd lost touch with much already. The failure to find a middle to meet in. The fight to keep their sex life breathing. Subscribing to Cinemax and watching soft-core porn together on the telephone. Timing the chemicals: they took her halving her Ritalin dosage, him knocking off his Zoloft dosage three days before he returns from long trips (and resenting the sluggish feeling he fights through when his clients look over and accept his photos at dinner), all so they can come together. But there is more to chemistry than chemicals. There is expectancy. History. The possibility of a life lived with someone whose presence in it both quickens time and elucidates its passage.

"I mean Kate, what can I say?"

"You say it's nothing, and you'll be in Tucson soon."

Careful how you answer. Only he really does believe it now. Words of the present, like *are* and *is*, float through him like a sane piece of music. His arms, when he next sees her, will be filled with negotiations. *But careful with the answer. Don't describe, or question, or even think about, the feeling you feel right now sinking to the back of the throat—what to call it?—the gnarl of undeserved redemption.* But he will make it good. He swears. The wanderer in him will die in the flight out west. *Only careful how you answer.* "I'll be in Tucson soon," Benny says, his eyes running over the break in the lamp, this portable past, "and it's nothing."

Observing the Sabbath

That was a lark; this is a dial tone. And those must be sanitation men clicking garbage cans together. Marie is intimate with each sound surrounding her secret. Some are ornamental (the lark's song); some threatening (the sanitation men—why do they do their job with no regard for the sleeping, or the waking that need the sleeping to stay asleep?). Some sounds serve as signals to the self: her own knuckles rapping at her pack of Virginia Slims, the breath of Mister Coffee as it percolates and pops. Signals reminding her of her subterfuge, and the doubts that dig into it like ivy into brick.

But yesterday was Sunday...

Doesn't matter; this is Monday. Both start and finish of her work week. For the past few months of Mondays, Marie has been buying clutches of a pharmaceutical stock—five shares here, another ten there—listening to analysts report back its success, speculating on its future growth, collecting in last week's mail her first dividend, $31.84. This Monday is different, though. It is her last. This Monday is the culmination; she has a script. Four hundred fifty shares please, in Advances/Neogen.

To get to this day she has had to keep her script quiet. It was important for Marie to purchase certain things: disposable calling cards, a cordless phone, a West Coast edition of *The Wall Street Journal*, personal copies of *The Los Angeles Times*. Slippers with soft pads, which helped Marie make light footfalls in the morning. Without those slippers, the steps Marie made on Mondays would've woken her youngest daughter Ellen—Ellen liked to help her mom fix breakfast. Children's Contac for Ed—a much weaker medicine than Ed's chronic cough warranted. A mix whose taste neatly mirrors the maximum-strength, doctor's orders stuff Marie administers to her husband on six of seven weeknights. But not Sunday nights. By Monday morning the Contac wears off, and Ed's coughing fits alert Marie to his presence the moment he first stirs.

It was also important to find a trader on the East Coast, with whom Marie could place orders at sunrise. One who wouldn't flinch at the intricacies of the situation. Trader Brian. Brian has been with Marie through all of this. He has had to go on faith. He has had to respect that when Marie hangs up mid-transaction, it's nothing personal. "It's me. I'm back. No, you aren't rushing me. I heard noises. I thought it was him."

And Brian has had to screen and disguise all their business transactions, and all their correspondence, and respect the protocol. Marie and Ed are married, united nearly twenty years ago, in the backdrop of holy vows, in the Catholic Church, with the Pope's abstract approval mixed in somewhere. And now on Mondays Marie is making deals, getting in on the ground floor with a commercial enterprise that happens to be promoting, as its primary venture, the American distribution and sale of mifepristone, RU-486, the abortion pill. If Brian's brokerage firm were to send letters and earnings reports bearing the corporation's logo, Ed would suspect, and then he would confront, and then he would know. And it's not that Ed would become violent if he knew—but something violent would happen. Ed's torso and forearms would sag when it sank in, like a marionette marooned by its puppeteer. That Marie could do this thing in the home she and Ed share would name, irrevocably, a separation that has been widening between them, without comment or resistance, for years.

That is the dark wet cough owned by Ed, owning Ed. That is the doorknob turning as Ed takes a walk up Sepulveda to clear his head of its ritual morning lassitude. Yes, he actually walks up smoggy Sepulveda to *clear* his head, and to loosen from his throat the liquid colored like sycamore bark. Marie must place the call quickly. Ed's walk to the corner grocer—for the beer he swears he waits until noon to down, and the newspaper he skims before leaving to Marie, not knowing she disposed of her own, private copy almost an hour before—will take him twelve minutes, thirty seconds. Enough time to make the trade she's put off so far. His shower will take ten minutes, and that may not be enough time. Doing it now is crucial.

But yesterday was Sunday...

And there was the doxology. The pipe organ at the cathedral's rear, circa Korean conflict, whistled dense beacons of *On Calvary*. The hymn's final measure lingered in the rafters, a scar of the original sound. Not the same sound as a receiver off its cradle— though there is some crossover in pitch and tone between the two. Enough to get Marie thinking about the oncoming day. As she sat in the pew she considered what she was about to do, and the stones she'd stepped over to bring her to this moment. To buy the first shares of this stock, Marie had skimmed money from her eldest daughter. Rebecca is a freshman attending a UC in central California. Marie had joint access to Rebecca's checking account. Ed was forgiving, when his daughter called for more cash earlier than expected. Ed figured it would take her time to learn to budget. Marie listened silently on her end of the phone, wondering whether her deceit was even necessary. She might be stealing from a kindred spirit. Ideally, Rebecca would support her mother's decision. But there is no way of knowing. This subject was always bowdlerized at the dinner table...and now it seems actually mutinous to examine the roots of faith and the flashpoints where divergence occurs. At an early visit to the UC campus, shaking the warty right hand of the campus minister, Marie recalled thinking: Do not set my girl back twenty years from where she is.

In the winter Marie made a play to speed the plow. She suggested taking on a job of her own, to help keep cash flowing. She suggested waitressing, an idea Ed refused; he'd been on too many demolition crews whose men, after holding down jackhammers all morning, looked forward to one hour in a diner grasping at asses. He'd coveted such women in such ways at such diners himself. They settled on a job Marie was qualified for, and one that would allow her ass to remain hidden behind a desk: reception clerk at the YWCA. Half the money went to Marie. The other half she deposited into Rebecca's account, of which Marie then circuitously funneled a third. After a few months, Ed told Marie to quit—his wounded provider's pride had taken enough hits and taunts from friends. But by then, Marie had scrimped up enough to go through with her plan. She'd also purchased new bedroom curtains and a dress of mild extravagance, to promote to Ed the notion that she was properly shopping her clutch of cash away.

Speaking of things proper, yesterday was Sunday...and Ed's left temple slid along the pillow as he curled into the contours beside Marie. The minute hand was barely left of midnight and the two of them had just made love. Ed's pants were in a ball, like a sleeping toddler on a rug. He'd whispered, "Wasn't sure we'd ever be up to *that* again," and this summary had been Sunday's second bookend. The first bookend was harder to identify. Maybe it was Ed sipping ginger ale with Sudafed, telling Marie he could feel his strength returning. Maybe it was the way he wiped dishwater on his pants and rushed from the kitchen, coughing shards, when Ellen cried, "Angel's walking funny," as though the family cat were more irreplaceable than he was. Whatever it was that had first stirred Marie, from that point on she and Ed had shared ten hours unlike any shared in ten years. This couldn't be them, laughing (without wine), springing for a sitter on Sunday night, stepping down a dance hall staircase like tightrope walkers, not caring whom they bumped or what lay below, just so long as their hands remained together. As the evening progressed, she kept checking the clocks in store windows, and strangers' watches. For a signal that this wasn't real. She'd heard somewhere it was impossible to dream about increments of time. And surely this was a dream, this wasn't them.

Once—twenty years ago—Marie had been keeping another secret that felt like a dream. The sound of a boy cheering in the background had been her signal that it wasn't. Marie had called a man named Jack in Massachusetts. Called Jack to inform him that Ed, her fiancé, had just put his house in Somerville up for sale. Ed was moving to California. But whether or not she went along she would leave to Jack. She wanted to know what, or when, Jack would leave for her. Then Marie heard Richie, Jack's adolescent son, yelling gleefully from the den—his basketball team was savaging the opponent. She hung up. She was ridiculous. Heart pounding like a crush victim. Not knowing where she stood, her intent was to make things shaky for others. She yanked the line out so Jack couldn't call back. The exposed wire was the color of a hamstring.

So. Marie now forms a prayer and dials Trader Brian. Brian whispers "Morning." Marie hangs up. But it's a cordless phone this time, and there's no line to yank. So she dials again, hears "Morning..." again, and then, "We'll go slow Marie. Your speed and no faster. Just say when you're ready to buy." But she isn't buying. She's bargaining. Between the God she entered into covenant with and the one her husband has.

Could she convince Ed it was something other than conscience steering her to buy the stock shares? That it was only about the money? History after all is filled with poisoned principles. The janitors at the Tuskeegee Institute. The nurses at Chernobyl; their chemical-coated fingers working overtime. Everyone at one time makes his or her bread from the mill of human misery. Even you, Ed. Even the workingmen of union 4011, who imbibe in the morning coffee grounds, being beans before, plucked by the numb fingers of migrant farmers in Guatemala; coffee grounds which give your local in California the drive to work ten hours beneath surgical masks and corduroy gloves, cordoned off from open air, scraping the sagas of asbestos from tenement halls in Watts. Yes. She *could* convince Ed it was only about money, but what would she be if she did?

Those are Ed's keys, ringing briskly as they dismount from the door lock. Those are the keys again, muffled ringing now as he thrusts them into his trousers. And that is his cough. In a moment its sound will fade as Ed enters the bathroom and runs the shower, but its echo will last. Just a minute ago, Brian's voice had confirmed the latest transaction, and the total number of shares Marie now owned. This, too, will echo.

Oh, to commit one perfect act of charity. One untraceable to the self, whose pure end result is joy, an act which wounds no one in its wake. But even the lynching of Christ, the redemption found in his bloodletting, was imperfect. His love for us separated us from Him. That is the showerhead, the snare drum of first droplets against the curtain, the water gushing out. That is the whooping hiss as hot water makes contact with her beloved's skin. All at once. She is alone. She has the day to wait and make as many or as few moves as she likes. She will switch on CNN once he's gone and watch the stock market ticker scroll from right to left, waiting patiently on the sofa for her investment to compound.

Outpatient

What Anne did in the bedroom she had to do in the dark: Step across the floor without bumping chairs, take off her clothes, softly set the spare house key on top of the dark brown bureau. After this, Anne crept beside Nefa to touch her—and even then, she had to be careful not to disturb the bandages wrapped around Nefa's shoulder, careful to let Nefa sleep on. Anne's dress and stockings—drenched again by rain—were hanging on a chair, one bath towel beneath the dress to keep the chair dry, another bath towel on the floor to catch drips.

After a few minutes, Anne shut the bedroom door and walked to the kitchen. With one hand she opened the refrigerator and, with the other, she dialed her doctor. Pain yawning through her knuckles, Anne studied the milk carton she'd pulled out of the fridge, making sure it was the right one. Nefa drinks 2%; Nefa's husband Frank only drinks skim. If Anne poured the wrong milk into the kettle, Nefa warned, her husband would notice how much was missing.

The doctor's receptionist had put Anne on hold, so she watched the milk heat up on the stove. Nefa liked to drink milk at a boil, liked the scald of it on her tongue, liked it being so hot in her mouth her teeth felt absent.

"Yes I'm sure," Anne said into the phone. "The doctor said to call today. Because I was sure when I called Friday that he said *definitely* Monday...but I shouldn't *have* to call back again tomorrow; this should fucking be *over*, already...Fine, goodbye."

Nefa appeared naked in the kitchen door's frame. When Nefa was naked, Anne noticed her eyes, her hips, and her stocky fingertips. In the hospital, where the two women first met, Anne had noticed Nefa's platform shoes—shoes that made a tall woman taller—and the four elliptic wooden earrings like eldest rings of a tree, clacking and smacking for attention. "Hi, baby."

"Hi, baby, back," Anne said, shutting off the stove. "You're up early."

Nefa scrounged two mugs. The first came from the shelf—it was embossed with the university seal of her husband's alma mater. The second mug was Anne's—Nefa hid it in the dumbwaiter, behind the extra detergent she used to wash Anne's presence from her sheets in the afternoon. "Not early enough to help out with breakfast. Sorry. Between you and the rain, I'm losing the battle to leave the bed."

"I'm not complaining." And she would not, Anne promised. Even to herself. Or when her heart knotted like a clenched fist each time Nefa sipped milk from her husband's mug.

Four mornings later—four more pair of wet stockings and shoes. The steady rain played havoc with Jackson Heights, pocking at the ground. High winds bled leaves off the pruned aspens. Branches cracked off, triggering motion floodlights. There was not much space to hide in this neighborhood, just the canopied driveway leading to Nefa and Frank's house. To keep their affair quiet, though, Nefa instructed the car service to let Anne off a block away from the house. So by the time she made it to the canopy, Anne was already soaked.

Anne eyed a bag of fresh English muffins, barely resisting the urge to undo its knot. She wasn't supposed to eat here anymore, but felt better when she did. Eating at her apartment was hard. Breakfasts alone were difficult, muddy: Coffee to the lips instead of a kiss, forcing herself to forget last night's dream because Nefa was not there to retell it to. Fighting the urge to dream awake, dream, for example, that the lap she touched was her lover's, not a chair's. That tapping raindrops were Nefa's fingernails; the idiotic radio chatter, her grumpy morning patois. What Anne missed from those breakfasts alone was inconsequential, saccharine, but also, she was learning, enormous.

While she waited for the milk to boil and Nefa to rise, Anne watched TV—the latest coverage of the Park Slope Pariah Parade. Assembled in response to a series of attacks in Brooklyn—the last straw a gay teen who had been pistol-whipped and bound to a chain-link fence—the Pariah Parade had grown in size and anger. Its members pledged to plunge into any community where violence occurred. They walked mornings. They'd gone west to Cobble Hill. Now, spurred by gay-baiting gang tags, they were on the move east to Far Rockaway.

Anne raised the volume of the TV slowly, one notch for every five minutes Nefa continued sleeping in the next room. The sound was still soft; Anne could hear Mr. Fallon from next door, hooking a leash to his dog Federal's collar. Mr. Fallon was a postal inspector—Federal, a hero turned pet (he had sniffed out a crude pipe bomb in a Priority Mail package. The inspectors had fled; Federal had not. Federal had remained there barking, long after the bomb detonated and he could no longer hear the barking sounds coming from his own mouth).

All this was part of Anne's world now. Was it part of Frank's? Had it ever been? Did Nefa's husband care to know his neighbors' lives? Nefa painted a kind picture of him, not just as a provider but as a partner—a picture that revolted Anne, because it seemed impenetrably amiable. Anne was certain the devil was in his details. Frank was one of those people lost in the forest of his own success. What right did he have to saunter in from that forest a few hours at night, fuck his woman, and then saunter back out the next morning?

Anne ran her finger, curled like an apostrophe, down Nefa and Frank's remote control. She pressed a button which listed the three most-selected channels of the eighty-four they subscribed to: CNN, TWC, ESPN2—news, weather, and sports. The Weather Channel was reporting from a local laundromat—the dryers were in such demand they had waiting lists.

"I heard a car," Nefa said. "Mr. Fallon leave?"

"No. He's still walking the dog."

"Damn thing's so antsy, no wonder walking it takes forever. Probably fills with piss every three minutes." Nefa peered through the blinds. "Around midnight it decides it isn't deaf. Barks louder and louder and won't shut up until it hears itself. Last thing I hear at night, first thing you hear in the morning."

What Anne first *saw* in the morning, when she entered the bedroom, were the neckties Frank had decided against. He tossed them in stacks: yellow, green, bold-striped power ties, crumpled and curved like misshapen spines. Anne had to hang them up before she could touch Nefa. She hung them on another chair in the bedroom, this one older and smaller than the first, a wedding gift from Nefa's grandmother, its back shaped like a heart and one leg chipped, which caused it to tip restlessly from the small weight of Frank's ties.

This was supposed to have been simple. This affair. This infidelity. This whatever. They'd let it happen; so it followed that they could make it stop. But desire was not simple. Desire cut its teeth on certainty, itched when comfort was needed. It doubled-back and double-crossed at its own discretion, the itinerary seldom traveling clockwise, when you wanted, or with whom.

Nefa threw back a finger of hot milk. "What's this on TV?"

"Pariah Parade."

"Do we really have to watch those people again?"

Just last month Anne would have asked herself the same thing. She lived where she did in part to avoid "those people." Chinatown was cheap and wild, minus the sucking and tongues, leather and chains, the sexuality on steroids that infested the Village. The closest Chinatown came to sexual politics was a banner in the fifty-cent hot dog store (*"President Clinton & Gray's Papaya—We Both Curve Left"*). Anne took to the rats and grime on Bowery far better than the agitprop of the gay and lesbian "minority group." She didn't hold anything against them really, except that she couldn't believe they were deserving of special privileges or protection. If life was really so hard on them, why did they have so much fucking time on their hands for marches? As far as the harassment, it was wrong—but you know—reap what you sow. Anne had always sided with her father's logic: If you wanted to move up in the world, you had to count on someone trying to knock you back.

But wasn't it different now?

The Parade's spokesperson was being interviewed in the rain, in full drag. He was supposed to be Bacall, but his smudged mascara evoked Dunaway as Crawford. "Weather permitting, we've got a softball tournament in Queens this morning. That's to raise money for a new hate-crime legal defense fund. After that we'll stage a protest at Eleanor Roosevelt's house, with our flyers and posters and our bad-ass selves. So anybody who wants to take a piece of me can come out and take a piece of us all."

"Describe the mood of your march. Frustration?"

"Fuck that, baby." The fuck was bleeped—but this was a female impersonator; he made certain his audience could read his lips. "First, this is a parade, not a march. Second, frustration is a kitten of a mood. This is rage. Sadness may bring us here, but rage will bring us out."

Nefa took a last swallow of milk. "Freaks."

"I'll change it, I'll change it." Weren't they two of the freaks?

"You want me to say I sympathize?" Nefa asked, turning her face to Anne. "I do. You want me to say what goes on mornings in this house has anything to do with that parade? I won't."

"I want to hear that what goes on in this house means enough to you to protect. If it came down to that."

Nefa's face went standstill, a stationary front. "Lord. Tell me," she said, "is it always such a pain in the ass being with a woman?"

They both knew the answer to that: They didn't know the answer. This was the first time they'd had to consider the question.

Nefa and Anne had met in a hospital waiting room four weeks ago, the first Friday in October. Anne had sat through her entire lunch hour, marked by cream soda, stale crackers, and anxiety. She was already supposed to be back at work. Not that they'd miss her—she was only a temp—but she'd miss the money.

When Nefa and Frank first came into the waiting room, Anne barely took notice. Nefa had closed her umbrella and set it against a table between two couches. She'd sat on the couch closest to Anne, eyeing the upholstery as though perhaps it were predatory. It made Anne tense watching this woman, made her hope that at least the woman's husband would be a little more in control, so Anne shifted her gaze to him.

Frank shimmied to the TV. "Mind if I change channels?" Anne shrugged from behind him. "There's a big storm hitting Key West. I'm worried about the damage it's gonna do."

"Do you have relatives in Key West?"

"Property."

Nefa turned to get a better view of the TV screen. When she did, her knee knocked into the umbrella, which violently mushroomed open, like some strange flower in time lapse. Water droplets sprayed Anne's face and clothes.

"God, damn!" Frank closed the umbrella quickly. He pulled a kerchief from his lapel and handed it to Anne. "Hundred-percent chance of indoor rain, huh? We're terribly sorry for this."

Anne shook her head and wiped her face. "It's okay." As she spoke, though she had no reason to, Anne touched Nefa. Nefa's skin had the memory of strength. As if, for years, she'd worked out rigorously, but had since granted herself permission to indulge the splendor of new vices. Her legs were coiled beneath the couch, conscious of being seen and touched, like garter snakes. She kept to herself, so Anne struck up a conversation with Frank. He had a handsome way of asking casual questions, and maintaining eye contact through at least half of Anne's replies. He explained how his father had taught him the value of land as a child. Each property he owned in Jackson Heights, he proudly revealed, had been in his family for four generations. The two spoke breezily, though Anne felt contrite when Frank asked where *she'd* been raised, contrite enough to lamely offer that her father had always hoped to live where Frank did. And that was true enough; Anne's father had hoped to move his family anywhere from where they'd been forced to go when his small restaurant went belly-up.

Frank excused himself to fill out forms at the registration desk. Anne listened to the TV, her gaze fixed on Nefa. Anne had never had cable, one of the few hospital amenities that seemed to have patients' interests in mind. On The Weather Channel, correspondents were analyzing the surprise tropical storm. "We hoped we'd get through this hurricane season without catastrophe, but it's not to be. With a report on Allan, here's Len Lilogrew in StormStation One. Len?"

"Brenda, this shouldn't come as a surprise. Mother Nature's a bitch."

Nefa looked up from her *Time*. "What did he just say?"

Anne's eyes sprung quickly to the TV screen; Brenda's face said it all, the contorted efforts of a woman trying to mate anger with decorum. "Sounded like, 'Anyone want my job?'"

Nefa studied the bandages on Anne's wrists and palms. "I heard you tell Frank you don't live here. Is that right?" Anne nodded. "If you don't live here, why get treated here?" Closest place to work, Anne answered, trying to stop talking, but continuing to chatter. She felt she should keep her voice low, keep what she said from carrying, as if her words were state secrets. She told Nefa she lived in Chinatown.

"I don't envy you your commute; especially in the rain. Mother Nature being a bitch and all." She grazed Anne's hands with her fingertips. "Kitchen accident?"

"Carpal tunnel."

Nefa touched Anne again, holding her fingers as if to weigh their value. She casually stroked the gauze. "Does it come off today?"

"I have my fingers crossed, or I would, if it didn't hurt. I've been sitting here so long—maybe I'm better already and don't know it. And you? Anything coming off?"

"No." Nefa opened her purse. "Something coming out, then bandages coming on." The subject shifted. Nefa wanted to know where Anne worked, what hours, when they expected her each morning, did she have a car. The barrage of personal questions caught Anne off-guard. She wasn't used to strangers caring to know such measly details. Especially not this stranger, who, a minute ago, couldn't have cared less. She hadn't joined in on the small talk her husband started; it didn't even seem she'd been listening. Now she was showing concern about Anne's injury, commute, and job. She'd even handed Anne one of Frank's business cards, pointing out the handwritten digits written on back. That was her home number, she explained. Feel free to call, come over for breakfast. It'll be an excuse to put the house in order.

Anne turned the card over. "Your name is Nefa? Beautiful."

"It's short for something. And you're Anne?...That's pretty, too."

"Pretty common. All my parents' creativity went into calling each other names." Anne thanked her for the invitation and pocketed the card. She felt suddenly distressed; had the invitation made her awkward because it had come from a woman of money and means? Or was it because it came from a woman Anne would take much more from, were it offered?

Just then Anne's doctor, an endoscopic specialist, strolled out. "Okay. Let's have a look at this mole." It wasn't a mole—Who said anything about a mole?—but then Nefa and Frank, who'd just returned, shuffled forward. The doctor clasped Frank's hand; Nefa halted before the handshake. "How are you, Frank?"

Frank smiled. "Six sand traps short of par, buddy."

"Well, Nefa's in good hands," the doctor said, ushering her in. Anne blinked; how did golf segue into minor surgery? How is it that a couple waiting in the lobby for fifteen minutes gets treated before a woman waiting four times longer?

The couple is from around here. Their doctor is a member of their country club. Friends in high places. Money even higher. That is how it is.

And for a mole. No wonder Nefa had offered breakfast. It was throwaway charity. Nefa knew she was about to get preferential treatment, and it embarrassed her. *Noblesse oblige*; what a crock. Anne's chronic pain took a backseat to plastic surgery.

Then Anne softened, telling herself it wasn't Nefa's fault; getting the mole removed was probably Frank's idea. It was getting close to Christmas, and he wanted the gift of an unblemished wife, and there was that money in his health insurance he hadn't used. So take it off. Get it done. Make me, hell, yourself, happy. No, Nefa was an innocent, and Anne longed again for her company. It was depressing having to face the banter of the orderlies alone, their ninja sexism creeping around and pinching nerves. "That girl in curtain two?" the first remarked. "Hot. And hot for me. She's about to get an organ donor." The second orderly hitched up his pea green trousers, the little bow dangling at the groin: "Then I'm gonna give her a bone marrow transplant." One of these men, Anne thought, will draw my blood in a moment.

Anne lifted her purse gingerly—suddenly conscious of the small damages she inflicted on herself in her daily routines. Gingerly she slid her left hand into her pocket. It brushed across the card Nefa'd given her.

Another hour passed before they finished. Frank emerged first, his wife leaning on him. Once he was satisfied Nefa could stand on her own, he brought her a cup of water and said he'd bring the car. Nefa stood at the bathroom door; she seemed wearier than before. "You've had to wait a long time, haven't you?" she asked.

"No." That word by itself was never enough of an answer. "I hope it was easy for you in there."

"That's a nice hope. Will we be seeing each other?"

"I'd like to. I'll call maybe in a week or two. After you've healed."

"Please. Don't insult me with politeness. Come tomorrow. While we're still walking wounded."

The architecture of the affair was in place; its inception came easily. Or perhaps they made it easier on each other by not voicing what it was they wanted. Taking without asking seemed implicit. During that whole long commute the first morning, Anne refused to ask herself questions. It helped that Nefa had led the way. Had kissed first. At no time did Anne feel confidence in where she was or what she was doing, but none of it felt shameful or unnatural. It flowed like morning fog. By the second week Nefa had rescinded the breakfast offer. Anne railed: "Frank will never know. I'll eat like a bird."

"It's not how much you eat that worries me. He'll get suspicious if we eat what he wants. Problem is, he changes his mind and his menu on a whim." Anne sighed. "Fine," said Nefa. "We'll compromise. I'll steam extra milk in the morning, and we can share. Satisfied?"

Anne nodded. She could do nodding if it would keep the affair intact. A nod was worth a kiss, worth Nefa's hands sliding beneath her denim. She was willing to compromise for affection. It was a trade, she felt, of a very wise kind.

At work Anne made friends, small, scattered friendships, which, like pressed lips or heat, threatened always to recede. Anne was grateful for the people who stooped low enough to chat with the temp. But in their too-captive stares and overplayed nods—Anne could feel it—they were already forgetting her name.

It was a plainclothes office, brimming with Celtic music, Guatemalan coffee, Swedish furniture, safe imports from faraway worlds. She would be downsized from it in just a matter of time. They only kept her a few hours each day before releasing her, but she was grateful for the income, for any work she could get while waiting to heal.

Two employees walked past, the older one describing to the other Anne's job: "The shit work Peters is supposed to do. But Peters is new. We figured we'd give Peters a break before clocking him with shit work. We'll tell him next week or the week after."

What if Nefa did tell Frank? About them? How would he take it? He might fly off the handle; he might want to watch; he might just laugh, finding the whole thing funny. Anne picked up the stapler on her desk and nodded; yes, laugh, that's what he'd do. *The girl from the hospital? That's my competition?* He would disarm Anne's body, pointing out its flaws. He'd start with Anne's chin, joking how it just kind of puddled into her neck with little resistance. And what about her dry, cracked lips, they're like weathered church steeples. Her squint, the thick eyebrows, and that thin chest. Plaster-of-Paris skin—nothing but white trash. He'd sneer, briefly but enough, *You're slumming, baby.* But Nefa would hear only charm in the voice, the measured snake oil. Stop it, Frank, she's beautiful. But Nefa would be suppressing laughter. She would let him go on.

One morning, while staring at her pain pills, Anne checked her messages from Nefa's house. The nurse had called; they needed more blood. It had been three weeks since they'd drawn the first blood; what was wrong with it? Had it expired? Withheld information?

Nefa walked into the kitchen, threading her fingers between Anne's, a latticework of skin. "Tried to go back to sleep but I couldn't. What we do is not very relaxing. How you just clutched my hair when we...?" Anne grinned. "That image won't fade anytime soon. Your fingers in my hair. Pulling at my scalp." She shut her eyes. "Any messages?"

"My health care provider called to provide me with excuses."

Nefa lifted Anne's hand with the strength of her own. "Any *good* messages?"

Sometimes, alone at her apartment, Anne watched footage of the Pariah Parade. She cooked rice, or bought squid from the market downstairs—the squid felt heavy, like a soggy newspaper. Compared with Nefa's eighty-four cable channels, the local station's coverage was skeletal, but Anne listened to what was there (the chanting protesters, the drag act working his microphone like a carnival barker), watched as though it were instructional. Watched the cute, strong, lifelong lesbians. They seemed to be gaming it: They loved the ones they were with, but their eyes remained open, straying for more possibilities. If what they had now fell apart, they would have a future to lean on. They would go through a box of Kleenex, go to a new bar, then get back in the game. She wondered if she could have their safety net: Would they take Anne in if she asked?

These were Anne's weekday mornings: hot showers, cold cream, black coffee, steeling herself for the travels ahead. At 5:15 AM she trekked from Division Avenue in Chinatown, up Bowery past Confucius Plaza, to the J, M, or Z (she left so early there were still ammonia suds on the platform where maintenance had cleaned). She then switched to the F at Delancey Street. At the Bleecker Street station she caught the 6 to Midtown. With Queens E service in interminable disrepair, she was forced to transfer to the pokier 7 train at 42nd. Then it was a straight shot to Queens, to Roosevelt Avenue, and to stairs that led her out from the underground. Finally, she waited in the rain for car service to 3 Sycamore Circle. At some point the bloom fueled by Anne's first coffee faded. She tipped her driver (with Frank's cash), ran one block through the downpour and, under the canopy, reclaimed her breath. Deactivated the security code, turned the key, steamed the milk, brought the mugs into the bedroom, drank, disrobed, made love if she was lucky, caught TV and a shower, cleaned up her tracks, backtracked to work for half a day, and returned to Chinatown. Sometimes she looked at herself in the subway windows, those casually accurate mirrors, to see a woman giving more—nothing new—than she gets.

Still. She was getting *something* from these clandestine meetings— the repetition of the routine had begun to feel like a form of love. Anne was made of so many disposable faiths; here was one she had begun to trust. She was familiar with her tendency to find comfort in depression: She'd picked that up from her father. Guessing how good luck would end was how Anne unwound at night—*now I malaise me down to sleep*—and she found this new offshoot, comfort in joy, so tempting, so eager to be believed.

Some mornings they wanted so much of the other it seemed they had toppled shame. Like Halloween, their four-week anniversary: Anne studied the clothes in Nefa's closet; she *had* been a thin woman, once. Anne held a blue tube dress up to her body, costuming, vamping, thinking, *I want to be me now for Halloween. The happy woman in this room.* "We should get you a whole new wardrobe. All this money he makes, and you don't take advantage. You don't like to shop for yourself much, do you?"

Nefa shrugged. "Why do *you* like it?"

"It's fun to buy. It's fun after you buy, to wear it, to stop people in their tracks."

"Exactly. I don't do that anymore."

Anne crossed from the mirror to where Nefa stood. "Maybe not his. But mine." Nefa's throat was tight. Wind tipped through the window. Anne touched Nefa's blouse lightly, then ripped it in two. Buttons fell. Anne could feel Nefa reminding herself to pick them up later. She wished her fingertips were lit like cigarettes. She could burn the clothes he'd bought for her, burn through Nefa's bandage (Why is it still on? Anne has called doctors. A mole does not take a month to heal).

She let Nefa control the next moves. Let her shut off the lights, let her tongue play along Anne's stomach, neck, elbow bend. Then the bedroom door slammed shut, and they bolted upright. Anne watched as Nefa gathered up their clothes in a flash, dragging Anne expertly to the walk-in closet, like a teacher scuttling students through a fire drill. "Was that wind?"

"It was me, I think, just me." Though neither could believe that Anne's damaged hands had slammed the door so hard. When those hands returned to Nefa—gripping her skin, reeling in, claiming—Nefa, still rattled, pulled away. But experience had made Anne a wilier lover. She knew what would calm Nefa, make her forget the close call. Anne only had a stake in three hours. When she had access to this skin, she had to surfeit it. Her time was precious. She could not afford to be patient.

"I want what I had yesterday."

"The zinger?"

"Oh right." Booming laugh like subway doors splitting open in an empty station. "Well, not that."

"How about Captain's Monologue? Imagine Earl Grey in a slinky dress." They were switching from milk to tea; less trouble. And that was fine, Anne thought. Tea was fine. Anne did not want to shake Nefa's confidence in the success of the affair.

"You want to watch TV?"

Anne shook her head. She had already watched TV this morning. Eighty-four channels were tiring. The Financial Network? That was like drinking before noon. ESPN2? The stoop sale of sports? She'd watched a few minutes of a talk show, and then a few minutes of a soap opera. Watched the Pariah Parade move into Morningside Heights; kept switching. Turned it off when The Weather Channel did a piece on the poor commuter traveling conditions. She was already familiar with those.

She wanted Nefa to know what a toll the coming and going had taken. She was turning into one of those women she used to feel sad for. A woman who scathes herself for drifting off in a not-quite-empty subway car at night, who seems only to have herself as a companion, who is so jumpy and cautious in where she looks, when she speaks, and to whom, that it seems as if a pickpocket has lifted her confidence. A woman smartly dressed, who regards the subway as her uneasy home, the overheated platform and the cold seats her climate, and who regards every scrap of cruelty with light sarcasm, who must do so if she is ever to shower and sleep the long trip off. Otherwise every loose insult, and severe sexual gaze upon her, would feel, somehow, stapled to the skin, sutured to the body like treads. One of those women. "You know what I want? I want breakfast. I want food."

"I told you: Frank notices what's missing. The more of a mess we make, the less chance I have of keeping you a secret."

"Well. Your secret is going hungry."

Nefa didn't speak. She took out a cup, and four eggs, cracking the equator of each against the cup's lip. Anne tentatively searched for a cutting board, a knife, oranges. Nefa smiled, shoveling butter onto a frying pan. Anne poured 2% into the kettle. The meal formed around them without words. Soon there were pancakes, there was sliced fruit, poached eggs billowing on a burner. Thickening layers of jam on toast. "Thank you."

They drew closer, but not much. A kiss tried to carve itself out but didn't.

Anne brushed Nefa's shoulder, dodging the bandage. She thought of Frank at the hospital a month ago, at Nefa's side. She hated the thought of his hands comforting Nefa, hated that she would never see the mole, or run her hand along it. Smoke curled beneath the pancakes when Anne flipped them. "I know you think you can't tell him about us. And I understand about security. But you know: So what? So what if he knew you had a friend from the city who visited you sometimes? Would he care? Would he even put it together?"

"He just might. He's smarter than you give him credit for."

Anne salted the eggs. "And less concerned than you believe."

Silence was needed here, but Anne stepped on the prospect. Was it the need to make a mess, or just the promise of food making Anne brave? "I mean he keeps redressing your bandages. But you and I both know that you don't need them anymore."

"Oh I don't." Nefa turned down the stove; the pancakes were scorching. Another thing to clean up. Hide. "What makes you so sure?"

"The mole's healed. It healed a long time ago."

Nefa lifted her nightshirt, and with the kitchen knife still sour with fruit pulp, sliced through the gauze. "This mole was trouble."

"For what, the marriage? The sex? His ego?"

"My life." The evenness of Nefa's lips beckoned Anne over. She took her first look at the wound. A layer of skin meshed like a screen door. Discolored flesh, pinkish-white, purpled edges. The skin was not quite in place, like a blanket over a body. "This was a malignant melanoma. Get it? Something that spread fast and is healing slow." Nefa cut off the stove. She filled the sink with water, started to wash the kitchen knife, and then unstopped the sink. Water pinwheeled back down the drain.

"Where are you going?" Anne asked.

"To watch TV."

"Not alone. I'll join you."

"Fuck it, have your breakfast. I owe you all this." Nefa walked into the sitting room. Anne picked up the shredded gauze and followed. Carefully, she reattached the pieces to Nefa's skin, tightening the tape. Anne was aware, suddenly, hopelessly, of how loss outmuscles what fights it.

"You never told me how serious this was."

"Serious?" Nefa shrugged. "Who's to say it is?"

"You should have told me. You should have filled me in."

Nefa picked at the belt around her robe. Next door, Federal was barking wildly, barking itself hoarse inside of his tiny doghouse. "After you go to work, I go to work too. You know? While you're on your train, I'm here dusting your fingerprints. Burying you. It takes a trip to the grocery store, paper towels, trash bags, detergent. Milk, eggs, the little messes you forget to tell me about. It takes a lot of lies to make everything around here look so goddamn squeaky-clean. So if I strike you as tight-lipped, maybe it's because I'm not sure which secrets I can and can't say around which lover. And another thing. Pushing two people I care for out the door each morning has gotten a little old."

"Eventually you're going to have to tell the second person he's a second person."

"Stop. I don't tell you how to live." That abraded Anne; she stiffened in her seat. Wasn't that what people in love did—presumed to tell the other how to live their life?

A phone rang. Nefa retied her robe. Anne took a single step backwards and watched the conversation, not listening in, not breathing until Nefa hung up. She turned too quickly and knocked the receiver off the lamp stand. "It's him. Oh Jesus—it's Frank—on his cell. Jesus."

She took cautious steps one way, then another, in no clear direction, as though her eyes were shut and if she moved too far too fast she would hit a wall. "He's in-between meetings. He wants to stop and check on me. For lunch. He's on his way."

"What do you need? What do I do? Help you clean up?"

"There's no time. Just get out."

"I'll help you."

"No. All you can do is go."

Suddenly, all of this is now.

Anne is at the side of the house, crouching in the rain. Her lover's husband has just walked in the door that Anne ran out from. In confusion toxic as bleach, a thought surfaces. The card she holds is four weeks. Frank holds all the others. It will take so little for him to win. Just a dance on the porch after dinner—the right piece of music too late at night—one ace played to remind his wife of their history, and Anne will be deflected.

She walks to the canopy and waits beneath it. Waits to dry. Waits for the rain to let up, waits for a sign. She is chilled, but she keeps her jacket at her side. Sheets of water blur the house. She feels warmth from Frank's Mercedes, and places her fingers near its engine block.

She turns her head to the open window. A thick shadow fills the frame. Hands; glasses; a nose. Signs of life. Anne squints for a signal to catch. Tell me when it's safe to come back to you.

Nefa closes the window and draws the shade.

Anne doesn't scream, or smash the car hood with her fists. She gives the scene time to correct itself. But it doesn't. Anne thinks about how the front window squealed when Nefa closed it, and realizes that the water in the kettle was still boiling when Frank called, when he shattered the morning. It might be boiling still. How she wills that it is. If liquid is capable of a place hotter than boil, let it happen. Let the whistle moan fiercely and rouse the dogs, even the deaf one. Let every room in that house echo with evidence that there is on the premises one woman more than there should be, one more mouth to feed, heart to fill.

She is conscious of feeling alone in this neighborhood, weak on this street. This feeling won't subside even when Frank heads back to work. So what she must do is leave. She marches away. The bandages on her hands are soaked through. They were supposed to be off by now, the minor surgery finished. Now she was having another round of tests at the hospital, a consultation, then possibly staying overnight. Nefa's mole was supposed to be cosmetic. Their procedures were supposed to be outpatient.

Strange sound spills over the hill; she's close to the center of the neighborhood. How far has she walked? To keep from noticing how miserable she feels, Anne moves on to a determined game: Find ten things wrong with Frank. His hairline, laboring to stay low, the nose like a halved mushroom, his teeth, jagged and yellowed, like a latchkey's... Oh what's the use? These things were only what she saw.

She needs solidarity. She's only been this word—this lesbian—a few weeks. But she is already an activist. In that she craves an end to this architecture that erases her. In that there is no room for castaways to be mute. In her silence she crushes herself. She must voice her particular evangelism for all the world to hear.

As her walk continues, Anne hears more dazzling noise than the neighborhood can hold. The world has become loud without permission, as though she has been yanked suddenly from the East River's mottled bottom into a bright syrup of carnival sounds. A mass of people approach; or is she the one approaching? As with a magnet, Anne cannot tell who is pulling whom. But in a moment she will be in the thick of the noise, the thick of the bodies. The thought gives her courage. It distracts her into shaking off the imagined images between husband and wife in that house. The kettle boiling, Frank skewering eggs meant for Anne and tearing off pieces of what was to have been her toast. Nefa's stare at the window. Even the image of what Anne's own face must have looked like beneath the canopy, still, expectant, as a woman in a portrait studio waiting to be made permanent.

The Pariah Parade needs shelter—the Eleanor Roosevelt house has issued an injunction legally barring them from the premises. Anne and the female impersonator speak quickly. An appraisal flickers between them.

"Most places we get, you know, one sympathetic librarian. Who lets us warm up in the alcove. Or a gay-friendly pub. But here, nothing." His hand pans across the neighborhood cinematically to make the point. "Is cruelty part of your neighborhood's birthright, or does it live in the tap water?"

"I'm not from here," Anne says. "I live nowhere near this place."

The group circles around her; some eat, some talk, most complain. She feels the heat they give off. The primitive huddling. Watching them, Anne feels hungry again. She squints; her eyes narrow and sharpen as though spinning on teeth. "But I do know the area well."

They are looking for cover, for protection. Anne knows she will not be able to resist bringing them into Nefa's neighborhood; directing them down

Sycamore Street to Sycamore Circle, and under the canopied driveway. She'll lead the parade into the kitchen window's sightline. If the window is closed, she'll let this beautiful cavalcade encircle the Mercedes: Hairdressers and heart specialists, flaming women cooling themselves with feather fans, cold men keeping warm in red stoles, a transsexual who fronts a minor league baseball team, a hermaphrodite who works in soft-serve. Bisexuals who bristle around men, lesbians who negotiate friendships with frat boys and investment bankers. Eighty-four channels, all of them loud, all of them demanding attention. This dizzy blizzard world, Nefa, that you know as well as I, the last, best storm of the season, is on its way to you and yours.

The Whole World Over

Receiving the invitation on the answering machine hurt, and that it took two years to get it at all hurt more. Still, when their old friends asked them to visit, Harvey and Sue jumped at the chance. It happened quickly; they didn't have time to catch their bearings. Harvey wasn't even sure what he'd packed. Moat had already booked the flight, leaving an open date for the return. Had paid for it without even affording Harvey the gesture of saving face, of offering to split the cost. Of course the trip was out of Harvey's means, but that wasn't the point. It was presumptuous for Moat to take care of everything. It was presuming a lot to take two people away from their home, without a moment's notice, without even their blessing, after having been absent so long.

"Sir? Care for a cocktail?"

Harvey smiled at the flight attendant and regarded her cart. "No. I know all about your cocktails. Seven-dollar glasses of sugar water. I could get looped quicker from cough syrup." Once they'd landed he would have plenty of time to drink his worries away. The attendant asked Sue, with the same doting, placid face, the same question. "I'm not above sugar water," said Sue. "A Rob Roy, please. No. Change it to rum and Coke, rum and Diet Coke. After all we are headed for the islands."

True enough, Harvey nearly added, *but why we're headed for* this *island...*

And if he had, Sue would've begun, but not finished, a follow-up speculation: *Oh I'm sure it's gorgeous, and bright, and maybe simpler, too...Still. Why Anna and Moat moved there, how they even knew there was a there to move to...* Here she would have folded her seat back, as if allowing their gripes room to breathe.

But in fact they didn't voice any complaints. Not during the initial flight, nor the JFK connection, nor the series of hop flights that followed. They said little at all, only mentioning Anna and Moat once: a comment about how their friends seemed to be making quite a life for themselves after retirement, and they must be more than happy, and the island must feel like home, since they hadn't mentioned any possibility of leaving it.

Not that Anna and Moat ever explained themselves anymore. Since the abrupt move, they'd sent just one card and a telegram. The answering-machine invitation had provided a phone number, a street address, but it had not suggested even a bare thread of the loneliness Harvey and Sue felt in the two years.

Anna and Moat weren't there to greet them at the airport. "You'd think at least one could show," Sue muttered. In fact, no friends or family were there for any of the passengers, no heraldry at all. There were suitcases and bloated duffels lying around, but no one came to claim them. It hardly even seemed like an airport, what with the low ceilings, the absence of vending machines and duty-free shops, the filthy carpeting. There weren't even those groups of men, usually thin, usually mustached, in white dress shirts rolled to the elbows, holding placards bearing the names of those they were supposed to drive to resorts.

"They'll be waiting for us once we clear customs," Harvey chanced.

But they weren't. Harvey swallowed his bitterness. A single officer, wearing, among other regalia, red and gold shoulder ribbons, smiled as they passed with their bags in tow. That was the extent of security. Harvey was ready to tip the officer with American dollars, but was ignored. The sky was a greenish, flat haze, a waste of sunlight. As they fished for sunglasses, they felt as though they were waking from a deep sleep, but into a silence so pleasant, breezes so mild, that the waking world seemed more comforting than the dreaming. When Sue hollered to hail a cab, she thought she saw her breath. How high up were they, and if they were high up, why wasn't it cooler?

"So your car doesn't have A-C, I'm guessing?" Harvey asked. As much as it embarrassed Sue, that side of her husband that would assume a driver in a foreign land would speak English, it pleased her greatly, the side of him that would assume that a driver in a foreign land would want to make friends.

"No, of course not, no. But you get used to it."

"Hah!" Harvey exclaimed. "That's a typical local response."

"Full truth," the cabby swore, his finger jutting up. "One adapts here. Don't believe? We make bet. If you still sweat when we get to where you go, you owe nothing. Now. Where do we go?"

Harvey checked his wallet. "Tell me if this makes sense: Kotanga C46, uh..."

"Actually," asked Sue, "could you take us to the center of town?" Harvey eyed Sue, who shrugged. "They don't know we're here, so let's have fun first. Besides, I know you. You'll be in a lather over getting snubbed, and you'll pout for an hour. You might as well pout with me. Over dinner and drinks. I'm famished."

"What kind of food you looking for?" the driver asked.

"Doesn't matter. Whatever's closest."

"Please. Name what you like." When they did, the driver only grinned and told them they weren't being specific enough. Their second effort received the same admonition. Sue noticed how high the hair of his beard was, how it touched the corners of his eyes when he grinned. He clicked his radio on to a reporter in midstream tragedy: *The bus overturned, trapping all thirty passengers under four tons of metal.* Frowning, he switched off the story. "Nasty news here, all the time." He squealed up an alley and parked beneath the terrace of a restaurant, which bore to Sue a hapless resemblance to the day-labor site in Boor's Bend, the small town she'd lived in her whole life. Pedestrians and bikes lit the dusty thoroughfare, which was spoked by creeping ivy and paved only by occasional protruding stones.

"So you recommend this place?"

"I recommend for you."

"I mean, do you like it?"

"What matters is you will."

Harvey smirked. "Your enthusiasm's talking in circles. There isn't much in town you'd recommend, is there?" The cabby wasn't sure about that. But he knew that what he did like here he loved, and what he'd found here he'd found nowhere else the whole world over. Harvey was satisfied.

"So now. Is this free ride for you?"

Harvey touched his skin. "Goddamn. You're right. I am getting used to it." He paid up happily, but his attempt to tip was again refused.

After dinner they arranged to meet Anna and Moat near the shore. On the phone, Anna and Moat had kept them reeling with questions. *We took a cab, yes. Yes, we already ate. The food? Marvelous. Well, we hadn't asked what it was...something like duck but not duck, lighter than duck, lighter than pheasant, lighter than quail. Tangy tomato, green rice glazed with lager, a bay leaf as big as a teaspoon in the mix.* They grew hungry again simply fumbling through the description. We can't wait either. See you then, see you.

Harvey enjoyed their chat. He *was* in better spirits having eaten, and laughed at how well his wife knew his tempers, knew him. He wasn't sure it was a question of love. Usually he felt he always would love her, though at times it seemed to him he never had. But Sue wanted and deserved devotion, and Harvey felt he'd honored their union by providing the providence of steady work. He'd worked hard for four decades; numbed away exhaustion and a gathering sourness over his contracting business; had lost dreams, sleep, and time—and in time, stamina—to keep Sue's hands idle and their house filled with goose-feather pillows, Chablis, crystal serving bowls, purchases that, in Harvey's estimation, framed love better than words.

Or at least those things were solid, and didn't require memory and imagination to conjure them back. Harvey didn't need to replay words Sue had said. He knew where she stood: when she'd bought ten bottles of that perfume that still made him a little crazy, just as the bankrupt manufacturer was pulling its stock off the shelves—that was love, or at least a tribute to it. Words were by nature both gummy and slippery, and Harvey had little use for them. Even Sue's old love notes were for him more attractive in the reedy feel of paper on fingertips, the veined ink joining one letter to the next, than they were in the messages themselves. When he was twenty-one, Harvey didn't have the money to give Sue an engagement ring (not even close), but he did have his hands and a stubborn idea. He had purchased a few ounces of an alloy called Inconel, carrying it around in a jacket pocket for a week, not sure where to turn for help. Finally, Harvey ingratiated himself with a supervisor at the tool-and-die plant in Boor's Bend, who agreed to let Harvey use their tools in exchange for off-the-clock janitorial work. Harvey had taken the bar stock, drilled out its center section, cut it on a band saw, sanded it, smoothed it, and, most of all, ausformed it. He'd abused every square millimeter of the ring-to-be, fed it to fire and left it soaking in fish oil, until he'd made it immune to any tests it might face through the years of days to come, to the challenges to longevity.

On their way to the shore, they walked by a group of musicians rehearsing on a bandshell stage. The performers were acclimating to the heat, playing awhile, resting, and playing again. Harvey carped about the time, but Sue stood still. The melodies enchanted her. They were airy, full; every other music in comparison seemed miserly, even Buddy Holly and the Crickets in her parents' basement forty-five summers before, playing "Not Fade Away" while she and Harvey played at the not-so-clear line between chastity and ecstasy in the muggy, mildewed heat. "What do you think that instrument is?" she asked. "I thought maybe a balalaika. But the sound's not the same, this is much rougher, or something…"

"Sue!" Harvey hissed. "Is it the lager talking, or does that look like Sid?"

Sue sighed in surrender, and asked where he was looking. Up the avenue, there were pylons connecting crackling chicken wire. "Where the wires end? See?" Sue stared, stunned. It *was* Sid. How long had he been here? Was he on vacation? Harvey, wondering the same, added, "You don't think he actually lives here? Do you? He isn't holding any maps, guides, nothing..." That was true—but they didn't have that kind of literature either. Still, something in the way Sid moved—how he blended with the environment—convinced Sue that he was a resident. Well, if he was, they'd have to introduce him to Anna and Moat. Sue watched Sid walk toward them, down the sloping street. He looked bright. His tight, curly hair had lapsed to gray, though his mustache was holding serve, still as dark, or darker, than his skin. And he still stepped with a long gait, as though he were just a few steps from home. Sue moved quickly, anticipating the reunion.

So had Harvey, although now he slowed, with a few hundred feet still between them. Sid looked different. He'd lost weight; had his penchant for weekend drinking caught up with him? His body was an echo of its former girth. But his nose had never looked that way, quite that big, hooked so sharply! And when had he switched from contacts to glasses? Harvey cleared his throat and clutched his wife's arm. "Do you know, that isn't Sid? That isn't Sid at all."

"Don't tease." Sue twisted out of her husband's grip, though now she too had doubts. Harvey was right; it wasn't Sid. Not Sid, but someone else they knew. That woman whose cheating rat husband ran out on her and their children. She and Sue had shared sitters. She had—shit—she had one of those Old Testament names...

"It's Sarah!" Harvey exclaimed. "The Sarah who wrote speeches for senators."

Harvey felt foolish thinking it had been Sid. But Sue had seen the same thing. Maybe the light here was tricky; or it had been Sid, and he'd slipped into the crowd... No, that was desperate talking. And it didn't matter besides. It was Sarah. Not Sid. Not a man. Sarah.

"Looks like her hair never completely grew back in after the chemo," Sue said. Harvey peered in. Yes. They'd heard about the cancer through the grapevine. But a grapevine with rotten roots: The rumor was that Sarah had died. Clearly, that was wrong. Yes, she looked tired; yes, her hair was short and brittle; but things could be worse. The closer they came, in fact, the fuller and darker Sarah's hair looked. The healthier she became, the younger she looked. Sarah's lipstick went through a thorough erasure, disappearing even as her lips widened, and an underbite developed. Just as they were about to greet Sarah with a hug, the man who was not Sid and who had become Sarah became not the woman who was Sarah but another man, a man with black bangs flopping over his eyelashes, a young man, younger than most of their memories, whose eyes pierced Sue and Harvey without even slight recognition.

He passed by oblivious to their presence. They didn't dare look back. An addled tenderness surfaced on their faces, as a patio conversation curved behind them. "Right into a corner, right into a corner. Never saw it coming." Harvey was worried the people were talking about them. He and Sue could find no safer or more comforting thing to do than bundle together, hold the other's waist without speaking.

This embrace could have gone on and on, but it lasted only until Moat called out a happy hello, carrying a bundle of flowers—cockscomb, zinnias, sunflowers, and statice—that all held the packed scent of fresh earth. "I know I should be bearing gifts."

"Nonsense," Harvey said, although Sue had shopped for hours for Moat and Anna, bringing back sundries from the States. "Let's get a look at you, old man."

Moat turned for them twice. He looked rested. His eyebrows were busy and black, features that somehow both quieted and dignified his baldness. His long face widened from bottom to top, like a hand fan. Harvey stared; he wouldn't hesitate to call Moat beautiful, right to his face, given the right situation. It was good to shake his hand, to wrestle with it playfully, to pretend to be young. Sue only gathered their suitcases.

Moat grunted as he lifted one. "My luck to get the one with the kitchen sink."

"We packed light," Sue responded sharply. "Not everyone can leave in a rush." Harvey knew Sue was peeved Moat hadn't brought a gift, and wished she'd get over it. "Not everyone can live like you."

"I'll give you that, Sue."

"We can't wait to see your vacation home."

"Hmm. Sorry if I misled you with the phone message. This isn't a vacation home. What we have now is all we have."

"You let go of your place on Ninetieth?" Sue marveled. "This place must be hot."

Harvey tried flattering Moat, a formidable talent of Sue's, but one Harvey never could seem to mimic, no matter how long he'd been her understudy. "It really is like heaven here," he offered, though based on the early returns, he hardly believed this.

Moat smiled thinly. "Come on, I'll take you to the boat. Anna's there. The waves will look rough but it's smooth sailing today, I promise."

Boat? Sailing? Had Harvey heard right? It had to be a joke. Moat was deathly afraid of water. Had been ever since he was a kid. His parents had once taken him to San Antonio, where he'd walked too close—and carelessly—to the edge of the River Walk. He had gone down twice before his mother could jump in and save him, had felt something slimy and hard brush his chest. He swore it was an eel; it had probably been an oar. In any case, Mitch became Moat after that, and his phobia stuck. Yet here they were, on the dock. There was Anna, biting a piece of dark bread and looking firm in her swimsuit. Moat yelled at her to start the engine. "What do you know," Harvey said, once he saw Moat step off the shore and commandeer the wheel. "Facing your fear really works."

"I'm not sure I get you," Moat replied. He pointed to the waves. "See those fish? The ones with red stripes? They don't surface unless a storm's on the way. When it hits, they feast on the dead remains."

"After which Moat and I take the boat out, cast our lines, and feast on them," Anna finished. She offered bread to the group; the casual copper in her hair glimmered as she tore off pieces. "All the fish here cook up pretty good. Poach 'em, add some lemon and butter, you'll pray for storms every night!"

"A sailor *and* fisherman, Moat?" Sue asked. "When did you decide it was safe to go into the water?"

"Having a boat saves time," Moat responded obliquely. Sue backed off, trying to catch sea spray in her mouth. Neither Moat nor Anna seemed to want to address the old phobia. Moat had probably undergone some kind of therapy, and blocking out conversations about the fear was part of the cure. Harvey was more suspicious. Moat had always been a braggart. It wasn't enough for him to recount the long process of dismantling his fear. No. Moat was acting as if he'd never been at the fear's mercy in the first place. Unbelievable. What better way to puff himself up? Harvey slid his hand across vinyl. He wouldn't let it bother him. If Moat wanted to dismiss the past, fine. If Moat wanted to wait until breakfast to gloat over his good fortune, wanted to spoon out the permanence of his estate one asset at a time—here's my boat, beachfront property, propeller plane—Harvey would let him. He didn't need to feel threatened. He didn't need to grip the rail that tightly; he could loosen his grip and let his knuckles plunge back from white to peach. Harvey had a prize of his own, a prize Moat had once wanted too: Sue. They were in college when they met Sue; she hosted debate team parties in her parents' basement. Down there, Moat and Harvey learned to switch off their trust and friendship, introduced themselves to the miserable brunt of desire. But Harvey had been the one to win Sue over. Or at least wear her down. Harvey took solace in this victory over Moat. Better investments, a younger wife—not even the farthest ends of earth could erase it.

Sue took the pin out of her hair. She breathed in the air, let it unfold in her lungs. Air lacking traffic, lacking the stench of the mills from Boor's Bend. Nowadays those mills seemed to burn hotter than normal. The odor of refined rubber was thick, greasy, incendiary. Harvey's frugal nature had pulled their daughter, Kate, through college, kept them out of debt and in a home. But that home was, and remained, in Boor's Bend. Except for one year, she'd never lived outside the town limits. If she and Harvey could ever move away, she would want it to be here. Close enough to friends. And far from home. But what did that matter if she couldn't clear aside the images of home even when she'd left it?

Harvey was complaining about the hop flights, the endless string of islands. Anna chuckled. "It's a long damn home we got. And getting longer all the time."

"Is it all developed?"

"Much of it's not. Most places never settled."

"Uninhabitable?"

"Yeah, but some have tried. People pack up, leave their families behind. It gets hard here. You don't know their names, but you can guess their stories. They try to stake a claim. Usually over that thick ridge to the east."

"Any towns that way?"

Moat cut the engine and threw a mooring over the side. Anna struck a match, daring the wind to kill the flame before it could fuel her cigarette. "None. They don't last long, I suspect." As they neared the dock, Harvey held his hand above his eyes like a bridge: there was a construction site within walking distance. He'd have to check it out. He made a note of what it was near, the outline of the stand of trees. The shore felt cold when he stepped down. It was darkening quickly. The tide rising. One wave washed up a mottled Venus, then another recollected it. Some water slapped Sue's thigh as the sun descended. The ocean waves, which had spooned them from pier to pier so carefully, were now circling the boat like wolves.

Before they went inside the house—which seemed small from the beach—Harvey stopped at a bodega. "He has this habit," Sue explained. "Every time we go overseas, he likes to buy the strangest-looking piece of fruit he sees." This time, it was purple, waxen, shaped a little like a dumbbell. Its skin was colored with a thin net of white stripes. After leaving, Harvey counted his money. "He shortchanged me."

"Shrug it off," Moat said. "You'll never miss the money."

Harvey and Sue got the mattress. Anna and Moat slept on the back porch. "We don't want to cause trouble," Harvey said. He nervously offered to stay at a motel.

"Good luck finding one," Moat replied, trying to squeeze the luggage through the door's frame.

The house was roofed with a dour, grassy thatch, built with particleboard, T-shaped, cramped for even one couple. The ceiling sagged sleepily. Sue felt embarrassed for the conditions. The ancient stove, shabby sink, the vines of dust in the corners. A broken thermometer lay on the floor, surrounded by spilt mercury. Sue compensated with brightness, overmentioning the rich banquet of sounds from outside: the cicadas, the night birds, the frogs. Harvey couldn't think of much to say as they sat on pillows, his feet almost touching Moat's. Letting jet lag explain their discomfort, Sue and Harvey said goodnight.

They slept for seventeen hours, a restless, broken sleep. When they rose it was barely still daylight. Sue hoped they were alone in the house. She wanted to remain in the room and have another night to come up with things to say. She rolled over and faced Harvey. She hadn't known the two of them weren't doing well—had he?

"Not a clue. Moat's got pride, but this is ridiculous. We could have wired cash."

"Cash doesn't sound like the issue. For how they tell it."

"Then what's keeping them here?" Harvey asked. "Maybe Moat got rooked on the boat. He's such a landlubber. Probably gave away the farm to get into the ocean."

Sue looked around the bedroom for better explanations. Green mildew covered the baseboard. The bureau was raised on cinder blocks, for when high tide bullied its way through the floor. They couldn't have become attached to a home like this. "It must be simpler here."

"So is prison," said Harvey.

Sue watched him rub skin cream into the wrinkles around his brow and under his eyes. She couldn't help herself. "I love you," she said. She tightened the lid to the cream and touched his oily hands.

What she said disarmed him. He knew it shouldn't have, but after all these years, their *I love you*'s had become mainly the means to dampen arguments, to take the sting out of escalated moments, words to cool off by. She said it—and she meant it, he knew—but there it was; the words seemed displaced.

He turned the sheet down and stroked her neck. When he touched with such tenderness she felt bound to reward him. She held his hand to her breast, acquiescing. He shut his eyes quickly when he pressed into Sue, as though surprised by a beam of sunlight. As he did, Sue thought of what she *wasn't* thinking of. The sweat on her thighs. How hard the floor felt beneath her back. How slow time seemed to move as Harvey built momentum. Sue wondered not why she was tired even after their long sleep, but why this tiredness did not concern her. What was filling her mind then? The clearing of Harvey's throat, the bump of his hand beneath the small of her back, the gingery smell left by last night's rain.

They felt guilty for having risen so late, so when they left the bedroom, Sue and Harvey acted as though it were early, aping the cosmetic gestures of morning. They pressed pants with a travel iron. He tried reading the sports pages from the local paper, though it was hard following the pidgin literature, and he couldn't make sense of the games' rules. She used toilet paper to fashion a makeshift filter for two cups of weak coffee. They fried up plantains, and did it all quietly, as if Moat and Anna were the ones still sleeping.

Sue found a skillet and then a single egg. She held it up for Harvey's approval. Then, raising her arm, she struck the egg too hard against the countertop. The shell splintered; its yolk crawled out. The sound was that of metal impaling more metal, something more ambitious and ugly than an eggshell simply splitting against wood. Sue did not move to collect the spill; she just watched. Harvey stood idly. A drop of isolated blood that had been in the center of the yolk spread out and dripped down the epicenter, ambushing the yellow with crimson.

A moment later their friends returned, their arms full of cloth bags. Moat and Anna stepped over the mess on the floor without comment.

They'd brought back sacks of alcohol. Anna placed the hardest liquor on the card table. The rest of the bottles they stored in the medicine cabinet. Moat removed a deck of cards from a pantry, which was, except for a stack of citronella candles, otherwise bare.

Anna cut the deck while standing; Harvey offered to arrange the chairs, so he could grab a better view of her. He liked the swing of her ass. Who wouldn't? Anna reveled in her relative youth.

Harvey thought of this as he shook his highball glass in his hand, let his wife pour his first drink, watched his one ice cube rock left to right, stirring the rum and cognac.

Everyone was wrecked and still trying to look serious about their playing. The moon had been up for hours, and they were down for the count. "This game is Spit in the Ocean," Harvey announced, almost singing the last word. "Wait, wait, you can't deal yet. You forgot to collect my cards," said Anna. "From the game before last." No one could remember who had won that game. The truth was no one would have noticed if wind brushing through the open door carried the deck away.

Moat asked Harvey how work was treating him. "Don't ask," Harvey muttered, shuffling. "If it's not the housing market that's gone soft it's the homeowners. Cold feet, trying to change styles on me mid-design...I swear. Young couples pick up one book on feng shui and think they're fucking architects. Dealer takes two."

Sue admired the table, the ponds of spilt rum. *Like*, she thought, *little islands*. People raised, people folded, Harvey called. Anna revealed a royal flush. "I win!" she yelled. "A royal flush beats your hand."

"It would," Harvey agreed, "if that were actually a king in the middle of your hand, and not just some pathetic six of clubs."

"Wow, unforced error." The wind blew Anna's hair. "Ooh, you guys feel it? Sea breeze gets so thick here you can drown in it. Which reminds me—we need another drink."

"No, please, no more drinks," said Sue. "We need something sub-tensestive. Sub-stens-tive."

"You want substance?" Moat produced a bag. "We got chocolate."

"Chocolate!" Anna squealed.

Harvey turned to bite a piece off the block Moat was holding. "We also have plantains," Moat offered. "But only two, so I'll play you quarters for them, Harv."

"You're trying to liquor us up, aren't you?" Harvey laughed. "So we'll take this shack off your hands?"

Buried beneath mixed drinks, Sue was still in contact with her sense of propriety. "We've survived worse, Harv. What about our place in Midtown?" That lone glorious year in Manhattan, where Sue wanted to hide herself in the city's indifference. "We signed the lease sight unseen; the bedroom window turned out to face a fifty-thousand-watt sign of the Dow-Jones average! We had to move the bed into the kitchen to get a decent night's rest."

"Was that the place you got," Moat asked, "after the first baby?"

"After Kate. Our daughter. The only baby we had." Harvey broke off more chocolate. Crumbs fell into his highball glass. That was cheap. Moat more than anyone knew how Harvey had longed for a son. Someone to pass his contracting firm onto. Although he'd hated the company for half his life, it was half of a life no one understood but him, a half Harvey wanted to have shared with somebody.

"This chocolate is fantastic, Moat. Which store'd you get it at?"

"I didn't. You get it by asking the right questions to the wrong people." He smiled mischievously. "You have to know the channels."

"Are these channels legal?"

Anna smiled. "Para-legal." Harvey and Sue joined in on their friends' splashing laughter, though they didn't know why. It was clear their connection was strained. But they persisted in retelling old stories Moat and Anna seemed tired of, or oblivious to. That Fourth of July in London, the pigeon that made off with Anna's hat...*Remember how we got fined for letting our dogs drink from the water fountain?* Anna and Moat smiled, but contributed little. Giving up, Harvey said, "Guess leaving wasn't hard for you."

"Not true," Anna replied. Leaving tore them apart, but more the act than the aftershock. Having been gone from the States two years, they found there were things they didn't much miss. The beggary of the rich. The "do unto others before they do it to me" philosophy. Oh, they missed a few small pleasures (thanks, by the way, for the massage oil). But it turns out life back there wasn't *the life*; the best was yet to come.

There was a shrill birdcall from a treetop. "What the hell's that?" Harvey asked.

"Those are nenes," Moat replied. "It means it's late. They have to mate before dawn, before their predators wake up."

"You've got your bird wrong," Harvey said. "Nenes are extinct."

"Not here they're not."

Harvey sneered at Moat's confidence. "We can cross-reference it with Peterson's if you want," Moat suggested, sobering with each syllable. They heard the birds again, whatever they were, mercilessly crying for companionship.

"I'm going to the bathroom," Sue said.

"You just went."

"Well I'm going again. I forgot to do my business the first time around."

"It's like when I slept with you Sue," Moat offered. "I wasn't even sure we'd really done it until the second time."

Sue lifted her head. She rubbed her hands to her temples, and then her ears, as though fearing a gunshot or drill or some terrible sound. But there was only quiet. Then: the cicadas and night animals. The fan in the other room. Harvey rocked on the legs of his chair. The wood grooved into the floor and made a noise like a small bone breaking. He turned slowly to Sue with a deference she found both alarming and ugly. "Did you," he asked, "hear that too?"

"I did," she said.

But said nothing else. And Anna hadn't budged. And Moat hadn't offered a punch line. So Harvey unbuttoned his shirt, fingers rubbing against the bottom of his throat. Air—he needed air—needed to let it in. He had to say something. The longer he waited to speak, the more irrelevant the revelation seemed, the more he wanted to forget it out of pocket and just go to bed. "Fuck you for being the one to tell me," Harvey said to Moat. He turned to Sue. "And fuck you for letting him be the one."

He'd heard of this happening, secondhand. Kate had come back home for half a year after her own affair cut down her marriage. Sarah, whom they thought they'd lost to cancer and then, just yesterday, to hallucination. Now the secondhand had caught up with him. He rose. "I'm out," he said, and he gave Sue his last blue chip.

It wasn't until he began walking that Harvey knew he had nowhere left to go. There were no car services, no taxis; here, the cabbies went home to their families after midnight, they didn't remain in front of Plexiglas, at the beck and call of any loose traveler who whistled or waved. There was no pay phone, no red-eye, no flights from the island at all until after noon, and even those Harvey couldn't afford. He had no means of transport. No way to get away.

"Where will you go?" Sue had asked, following him into the bedroom. He was fumbling with his shirt and wouldn't answer. Each time he missed a button, he felt old. She kept up her goddamn talking until he said something back. *When did it happen? How long did it last?* The scene alternated between blurted questions and lengths of silence. He'd agreed to sleep on it before demanding a divorce. She'd agreed to let him go where he wanted, but she wanted to know where that was.

"Wherever it is, I'm sure it will be beautiful." He knew perfectly well where he was headed—the memory of the construction site had haunted him all day—but it felt so good to act as though he were wandering, to keep her guessing, to lie to her, to do just a little bit back of what she'd done to him.

Make her fear he might wind up lost in the darkness, and that it would be her fault if she never saw him again. "After all, this is paradise here. I might as well explore paradise." Outside, a rowboat knocked twice into the retaining wall. Harvey shut his eyes. The alcohol was like a splint in his head. *You don't know their names*, Moat had said of the people here who tried escaping from their homes, *but you can guess their stories...*

Fuck you, Moat. You knew my fucking story. Better than me.

When Harvey reached the construction site, he was vexed by what he saw. Or rather, by what he didn't. An absence of drill bits, forklifts, measuring tape. It was all abandoned; work had been stalled for months, maybe years. Maybe there'd been a strike. Or the money had dried up, or the interest. Harvey walked through the building's skeleton. Warts of tar had dried on the floorboards. He stepped over humps of dust. It occurred to him he'd never visited one of his own sites on a weekend, seen it this way. Without women and men on-site, the building was left to the mechanics of nature, which was always tracing its path, be it lightest erosion or heavy rains stabbing unprotected sheets of drywall. Was it still a construction site? If someone wasn't there working, measuring, or securing pieces every moment, was the site simply left to atrophy?

When he returned, the house seemed even smaller. Sue was on her side. For the first time in years, when he climbed into bed he realized he was climbing into bed. But he felt he had to be beside her. She clutched his hip and, to his surprise, he let her. A long while without words passed. "Did you take your medicine?" he asked.

"I did. But it isn't helping. I got too drunk."

"You had water, though?"

"From the bottle," she said. "I still don't trust the water here."

"I'm just beginning to," Harvey said. He wondered what he would look like in the morning to his wife, how she would look to him. "It was beautiful. Out there just now."

"I'm so sorry, Harvey. I'm sorry for all of it."

He didn't know how to answer. It was an apology he was expecting, but one he suddenly felt little need for. Still, Harvey took it with him to sleep. He dreamt of everyone he knew, from his baby daughter, Kate, to her baby daughter; from animals he'd thought were extinct, to friends he'd lost contact with so long ago he couldn't guess whether they were still alive. A dream that everyone was mute in the afterlife. There were rules, restrictions, borders. You could empathize and laugh with the eyes, but not the mouth. You could not describe your lamentations. You could not answer for yourself or plead your innocence, because here innocence had lost its allure and affectation.

Harvey woke to pieces of something brushing his face. He thought it was seaweed, that he was sleepwalking into the ocean. "Are you afraid of water?" It was Anna. Her elbows rested on his chest, and her hands were scooped around her ears.

"Only when I'm under it," Harvey laughed. Moat had fucked Sue ten years ago, when Sue was fifty, the age Anna was now. "Jesus, you scared the shit out of me."

"That's how wake-up calls go," she said, lighting a pillar candle. He watched the erection of the flame, the light dully gleaming off the brass cup. Sue wasn't in the bed. He had a wild thought of pulling Anna down to him, candle and all. "We want to swim."

To swim. Harvey figured it for three or four A.M. They want to swim. They were insane, the both of them. "OK, a swim." But first he wanted to shave the shadow off his face. He went to the bathroom; pipes creaked as hot water spat from the spigot. Harvey caught it with a rag, which he placed to his face. He could feel his skin getting supple under the heat. He held the rag still on his skin until it cooled, and he realized he wanted more. He thought of Sue. Harvey again covered his face. Their marriage was (and *was* seemed the right tense for the marriage; death or divorce, whatever would wind up killing it, it was nearly over) a good citizen—purchasing anniversary gifts on time, kissing goodnight, bringing home milk from the market. Certainly in the course of over forty years, the marriage had bled out of loyalty. But for the most part it had been timid. Stalled, as though waiting for a shove that had not come. The snowballing wealth of recent times hadn't helped. The gifts felt unearned. Harvey felt beneath the spigot; the water was cooling. He decided his shave could wait.

Moat was outside already, throwing rocks into the sea. After each throw his hand stayed outstretched, as if he expected the rocks to boomerang back once he'd released them. Sue was standing next to him, but she drifted away when Harvey approached. "You've got Crest in your bathroom," Harvey announced. "And Camay. I'd have thought you made your own shaving cream out of, you know, homegrown aloe and petrified cicada shells or something."

Moat was sheepish. "Nothing like that, no. No coconut radios, either."

Why were they discussing this, Harvey wondered, discussing anything? Shouldn't he and Anna be enraged? Shouldn't he be punching Moat's lights out? Harvey wanted to lift one of the black rocks at their feet, make Moat think he was going to bring it down on his head, only to heave it into the sea instead, watch the army of rings spring from the point of impact, feel the wave he created consume their feet. But he couldn't work up the restlessness. Had old age reduced him to this? Had what he felt for Sue declined so sharply that he gave others permission to touch her, desire her, take her to bed and live to tell the story?

They didn't wind up in the sea. Moat and Anna led them up a trail far from the house, climbing steeply over a ridge. When they reached the pond, they were overheated and out of breath, and it was a welcome sight. Sue treaded water, wondering if Moat would speak. The truth was she didn't know his side of it. Her side was desire and emptiness, feelings that came so doggedly and determinedly ten years ago, they'd decided to work together. Sue had calculated that night, planned it, and had lived off its high for years. Hadn't he? The four swam to a spot where the water was shallow and they could stand. "Where were you when it happened?" Harvey asked. "What season was it?"

Moat couldn't remember. Not any of it—what Sue had worn, who'd first suggested keeping the affair quiet. Sue realized it wasn't an act. Every fact of the night was lost to Moat: the scratch of AM jazz when clouds interrupted the rented compact's radio signal, the high memory of Sue's stockings curled around the hotel room lamppost, how she'd had to plow her hands in the ice bucket the next morning, so she could slide her wedding band back on. He didn't share her memory of the danger involved, the prickly thrill of shame.

Harvey kept pressing; even now, his directness was breathtaking to Sue. "It wasn't in our bed?"

"No," Sue whispered, as if she'd taken that precaution particularly to spare him, "never on our bed."

"The second time, you mean? The second time, were you still drunk, or sober?"

"Look," Moat said, "we had sex."

"So I've been hearing. That's the rumor."

"But it's less than a rumor; it's over. A finished fact. Old lust. Does it have to hurt you this much?"

It was not the sex that hurt but the history that followed. A history they'd constructed and he hadn't seen. A history they'd carried with them quietly in Harvey's presence, at parks, driving through tollbooths on their way to Prospect Beach, sealing inside the envelopes of cards they gave to each other on anniversaries. Harvey thought of the faces he'd seen when they first arrived on the island. Faces that seemed to be friends but were only strangers cast in a deceptive light.

"Is it going to keep hurting you?"

"You adapt," Harvey snapped. "Here, you adapt. It's going back I'm worried about." They were running out of friends in the States. Abrupt heart arrests, complications from triple bypass surgeries, and protracted cancers had seen to that. Some still lived in Boor's Bend, but were not up to visitors; it was all they could do to care for themselves. Others were healthy but were defecting: to the Sun Belt, to condominiums and planned communities. Sue had mentioned joining some of them soon. But that didn't sound like joining to Harvey; it sounded like chasing.

And Harvey knew a thing about chasing. He'd chased Moat for years. He'd minored in Moat's major, business administration. He'd moved to New York City right after Moat had. And while Moat settled in, thrived in his work, got the place with Anna in Westchester, the city grew exponentially harder for Harvey, and he left as soon as office space opened up in Boor's Bend. Even in college, Harvey considered now, Sue had caught Moat's eye before his own.

"I hate what you have," Harvey said. He meant it for Moat, but was looking at both Moat and Anna.

"This?" Anna asked. "This is swampland with a view. Everything here is provisional. Just enough to get by."

"That's beside every important fucking point I could name." He wanted to scream at her for patronizing his situation. This wasn't about one house over another; it was about who had made the better home with what they'd been given.

"What we have isn't glamorous," Moat said. "Spending hours each day with a shovel, in galoshes. Digging out sand and debris. Thoughts I don't want to have. You're going back to friends and family. You have the whole world over there."

Then, Harvey thought, *I want the whole world over.* His mind danced back to the construction site. The frame, still standing, but useless. Was this what hurt now, what kept him from asking anything more? Would any questions he pursued, or answers she gave, expose holes in their life they'd never bothered to fill?

He didn't want to ask Sue why she'd done it—out of fear he would recognize the reasons. Lust, the encroachment of age, a compound fracture of the two, or something more sublime. Kate was grown and gone, the deed to the house signed; they had settled their accounts. It would seem there was nothing in disarray left in their lives. Harvey was not afraid to talk about the past. He was afraid of the man he'd become—no longer one who wanted Sue so much he'd give up nights to make a ring so perfect she'd never want to be seen without it, but one who sighed through his teeth when she told him she'd been unfaithful, a man who would let something like that go.

They were at a clearing; could tell night was breaking. Sue saw the first peek of a sloppy peach sun and heard the tide, unendurably calm from this high up. No birds or clouds, yet; the sky seemed empty handed. "It's morning," she said.

"Morning enough," Anna answered. "We've got to find food."

"If it's open," Moat remembered, "I know a place. A little chophouse."

Sue turned to Harvey. They hadn't had a full meal since the first night, that light fowl, the rice. Since then they'd had only coffee and liquor, plantains and chocolate. Harvey hadn't even thought to cut up that dumbbell-shaped fruit he'd bought. Knots turned in their stomach. So little made sense on this island. It was hardly threatening, but they wanted to leave; and though it was beautiful only in pockets, they knew they would someday long to return, just as any dream, good or bad, begs completion.

They walked a little further, around a tangle of banyan trees, their pace picking up, and found the chophouse. But all signs suggested it was closed. The inside was dark. There was a hearth outside but no smoke. No scents of grease, fire, sugary dough. Harvey took Sue's hand. Later on, once they'd safely made it back, he would feel suffocated by that hand. It would take effort on Harvey's part not to turn from Sue when she looked her husband's way. They would cry and bungle their hugs; their bodies would feel blocky. And they would not know which damages to first attend to. But this could come later. Now they only needed their next meal. "I think we're in luck," Anna said, waving her arms to be seen. She'd spotted a woman in the window turning a sign over, turning on lights. The place ahead was opening up after all. They would be received.

Au Lieu des Fleurs

"Everything's fine in the world so long as I keep my head down."
Mouna Aguigui

Latin Quarter, Paris—May 11, 1999

My, was there a pall that day. Birds and bees were about but barely active. Their paths were aimless, their motions half-hearted, as were those of the red squirrels foraging for new nest material. The morning was clear enough, light-scorched, but that was a thin illusion. The sun rose sluggishly as if dragged from the horizon. Young children were in the park, but most were dozing or picking their noses. The playground was bare of their little hands and acrobatics—the jungle gyms were vacant and lonely skeletons of birds picked clean. Not enough wind to fly kites. Not enough energy in mommy or daddy to heft their children and bound around making flying sounds. Passing pleasantries between strangers lacked even seeds of sincerity, and the editorials in Le Monde were full of forced treacle. The student artisans seated on wooden stools on Boul St. Mich must have kept sketching—but what was there to inspire them? Probably all they drew that day were portraits of their own scuffed, untied shoes.

I was a simple failure then. My income was generous, my suits, solid, the trip to sleep from the moment I first shut my eyes, brief and uneventful. But let me say this clear, my head was going under, my mouth filling with salty foam, I was drowning. It can't be said that I embraced my routine, not quite; it's far more truthful to say that my routine was feasting on me, consuming me confidently. And my hand played the biggest part, as it was what each morning wrapped the fat, striated neckties around my throat.

That May Monday began just like any other. I woke. Ate grapefruit and hummed idle notes in the toilet. Toiled through a cheap cigarette and with a flimsy comb whipped my hair into a style disrespectfully imitative of a cockatoo. I arrived by car at work, where I balanced the books for the largest housekey duplicator in France. Sat at a cardboard brown desk at a windowless office on the seventh floor and pretended, pretended, pretended to devote myself. Prayed for the hours to pass. Unastonishingly, they did. Finally, lunch. I knew it was time because I watched my supervisor approach the elevator. I saw her tug at the elevator door's iron knob, which was hollow at the center like an open inarticulate mouth. Heard the door shut, saw the light disappear down the shaft, heard her strike a match as she exited the building. These acts amounted to my permission to leave.

I walked alone to the bistro where I had been dining without alteration for fourteen years. Two men who had finished their meals stood in front, smoking. An acquaintance of theirs bummed a drag. "What's the advance report?" he asked the two men. "Menu up to snuff?" The diners looked glumly at one another. One stood at rigid attention and covered his eyes with his necktie, while the second held his hands in a pantomime of a sniper in a firing squad.

It was indeed a disaster. The proprietor's wife was finishing two angry phone conversations at once, slamming down both receivers simultaneously. Whole shipments had not arrived at the bistro that day, and those that had were spoiled—forcing the proprietor to serve the only food that had kept from the night before: fish soup.

I draped my serviette over my lap. Without realizing I'd ordered, a bowl of the stuff was set before me. It smelled of clams and sewers. I recoiled at the odor. I wasn't alone in my distaste: Others turned from their bowls, trying not to inhale. Those patrons beside me who had already finished their soup settled up quickly to escape the scent—their francs, normally a frisky currency, lay limp on the countertop. My own gray spoon was turned away from the bowl as though insulted. And there was fish soup as far as the eye could see. Fish soup broken only by water glasses and occasional elbows. I watched a nurse seated next to me scoop up a snortful. She winced; her eyebrows had a terrible collision. Still, she ate.

Still we all ate. I grunted down sip after sour sip. When the proprietor's wife wheeled around to ask if I was happy with everything, ashes from her cigarette tumbled into my bowl. I was grateful, frankly, for an excuse not to eat another bite. Back on the street, I walked with my hat off. Took as always the long way back to work, through the crooked streets that led past Priscille's parents' home…seven months had passed since that terrible day, the day of Priscille's wreck…I took stock of my stumbling life…I would kiss the rough walls of her parents' home when I knew no one was watching...my lips would brush against the stone...return to my desk late, avoiding promotion...the week, then the weekend...luxuriate with the ducks on Saturday instead of finishing Proust... stroke the felt that lined the wooden box I kept my fountain pen in, not writing down a single word...I didn't mean to galvanize my life so divisively between the tended and the intended, but such a division did strike me as correct. What I did was not what I wanted to do, but only the pale suggestions of what I wanted more...

Cackles coming from the bottom of the street broke my train of thought. Two circus roustabouts were fighting in front of a three-speed bicycle, which leaned against the façade of a building foreign to me; fighting over the use of colored markers. From where I stood their cackling sounded muted, just a series of bitchy whispers. Yet I knew what it was—what it must sound like—where they stood: unbridled laughter, bellies of it. I inched forward, yet the sound seemed to have come no closer to me. I had no business approaching those clowns—my mind was already back on the seventh floor, entangled in cobwebs, ears filled with the dripping tick of our office clock.

Yet I rattled off, semi-mad, down the street. Only to see the roustabouts hitch up their pants, drop their markers and whistle away, as though they'd been committing some vandal's act which I had uncovered. Pulling up short of the bike, I examined their handiwork. They had scrawled messages on posterboard, which was glued to both sides of the bicycle's banana seat. The side of the sign aired to the street read: "Grab What You Can—JUST 5 Francs! Macho Meat-Filled Pastries, Raspberries, Rice, Pickle Relish Choucroute...We Don't Mind, Rob Us Blind! Inquire Within." I had to go inside. I was still so hungry, I couldn't bear to pass up the tempting offer.

Ignoring the consequences that my tardiness to work might bring, I opened the door, hung my blazer on a hook and continued in, past the lounge and guestbook.

Inside I waited fruitlessly. There were no busboys, no maitre d'. I wondered if I'd missed the meal. I peered out the window to read the backside of the billboard on the bike: "Always Serving."

Well then?

I strolled down the corridors to make myself more conspicuous to the waitstaff, and to steal glances at what the other diners were having. A group of three caught my eye. The first two I knew from newspapers: prominent spokespersons from *les Verts* and *Parti communiste*. For years I'd admired their ability to inspire and incite, to lead strangers to action by virtue of voice alone. In my more inspired moments I had concocted fantasies of quitting work and dashing to their side.

The woman from Green Party spoke, martini sip not quite settled down her throat: "Only death can engineer so pointless a silence." But it was the group's third member, a tall, enviably tanned fellow with a foamy salt-and-pepper beard and eminent nose, whose words stunned me. The tall fellow turned to the woman, smiling, as though he'd considered her statement the moment before she'd made it, and was about to bring everyone up to speed on its merit. He was dressed with cosmopolitan flair, in a purple flowing pullover shirt, a tailored navy blue jacket, with a brightly-beaded brooch in the shape of Africa on his chest (broadcasting that the condition of the suffering greatly dictated the shape of his days). "That is true," he said, consonants whistling past his teeth. "And yet only Mouna I think would have had the wherewithal to *violate* such silence."

Mouna?

Then this was not a restaurant's dining room at all—but in fact a funeral parlor, in which services for that old Frenchman Mouna Aguigui were being held. You'll forgive what must seem on my part blunt stupidity. But before I had eavesdropped on that brief conversation, I'd peered into what I'd guessed to be the banquet hall. Sure enough there was a rolling cart positioned at the center, lid peeled back. Though my view was obscured, I guessed the cart was the centerpiece to a buffet. Assortments of people had passed by the cart, looking inside—and while they weren't holding any knives or forks, I'd imagined they were simply sizing up their pickings, and would return soon with plate and saucer.

No. As I took a second glance, I realized my mistake. It was a coffin they were looking inside. I had thought that the people clustered around it were sniffing. And they were. But not as diners examining the bouquets of varied entrees—but as mourners overcome by the gears of grief. This was not a cart stocked with house specialties, but a miniature hearse, held steady by four gigantic bicycle wheels just like those I'd seen outside.

I approached.

I had heard a little of this dead clown, Mouna: He was a sloganeer, a snitch—and as such too dangerous a topic to introduce around the water cooler, too mercurial for journalists to consider an ally, too marginal for Mitterand or Chirac to have to engage in debate. And just extreme and eager enough to be an easy victim of historians, who play a game of reducing the passionate to footnotes.

I suppose we've come to the story part of things: my lover's sudden death. Priscille's death. When such a tragedy befalls the living, we wear our epitaphs publicly. Mine read: I am disconsolate but my smile tries to tell you differently. My own emotions? Couldn't catch them with a glove. I had spent the entirety of the night she died lying in my bathtub, water cresting at my chin cleft, refusing to accept any memories of her, as though they were unwelcome immigrants. I remembered how shamefully I'd acted...after I'd heard the news I had not come calling to her parents' house. I never paid my respects. And although I was given the day off from work, I had failed to even show for the funeral. I had disowned her family's anguish. Had excommunicated them...refusing to take their calls, refusing to revisit photo albums with them, to touch my face by way of conjuring her. A crime of abandonment that shamed me now no less than in the seven months since I'd perpetrated it.

My eyes blinked open, and their gaze returned to the scene at hand. At the coffin's head and foot were sets of chrome handlebars, given a recent polish by the look of it. Garish ribbons sprouted from the handles; there was a horn, little bells—how had I missed seeing these? I felt at that moment as though I were covered with sheets of glass—windows that all needed opening at once! I tried to dismiss this feeling, and concentrate instead on the deceased. Indeed his corpse was captivating, exquisite even. A short body for such a long coffin. Under his feet, as though to boost him, were stacks of newspapers, the headlines of which bore his own name. I marveled at the many dazzling artifacts embroidered into his person. Little posies threaded through the hinges of his eyeglasses; other flowers ran in and out like tinsel in his scraggly beard. A Guatemalan worry doll...a strand of rosary beads... and a noisemaker peek-a-boo'd from his shirt pockets. An outbreak of metal buttons, like cheery measles, were pinned to his cap and corduroys, their messages tilted at angles impossible to read without craning my head: "Full Retirement at 15!" "My Heroes are the Happy," and "Concerned Scholars for Bathing."

Not all his messages were festooned with such absurd mirth. There was a billboard tied to his chest pleading for a landmine ban. And all over his clumsy potato-sack pants were bumper stickers, one decrying the use of child soldiers, another reading, *"Hurlez à la lune, pas avec les loups."* I continued reading Aguigui's body, pausing only to wipe his still smudged spectacles with my handkerchief.

As I studied him I was possessed by a belief: that the bumper stickers covering his pants were serving as makeshift patches. I had to know if I was right, and if so, what the patches were concealing. I had to know. I bent down and yanked off one of the stickers. Instantaneously a fragment of cloth erupted from the hole I'd torn in Mouna's pants. The cloth rose a few inches above his body, then fluttered in suspension, refusing to sink from its highest point. I snared it. It continued like a butterfly to beat in my hand, its lacy edges tickling my palm like eyelashes, flapping gently against my fingers. I held it to my chest until its beating subsided.

Mouna's own handkerchief. Of course there was an inscription stitched into its fabric—*"Au Lieu des Fleurs Faites Quelque Chose"*—In Place of Flowers Do Something.

Then...odd. I felt I should leave, felt...rewarded...as one might after having driven many miles from home simply to secure the sight of sunset from an unusual spot. But my brow was moist, my eyelids heavy. I was no longer myself. I pursed my mouth and let the loops out from my belt, finding myself at once stricken with loose lips and a tight stomach. What was wrong with me? Could it be that rancid fish soup? Hunger? Or was it Aguigui's handkerchief—had I acquired some contagion from it?

I knew I was near Luxembourg Gardens, so I headed there, hoping the new scenery would improve my condition. As I turned from the coffin, I felt others' eyes. I was not so alone. Many of the mourners stood near me, impassively staring at the handkerchief I'd taken from Mouna's trousers...and then when I walked out the front door, several of them followed me. I took a glance backwards: Their eyes were sunspots, the kind of intense gaze rooted in either fascination or indictment. Taking no chances I picked up speed. My quick pace prompted sharper pulses in my gut. My pursuers remained just steps behind. I ran toward the arc which fronted the park; from there I darted into a throng of pantomimes and street performers, hoping these people would provide me with camouflage. But no matter where I moved, or what sharp turns I took, the mourners shadowed me. In fact, they were gaining ground, as though they knew my destination better than I. I sprinted for the park's toilets, further undoing my belt, further tightening my mouth. The sensation wasn't nausea...in fact it was a sensation to the contrary. It reminded me of other forms of suppression. How, for example, I'd had to resist sobbing until closing time on the day Priscille was killed in the wreck. I'd been told at four...my company's profit numbers for the quarter were due, and I was obliged to stay and finish, aligning decimal points and countersigning my own figures, before rushing to the morgue. But the feeling was contrary even to this. It was lighter, a sensation like you or I might have shared if we'd exchanged dirty jokes in grammar school—an intense suppression of laughter, practically crapping ourselves trying not to burst with giggles in front of teacher, as though we were carbonated canisters which had been violently rattled and shook...

By now I had reached the park bathroom. But just as I gripped the door, I was seized by the waist. I made no move to escape. The mourners had chased me down. The reason was clear. They were menacing me for the disrespect I'd shown in accosting Aguigui's coffin, violating his body, stealing the handkerchief that was rightfully his. Dropping my shoulders and lifting my palms I turned to accept my punishment, like a dog who cannot help but confess to a mess his owner has just uncovered.

I turned to face my attackers, but there was only one. I recognized her from the funeral parlor. She'd been kneeling by the flower arrangements lining Mouna's observation room like river tributaries. A mature woman, fifty anyway, old enough not to chase men into bathrooms unless driven by expectation. Her lips jutted outward, and her plum eyes pointed down...as though she were playing a child's game...trying to see what she could of her own face without aid of a mirror.

With her face frozen in this fearsome pose, she spoke: "This park is not, you could say, my favorite. For starters there's that odiously precious fountain. Plus, its visitors keep house casually. And those hard green chairs! They really take a toll on a person's rear..."

She drew closer, eyes squinted nearly shut. I somehow knew that she hadn't read the brief will and testament written on Mouna's kerchief—it was possible she'd seen me read it though, and wanted to know what the hanky had said. Well that information was simply enough imparted; I could recite the text back to her, it was only a phrase. Or I could just hand the cloth over to her outright and be finished here. I could resign myself to a docile position, curling up maybe like a hardened sponge on the park lawn. It was the lazy middle of May, after all, the start of spring; I had a right to resist thought, to waste my liberty where and how I chose; a right to bend my ear to the sounds of roots gobbling groundwater, of squirrels constructing nests, the sound of nature asserting itself—which seemed somehow always more soothing than my own efforts at assertion.

"Excuse me," the woman cut in, "I couldn't help but overhear your thoughts."

"Thank god for that!" I cried. "I couldn't help but think them." The woman giggled and I hiccuped. Now the tightness in my stomach attacked me in waves. "I want to apologize for my behavior, Madame, I do, but at this moment I find myself frantically sorting through the slop of my brain, trying to, you know, dig up a piece of etiquette to present to you, but I'm damn fresh out."

She lifted, for the first time, her head. Her neck was gooselike, both grand

and gangly. "You are above reproach, monsieur...for one, I'm expertly qualified to receive huge amounts of uncouth behavior at one sitting...and for two, this whole time that you've been speaking you've been speaking into my deaf ear."

"Marvelous soulmate!" I responded. "What you say fills me with gladness. With other attempted confidantes, no matter how much I want to tell them what feels true at the time, I find myself constantly covering my words with little Band-Aids. I have never proven an able forum for my own confessions. I allow nothing to vent through me. I am a plugged bottle when straight talk is in the air."

"But you'll repent now? With me?"

"Oh sweetie, indeedie, indeed! Do you realize that right now I'm missing work for you? Well," I amended, gleefully, "I'm not *missing* it at all, really, I'm just not there. But hang work! Tell me about yourself and what yourself is about. Show me to your name—speak just the sound of it, marvelous soulmate, and instantly it will become my mantra!" She did just this—she was Dawn—and her words were flurries of snow melting on my tongue. Our improvisations filled me with lightness. It felt like I'd learned a new magic trick, one whose secret I would lose again the moment I stopped practicing. The moment we quit speaking, I would squander this found lightness forever...and yet... with my stomach railing again, I had to leave Dawn behind. "But not without a parting shot," I said, guessing that she still had access to my thoughts. "I must momentarily take leave, but upon my return, we'll have a discussion, our topics ranging from Chilean refugees to the death penalty to fish soup!" Then I ducked into the bathroom. I vomited, caught my breath, let the blood splash and wade through my veins—a sensation like watching my little niece play in my office, putting paper clips up her nose, making believe the stapler was a second phone; creating a playpen, in other words, out of space I had long regarded as colorless.

As soon as I was able, I walked back out, only to find that Dawn was gone. Another woman had replaced her. This new visitor was attractive and stunningly poised; her long hair was clearly a prized asset, it gleamed in the little light left of day. She had full lips and unassuming eyes. Searching for Dawn as if for housekeys, I scanned the garden. The harsh gleam of sunset kept me from seeing far. And this new woman kept bobbing in front of me. She was as insistent as she was young.

"I saw her leave, monsieur. She was in a serious hurry!"

"The woman? The one here a moment ago?" I wanted badly to chase Dawn. But it was no use; she was not in sight. Besides I didn't dare stray too far from the bathroom until my stomach settled. Damn. In disgust I tore a piece off my thumbnail. What a fuck I was! Dawn had only humored me until she felt courageous enough to escape on foot. Escape from me did seem the wise choice. Fun as it was, what had my ramble amounted to? Gibberish, a few leftist heartstring-tuggers spouted her way, and then? Fish soup? Why did I say I wanted to talk about fish soup, for God's sake?

I felt like the bread bags and cigarette butts lying near trashcans, longing to be left alone.

But this new visitor wouldn't be denied. Like the first, she courted my attention with idle chitchat. Hers did not concern the conditions of the park, but instead, the new art installation she'd just come from at Centre Pompidou. Though this woman—a generation junior to Dawn, clearly of a different class, almost clearly not Parisian—outwardly seemed to share little with my experience, we warmed to one another, moving rapidly between topics. Some of what we said was inappropriate, even scandalous, fodder for public streets. We made more than one passing reference to anarchy, of poking holes of civil disobedience into the police state; the street riots of '68, which she was not born for and I not interested in until that moment. We were freeing ourselves from language's heavy boot—and from consternation, the tax levied upon we who question our leaders (which is supposed to be like doubting the atmosphere).

However, the tremors in my gut soon overwhelmed me, miserably mirroring the sensations I'd felt in Dawn's presence. Again I entreated this new sister, please wait for me, won't be gone for long, keep near: "And upon my return," I began, and this time I suggested we debate the horrors of the nuclear meltdown in Ukraine, the repatriation efforts in East Timor—and then, to my agony again, "Fish soup." I rushed into the bathroom, and again when I returned, I returned to a replacement.

The evening drew its pattern. Strangers took the place of strangers whose company I'd just begun to enjoy; we caught some robust oral and intellectual wave; I turned queasy, made a plea for what we might discuss at greater length once I had purged; and my suggestions invariably dovetailed into fish soup, always my last, inapt words to these brief kin. Words that couldn't be further from the ones I'd wished to leave them with: Not the delivery boy rolling up evening editions like sleeves to throw at professors' doorsteps...not the schoolgirl who dashed her head slightly askance as she summated her arguments...And certainly not Paul, my last visitor, a haunted man who'd just spent a year on business in Beijing. There, he'd witnessed several scorching human rights abuses. And he longed now to have a stage to prowl, to broadcast his testimony to the rafters of this world. I didn't even get a chance to tell him I would like to come along. "Sorry," was all I could muster before rushing to the toilet. "It's been like this all evening..." "From bad soup, you say?" he asked, but I had already slipped inside, and he'd already begun to turn away.

Finally it ended; moon up; park emptied, I hitched my trousers to the loop they were accustomed, sighed, and exited the restroom. It must have been past midnight. Petty crooks walked with territorial cockiness along the cobbled paths, not with the stealth they submit to in early evening, and the indigents slept soundly on their stone sofas. It was the beginning of the dead hours, the formless ones, the only hours that seem to belong to anyone who wants them. I walked home. The stars were still as dogs awaiting table scraps.

I spent the next few nights retracing my steps in the garden. Hoping to get sick again. Waiting for at least one of my cronies to reappear. Trying to decipher what it was that happened that night. If anything of significance in fact really had. As my despondency grew, the walks shortened. I read and reread the handkerchief. What had overwhelmed me when I first read it, what had I hoped to accomplish? I'd been a fool, soapboxing about abuses and tyrannies I knew little of, simply because a vague statement on a corpse's old snot rag supplied the fuel. It was as though a rocket had returned to Earth smelling of crocuses and grandfathers, and from that our scientists claimed alien life to have been proven beyond a doubt.

After several weeks I gave up my search, feeling foolish and overwhelmed.

Overwhelmed. I returned to that word, and knew it to be true. Since I'd first moved from the South of France to Paris, fourteen years ago, it had been true. You can do that, move your whole life to a city with abandon. Then you open your apartment windows, and the sensation that the city has already annulled you overwhelms. This is a city's supreme weapon, indifference, indifference bordering on the unreal, as though the Parisians had given me up for dead and were not officially recognizing my gait or odor or smile. It was an art form, a competition: Who could care least? Who could turn the deafest ear? You pretended not to see the person walking towards you or that you'd disrupted their path; pretended not to notice haggard women smelling of linseed shouting, *"Je suis drôlement emmerdé!"* (Christ— a few years of city life and you laughed open-mouthed at such women!); pretended not even to notice pigeons clustering round your brioche—the sound from their green throats the groan of plaintive stomachs. And you did not, under any circumstances, notice the pleas of panhandlers and pass-ersby. You learned to subtract those pleas from the range of your senses. Even pleas coming from your former lover's parents...whose house you finally reach out to, on July 12th, with a plea of your own, slipping a letter into their mailbox that reads, "I beg you—let me speak with you about her. Let us remember her together. Let me be to you now what I should've been then." The next morning, ungainly as it is, my plea is answered. Priscille's parents messenger a response over to my office. It reads: "We know you've meant well, know you've been meaning to meet us. It does surprise us that you have the time to see us now, given your sheer activity in recent days. But we are overjoyed that the silence between us is broken, and will call you the day after tomorrow, after the holiday." Though their middle sentence was cryptic, the rest was clear and comforting. My only wish was that we could speak at that moment, but I respected their wish to wait until after the holi-day. I would simply have to busy myself until then, like a boy who can't sleep through Christmas Eve but must wait out the sunrise.

Bastille Day had no business being the day the stuck stylus jumped its groove. But there is all that diverting noise, and blue white red confetti whirling, so that I cannot help but look out the window at least briefly when I hear fighter jets snap the sonic boom as they fly showoff routines above. So yes, I venture out, if only for the cheap thrill of feeling, for a moment, in the company of an electric crowd. No sooner have my eyes adjusted to the light then I am approached by an old woman, who, clasping my hand and pointing to the swelling parade, angrily remarks, "Look at them!" Where she points, two gleaming Algerian girls unfurl a banner. I ask the woman where I've seen them before. Seems in late spring they interned with the Parliament kitchen staff. While in this capacity, they made a point of carving chips in the ceremonial soup bowl of our nation's leader. So that when Chirac dined with President Clinton in June, he found himself wiping off drips of ptarmi-gan bisque that drooled into his lap. The old woman huffs to punctuate her contempt, then huffs once again when she gets a good look at my face.

Bravo to those girls! What a gorgeous trick! Yet that wasn't where I remem-bered them from. It seemed I actually knew them. But—no—it's an illusion, I say to myself, your mind is hopscotching from too much wine. Get some food and fill your stomach.

...From there I walk by the fish market, with no intent of stopping. Yet the display window captures me—moisture drips from the imbricate scales of grouper and trout, salmon levitates, sea bass too, all tied to an almost invisible wire, floating like a morbid trapeze act. And there's a face on the television set I swear I know. So I step in. Oh, it's no one. Just some actress doing community work while cameras roll around her. No...excuse me... come again—it *is* an actress, but not one I know from movies. She has a ladle in her hand; she is spooning out bean soup in Macedonia to a refugee family. She looks up only once from her work. Yet that lone look is enough to prove what I'm hoping for. That hair of hers? Unmistakable. Unbelievable! It's the young woman I spoke to that night in Luxembourg Gardens, just after Dawn, and just before Paul...

...Paul I see on the TV that night: an invited panelist for a political round-table in the UK. An ambassador from China has just bestowed some trinket on the British Prime Minister, a token of affection for opening up trade rela-tions. Now, Paul stands up and, walking over to the ambassador, says, "Let me respond with a gift in kind. For your record of human rights violations against dissidents, I present you this bowl of scorpion soup. A delicacy in your country. Enjoy! Just mind the tip of the tail. It's lethal, and I suppose in my excitement I overlooked its removal...I pray your removal isn't similarly overlooked." In *my* excitement, I nearly run into my TV set, rushing to turn the volume up on my friend's performance. On *our* performance—for Paul is doing his routine the very same way the two of us laughingly rehearsed it that night in May. He has perfected a delicious quality of showmanship. As he prowls the stage, I feel pride spiraling into my marrow.

...Next, just after the commercial break, comes Dawn. She heads a group of legal advocates who are advising death-row inmates to file frivolous lawsuits to protest poor treatment. Their first case? A suit by a prisoner complain-ing his chicken consommé was served "a tad on the chilly side." When the TV reporter asks about the inspiration for her creative outburst, Dawn arcs her shoulders in a humble shrug. "It happened on that spring night near Luxembourg Gardens. You know the one I'm talking about—I'd tell the story but you've all heard it by now." Yes. I know the one she's talking about too. But now I have to hear it told again: "This little spinning top of a fellow, only thing that could match his words in terms of tumbling speed was his sour tummy, starts to speak. Gives his take on everything dark under the sun. I listen, then give back. He turns pale. Fish soup, apology, he gimpily runs to unravel his guts in the toilet, and then I—just like everyone else from that night has testified—found myself quivering with purpose, unable to stand still or stand for stillness another minute longer."

After that, I found them everywhere, all my fleeing companions. Couldn't help but find them, even when I was not looking. I recalled my talks with them that mad night in the garden, what had enraged and haunted them, and so I knew where to spot them. Even those that I hadn't met myself—say those Korean students spearheading a hunger strike, sipping soup as a symbolic last meal and chanting, *"We are happy, we are very happy,"*—I knew. Each one I knew. And as I read on and witnessed and marveled at their grand breaches of order, I felt like a twin to them all.

Kokomo

Carla Attends to Her Son

Our boy was hearing hums again.

"Go get him."

Those first few nights he cried out and woke us, it caught me by my startlebone so bad, each move I made felt dislocated from the one it followed. I turned over. Mopped the sweat. Off my neck. With my pillowcase. "No, you."

The heat was a fat man lying on me. Each sticky July day hung around well past nightfall, the wind powerless to push it along. Our town was a closet for the sun to throw itself into.

"Who got him last?" my husband, Danny, asked. He is a faithful provider, but is a bastard at night. He wouldn't call a bet like that if he didn't like his hand.

"Fine," I said, already craning my wrist over the bed, in search of my panties. "I'm gone, I'm gone, I'm gone."

The Blanket at Breakfast

"What was he dreaming this time?" Danny asked, when I got back. I wouldn't say. I was mad. I let him sop in his curiosity. He could've drifted right back off to sleep in my absence but didn't. Why waste your big chance at peaceful slumber?

Hours later, though, Danny was standing shirtless over the stove frying peppered Canadian bacon and clamping fresh OJ with the juicer and everything was fine again. That's what mornings are for. Food, as a way to ask forgiveness and save face all at once.

"Tell you why the boy can't sleep through the night," Danny said, the calories making him confident and his voice gauzy from the meat in his mouth. "That damn scratchy towel."

What he was talking about was a tie-dyed heavy blanket that our son, J.J., insisted on wrapping himself inside each night. We bought it at the last live Dead show in Indiana before Garcia's heart gave. After one of his screaming fits, J.J.'s blanket would be sweat-soaked straight through, making the colors as vivid and tense as when we first paid for it.

Danny's timeline was lazy, though, a thing I reminded him of after a gulp of milk. "The blanket came later. We didn't give it to J.J. until after his nightmares started."

"Yeah? And whose idea was it to give him a blankie in the first place, Carla?"

It was a book's, but I passed on saying so. Danny lived life like it was tic-tac-toe, some winnable kid's game. Whereas, I'd reached a point where my big life decisions felt like things I'd done on dares. How else to connect the man I married (who calls food 'grub,' who's President of a karaoke club, who thinks Notre Dame homecoming games qualify as family vacations) to the girl I used to be, and those men she dreamed about?

That bacon was so heavy it sat like a stain in our stomachs.

J.J., by the way, stands for Joseph Joseph. After the Sonogram, mine and Danny's dads each pushed us to pass their first names onto their grandson. Whosoever we used, the other one would always be bound to feel like a lemon. But both of their middle names were Joseph, so that's how we closed the dispute. Our circle of friends found the whole situation pretty funny. Then again, most of them went to work, bed, even showers, stoned. So they found anything funny: Turtle Wax, Groundhog Day, turnips. I can't quite pinpoint the moment when our friends became more irritating than the lines of assholes I wait on at the bank.

What I *can* pinpoint is when we bought the blanket. A Friday. The Dead show. We set camp on top of a soft mustache of grass not fifty feet from the stage. Hippies next to us passed out pink bottles of soap bubbles. While Danny shook out the blanket, I blew into the ridged plastic halo that held drippy soap in place like a dream catcher; through those bubbles I watched the blanket wave in sunlight, in kaleidoscopic animation before my eyes. Colors formed, glistened, and dissolved through the bubbles' weightless windows. It got in my head that those bubbles were factories of color.

Professional Reassurance

Danny gazed at the framed degrees hung on the shrink's office walls as if each were a set of wolf eyes, or riot officers' cocked nightsticks. "You tell me he's a hopeless case, or that me or her are, or—or her or me are unfit, I swear I will walk out of here right now." He picked one of the shrink's contact cards out of a dish and flicked it for emphasis. "Or maybe I don't even give you the satisfaction of watching me go. Maybe I punch you first and then leave."

The doctor looked over at me. I got the feeling he'd dealt with men like mine for years, who needed their wives to sometimes play lion tamer.

Then the shrink, Dr. Farrow, took a deep breath. His hands circled over a manila folder resting on his desk, like he was rubbing an invisible spot off of it. "J.J. is bright, intuitive, and given his troubles, remarkably confiding. On the other hand, he's laggard, agitated, dizzy with dreams that to him seem as real as..." rapping his desk, "...this. And you say this hum has thrown off his sleep cycle for over a—what?—year now?"

"Yeah," I said. "July before last. July he turned seven."

"And it only happens to him at night?"

"Only at night."

Dr. Farrow gave me a distant nod and wrote something down. I didn't know I could feel bad after telling someone the truth, but as he moved his pen across the page, bad was exactly how I felt. Then he punched a blinking button on his phone. Asked J.J. to join us. Once J.J. took a seat, the doctor asked him, "Remember the talk we just had?"

My little man nodded.

"I wrote down some of what you said. So I could remember it better. You told me then that those things aren't secrets. Is that still how you feel?"

"Oh yeah," J.J. nodded. "I want everyone to know."

"Well, then I'd like to read your remarks aloud." He opened his manila folder. I saw him memorizing J.J.'s lines so he could watch Danny and me when he spoke. We were being tested. Dr. Farrow was a gumshoe behind one-way glass, expecting us to confess to crimes he ticked off. I hoped Danny wouldn't notice. "'I'm under a pond,'" Farrow read. "'I see bottom-feeders snatched up by soily pond muck. Then I hear the sky. Ducks circling the sky searching for food and a home to rest in. The ducks spot the pond and dive headfirst into water. They think they're about to eat bugs. What they don't know is everything under the surface is a lure. A few men and women near the marsh see the ducks coming, and start sneezing like beasts. Warning calls. But the ducks don't stop diving.'" Dr. Farrow glanced up. "Remember saying this?"

Off J.J.'s nod, I ask what pond. "The one here," he answers, flinching. Where's here, Farrow asks. Home? "Of course," J.J. says. "The pond is home. Kokomo, Indiana."

Studying the Sound

What got Danny agreeable to pulling the overtime we needed, so we could afford to hang from the lowest rung of Dr. Farrow's sliding scale, was how Farrow summed up J.J.'s tribulations: "Right now, your son is living his childhood on two planets. The one he talks, eats and rides the school bus in, and the one he's taken to against his will from 3 to 5 each morning."

That was true, but those planets had begun to bang together. J.J. dozed off in school, and tried to do book reports on his "purpose," which did not set well with most of his teachers. Year after that, while he was unsupervised, couple of assholes at the *Kokomo Courier* telephoned J.J. at home and quoted him for their April Fools Edition.

One day deep into J.J.'s third year hearing the hum, Kokomo City Council called us up. They thought they had some answers, and invited us to join them in their next general meeting. We got there. Waited for hours. J.J. fidgeted with, then yanked out, then lost, his clip-on. Finally, this square-headed fellow with an awful slicked haircut that looked like a bent candle went to the podium. Hung on it like the end of a slow dance. We taxpayers had been helping him, for three years, isolate the acoustics of the noise at night. "What the hum is," the speaker began, concluding, "what it sounds like, depends on different ears. Many mistake it for idling engines. Some compare it to sizzling butter. I've heard crackling wires, I've heard a constant gutter ball in a bowling alley."

To J.J. the hum is closer to grown men grumbling underwater.

"Paying people to study," Danny growled, pressing his hair down (the ceiling exhaust fans kept blowing it around). "Biggest crock of shit I ever heard." He looked over at me with sagging, rusty eyes. "Someone's heart stops, would you waste time studying what did it?"

I was silent. When I caught my first view of J.J. in labor and delivery—flushed, screaming, gooey—I broke into wild laughter. Nurses thought that I'd reacted bad to the epidural. But it was just joy. Aching, exhausted joy. I had never bothered, in all the months leading to labor, even wishing for a healthy baby. When J.J. broke my water four weeks early, all I thought was, "Time to lose you." I know Danny felt the same. We had each sprung from dark roots. He used to "dry-dock," what they call it when you chop up seasickness pills and snort them through your nose. And I'd gotten taken advantage of in junior high by the man whose house I cleaned after school. I won't say much about my miscarriage; I hear pounding in my teeth when I dwell on it, but some childless couple pressured a baby, who wasn't theirs to pressure, into carrying a baby, that wasn't theirs either; I'll never forgive them.

Shuttled Between Homes

After J.J. came to us hale and hearty, Danny began believing he'd escaped the brushfires he'd set to his life as a dumb kid. Few years later, though, once J.J. broke open our nights with his screams, once the knuckling hum began settling into our son's skull, Danny got scared, like me, that maybe our pasts were pinning us to a wall after all. Only I was ready to face up. Not Danny. Danny made a point of tracing J.J.'s troubles to any problem and product of the town but him. Farm machinery. Factory smoke. Flat pieces of tar on sidewalks that looked like squashed slugs, and were maybe fallen drops of jet fuel from Indianapolis air traffic. But these things, the sweat of progress, was why we'd come to Kokomo in the first place. Danny sold me on it being a small town close to booming; we'd leave when the boom popped.

Danny sure held up his end. It didn't surprise me *that* he walked out on me and J.J., just when. All men fix a limit on how long they're willing to stand bad luck, but never let you know in advance what that limit is. The months that rolled by were rough. Much as I missed Danny's lips and whispers, I missed just as much his way of batting mirrors off our mantel, the nutty but stale smell of his suntan lotion. When we'd meet in a neutral parking lot to trade J.J., I couldn't seem to stop myself from trying to trip his temper. It was like flirting again. Only instead of getting him hot, like as kids, I was trying to make him scream. Something wasn't right when he opened his car door to let J.J. come to mine.

J.J. had to start living back and forth between two apartments. He never found friends on either street worth a nickel. He got teased on account of the blanket he talked about and carried everywhere. As long as schoolkids thought he was clowning, they'd leave him be. But once it slipped about his dreams, the bullying began. Nights, when he tried to spell "leopard" and "nuisance," his pencil would slip from his shaky hands. Most dinners, he threw up. Headaches hit often and lasted hours. Certain sounds—me filing down a thumb blister or Danny eating Doritos—left him wincing.

Itinerant Talking

Each time I dropped new symptoms into Farrow's lap, he shut his eyes and rubbed his palms. "Let's switch from the physical to the social," he'd say. "J.J.'s run-ins with classmates. Have they curbed at all?"

"*Curbed?* Yesterday, boys in the grade above J.J. hopped a ride on his bus. Badgered him in the back seat, tore holes in his blanket. J.J. left two stops early and the kids followed. Shoved him into a well."

Dr. Farrow tugged his desk drawer. "Did he tell them about his dreams?"

"You know it's never gotten through to J.J. That it'd be better for him to stop."

"Before you arrived, I took time to review my recent notes, and compare them with J.J.'s earliest recorded nightmares. The dreams that he used to relay to us *sounded* like dreams. Shifting, shapeless. They feel lately more like proclamations. This one, for instance, from last night: 'God has almost ceased his work. Once He does, it's going to be up to us to keep going while He rests. Take care of His riches or lose everything. All of creation is in our charge.' Carla, after his episodes, you fall back asleep before J.J., don't you? You think he might sneak a peek at the TV after you nod off?"

Well I would, I said, if it were me. What's your point?

Farrow didn't answer directly. That'd be too easy. "Here's something else J.J. said to me in our last session: 'It's going to get rough after He goes. Might get so rough for so long you might forget you ever had it good.' There's a man on the North Side of Kokomo who tapes a TV show out of his basement. Calls himself a math-prophet. He sneers a lot. His show airs during predawn hours. Anyway, from what I've heard of the host's rants, he seems to believe Earth is entering its 'second seventh day.' When this happens, the host believes God will rest again, leaving us alone for centuries, no more interference, no more aid, until the next cycle begins. J.J. hasn't directly lifted this TV host's testimony, but there is a resemblance. Do you think J.J.'s nightmares may be slowing down? That he continues to say outlandish things because it's all he knows? And he's, well, maybe a little frightened, to lose the routine of their intrusion. To lose the attention they bring him. You see what I'm saying?"

Outside of Farrow's window—a rectangular window made of two rows of three circled pieces of glass, like a cupcake tin—I could make enough of the sun out to see it had almost had enough. I'd been in this office a hundred times, through all seasons—it was spring now—but for some reason I couldn't remember ever looking outside Farrow's window and seeing anything but the dry bone days of dead November. My throat got tight as I thought about night, another night, closing. "Sell the TV?"

Speaking to Shoppers

After the session, I drove J.J. to the mall to replace his ruined clothes. And also just to relax with him, buy him a peanut-butter pretzel and eat only the insides, grasp at one of those thin straws of a normal moment that used to surround us.

I headed to the drugstore first, to buy laundry suds. After his fight the day before, I'd thrown J.J.'s mucked-up putrid blanket in the wash. What do you know, this new brand, Flashfresh!, somehow killed the stains from the dirty well the bullies threw it in. Flashfresh! says they use some kind of triple-aggressive cleansing powder. I'm sold. It reunited J.J.'s blanket with its original shine. I'd forgot some of those colors had ever even been there.

Each time we left another store, he'd peer at the plaza in the middle of the mall. There was some commotion there, couple cameras, lots of stopped shoppers. After we left Fashion Your Seat Belts, I let J.J. grab a look. Our mayor, who was up for re-election, was sitting in this giant flimsy throne covered with plush cushions, its arms layered in dull gold paint. He was dressed as the Easter Bunny, for the most part. He had the whole white suit, down. The floppy feet and long pink ears. But someone had cut an oval hole out at the face, from forehead to chin, so you could be sure it was him inside. People renting suits aren't supposed to do that, but I guess mayors don't have to rent. For thirty bucks (checks only, made out to "Friends of Mayor Calhoun"), any child could sit on His Honor's furry lap and have a photo snapped. Every so often, Mayor Calhoun would leap up, hop over to a microphone stand, and yell out, "I'm here just one more night folks!" as he looked for more Friends.

"Mom? Just how many people are here right now?"

"I couldn't even guess, shug."

"Do you think a hundred people are listening?"

"Oh," I said, "two at least," though most were only rubbernecking. J.J. nodded, then gave the mayor this tidy but leering gaze. "Want to hop up there?" I offered.

J.J. wheeled around, wearing the look he gets when he sees it's carrots for dinner. "You mean and pose? On his lap? With that dumb ape?"

I felt light, grateful to share his gaze, like when you and some stranger watch the same funny thing unfold from opposite sides of a crowded room. "Wanna see something really dumb?" I asked, reaching into my purse to take out a colored egg with the words, *Friends of Mayor Calhoun: Politics Paired With Progress*, etched into its plastic shell.

We giggled. I looked for more eggs. "They're lying all over the carpet. All of them say different stuff, all of it stupid. You believe someone wasted weeks of time making these? They don't even have chocolate inside!" But when I looked over to enjoy J.J.'s reaction, he was gone. I heard the sound of a bracing squeal. J.J. had taken the stage, and was pulling the mike off its stand. A few people watched my loony son. One of the mall guards crossed over

149

to the Mayor Bunny, either to protect him or to check whether this outburst was on the schedule. Mostly though the shoppers were looking the plaza over, trying to figure out which mom this troublemaker belonged to. Then, to add weight to my misery, the mall speakers started in with that fucking Beach Boys song they always play at closing time:

"*Ooh I wanna take you down to Kokomo,*
We'll get there fast and then we'll take it slow."

And then an announcer's voice, cutting into the verses...

"*Just a reminder not to take things* too *slow, shoppers. Kokomo Mall will close at ten.*"

J.J. tapped the mike twice before speaking. "How many people can hear me?"

He got a thin, polite round of applause. The rubberneckers.

"How many people can hear *it*, too?"

The applause stopped, even by teens who'd been egging him on. But a few folks who weren't clapping before suddenly turned to the podium, and pointed to their own chests with fingers from both hands.

"After this, He's going to stop working."

The chest-pointers moved up, from scattered points around the plaza, toward J.J., forming a hip-by-hip line at the lip of the stage.

"But look at all the raised hands hearing it at this mall." He let this sink in, like a teacher telling you the one thing you had to solve if you hoped to move up a grade. "Just here at this mall. There have to be more of us in Kokomo. Even if there aren't more of us, I can't believe He'd sweep the whole town away. Even if it's only ten of us who hear the noise, I have to believe He'd spare us all."

I waited for people to yell, boo, storm the stage, drag him off. What I saw were nods of recognition. The take-charge mall guard, who was practically in the mayor's lap, was about to make a move. But he froze when the first lightning flash spread out over the skylight like an unfolding map. For a second the whole mall was an overexposed picture. I kept waiting on thunder to report back just how close the lightning had struck, but no crash came. J.J. seemed to expect the light, only looking up long enough to say, "And now we will know." Then he set down the mike, and came back to me like he was ready to go try on more trousers.

Babble On

"Doctor, I know you hate home calls, but..."

"I saw the mall coverage, Carla. The newsroom's second story, in fact, following the flash flood reports. I thought I might hear from you."

"He's gone even worse since."

"Worse how? Ill? Delusions?"

Seemed pretty pointless to go over what was wrong when what was wrong was standing right in front of me. "I'm gonna put the phone to his mouth, OK? The next voice you hear will be my son's."

"J.J.?"

"...racing no towel, from all this that's us but, armchair from his he overhears us, ruined nice, damage panic-soaked minutes! Um, O.K., O.K. Only all forms beneath us if we're caught..."

I took the phone back. "You hear that?"

"Does he ever take a pause?"

"No. Same bunch of words over and over, too. It's just the way he words the words that keeps changing."

"His syntax is jumbled. But I don't think it's babbling. If he keeps repeating himself, he may be sure of *what* he's saying. Just not how to broadcast it clearly. I'm going to phone a colleague in the linguistics department at I.U. as soon as we hang up. Try to come by Monday morning. Until then: you know that mini-recorder I tape J.J. on? Buy one of your own. Keep it running wherever he does."

Prodigal Homecoming

My new life, Danny told me, that night in my bedroom, stripping out of wet clothes and looking for where I've put the laundry hamper, is just one ugly scream. Since me and him split up it's just been him—never mind the new job and willing women he'd been bragging about before—screaming at his old life. The only life he really knows. It's like he's some grounded teen threatening to run away, but run away to what, he asked, twisting rain out of his socks. Spoiled kid looks around long enough, he's bound to see sneakers in his closet, bounty of food, the great CD player he got for his birthday. All of life's treasures are stuck in that house he got raised in, so he's gotta stick it out there too. So what if there's some burdens to shoulder while he's there? It's the least he can do. At some point, every screamer has to close his mouth and see that all he's doing is lashing out at his blessings. Danny looked up, naked by this point, the black hair on his moist chest all a bunch of curled scoops, to catch my eye and see if I wanted it, too.

"You believe this fucking weather?" he asked, his hand stroking mine.

For some reason, I thought of taking out the garbage. Each Wednesday night I carried trash out the door, breathed in crisp air, and felt utterly alone. The next morning, on my way to work, I drove past toppled trashcans, slashed plastic, gutted banana peels and yogurt cups. Raccoons probably watched my every move. You must believe in the undertow of the inevitable. "Yes."

"You think it's gonna let up?"

"Ask our son."

J.J. Testifies

Danny hadn't brought a change of clothes ("I had no idea this would happen," he lied, looking for his lighter), so, after we were through with our reunion, at the point when he usually gets restless anyway, he slipped back into his half-wet jockeys, and out my room, and into J.J.'s.

Later, I followed. Peeking in I saw J.J. explain the Web to his father, how thanks to a bundle of wires all the distance in the world means nothing. Danny asked what video games it gets.

J.J. waved at the question like it was some moth. "'Til I learn HTML, I mainly use the computer to talk. In Taos—this town in New Mexico—a bunch of people who heard their own hums set up chatrooms. They had fire, not rain. Thousands of acres burnt. So bad kids got used to falling asleep with the glow of redbuds and aspens burning through the windows." He paused a moment. "Taos can't tell Kokomo what's in store for us, of course. But it's nice to hear from other folks bearing up under the brunt."

Prompted by a beep on the monitor, J.J. typed hello to a Kokomo kid who'd logged on. Then he slumped in his seat and asked: "Are you back with us for good?"

Danny gawked at J.J.'s bedroom window, like he couldn't figure out what to make of his reflection. Your kid blurts a question like that, you feel your heart expand inside you, and you must blurt back. "I am, I'd say."

"That's good to hear, Dad. You're safer here."

The Town Through Its Toils

After the third week of rain, J.J. told us to stock up on water and non-perishables.

And we did, Danny doing the shopping as I closed out our bank accounts. What followed was a storm that all you, of course, saw covered from a dozen different angles on the national news. But I say if you don't live here you don't really know, not yet, the degree of the rain. You got a cousin in the National Guard, maybe you understand a little. Maybe that cousin told you about clogged drainage ditches, snaky rainbows of oil floating on flooded streets.

How the ground's given way in places, and both the cotton and chemical factories have slid happily down muddy hills like kids on slip n' slides. And how more of the town leaves each day but J.J. tells us each night not to follow. How teenagers gather at Kokomo's lowest plains playing chicken with flash floods, daring the waters to scoop them up and carry their cars away. At some point the water starts playing dirty, grabbing by the ankles, and the teens hightail it to Food & Fuel, where they regroup, wring their collars on the tiles, and burn through sacks of Wise potato chips.

You can't know this town truly unless you've been here for years, and have chosen to stay, and own an 18-foot ladder with sandbags tied to the support struts, and are surveying it from your rooftop. Then you know what's happening, how little of your own world you own. How your hours are all now hazardous. Are all now alien. Are all now singed with energy that seems at once vital and vengeful. Trouble is, we've nothing else to use and go on but those hours. So it's either suicide or stamina, that is all we have to decide.

J.J.'s dreams stopped—he hears what he needs to during daylight now— but my own are just beginning. In one, we're running through the Kokomo Mall when I lose sight of him. Suddenly all these handheld Nintendos and pagers and cells and all these Palm Pilots and electronic security horseshoes begin letting out, at once, this god-awful vibrating wail. The digital chirps char my skull. I stop, then bite down on my tongue, because I know the Beach Boys song will be starting up any second. J.J. keeps running. His steps are small but he's taken enough of them to build a head start on the terror. I'm still still. I don't bother to run. For me it is only a matter of time, so I just study the noise like you always mean to study, but never quite do, your life.

Matthew Pitt was born in St. Louis. He is a graduate of Hampshire College and NYU, where he was a *New York Times* fellow. His work has appeared in *Oxford American, The Southern Review, Colorado Review, New Letters, Best New American Voices*, and elsewhere. Stories of his were cited in both the *Best American Short Stories* and *Pushcart Prize* anthologies, and have earned awards from the Mississippi Arts Commission, the Bronx Council on the Arts, and the *St. Louis Post-Dispatch*. He has received scholarships from the Bread Loaf and Sewanee Writers' Conferences, and has taught at NYU, Penn State-Altoona, and the Bronx Writers' Center. He lives with his wife Kimberly and their two young daughters.

The Autumn House Fiction Series

New World Order, by Derek Green
Drift and Swerve, by Samuel Ligon ■ 2008
Monongahela Dusk, by John Hoerr
Attention Please Now, by Matthew Pitt ■ 2009

■ Winner of the annual Autumn House Poetry Prize

Design and Production

Cover and text design by Kathy Boykowycz

Set in Lucida fonts, designed in 1987 by Kris Holmes

Printed by BookMobile